CAN'T TAKE THE HEAT?

HAILEY SHORE

Copyright © 2023 by Hailey Shore

All rights reserved.

No part of this book may be reproduced in any form or by any electronic or mechanical means, including information storage and retrieval systems, without written permission from the author, except for the use of brief quotations in a book review.

❦ Created with Vellum

1

Calico Cove
Spring
Birdie

Mistakes were made.

I'm a grown-ass woman so I had no problem admitting that. I have made some mistakes.

First mistake, thinking things with my father would be different this time.

Second, that I didn't break up this trip in a reasonable way, so now I was strung out on caffeine, exhausted and rattling down a gravel road in Old Blue in the middle of the night.

Third mistake, and maybe the most important. I forgot to text my aunt to let her know I was coming.

My aunt lived alone in a trailer on a dead-end road in

Maine. Stephen King country. Showing up close to midnight, I was going to give her a heart attack.

Should I flash my lights? Would that be worse? Honk? Would she recognize the general size and shape of Old Blue…I hit another pot hole and all the drawers in the back escaped their tiny little latches and banged open. I hit another pot hole and they banged closed.

This had been happening for a while.

My left eye twitched. From the residual effects of my fight with Dad? The stress? The seven hundred cups of coffee and no sleep?

Yes. Yes to all of the above.

Like I said – mistakes were made.

Every shadow on the side of the road I was sure was a bear. Or worse, a moose. I was hallucinating. If I hit a moose, Old Blue would crumple like a tin can. Also the bear would eat me.

This was Maine. Shit like that happened.

Another pot hole.

Bang-Bang.

I came up over a little rise and my headlights finally landed on my aunt's trailer, nestled into the woods.

It was like a fairy encampment. There were hundreds of lights, comfortable seating around a fire pit. A garden surrounded by netting to keep out the deer. A barbecue next to her really swanky vintage Air Stream and a picnic table inside mosquito netting.

There, in the middle of the road, was my Aunt Za. In a robe and fuzzy slippers. Her steel grey hair up in curlers on her head.

The knot in my chest abruptly relaxed.

Home.

She put up her hand and I stopped.

"If you're not my niece," Aunt Za yelled, "I'm going to put a hex on you."

"You don't like hexes. Too much dark energy," I shouted out the window.

At the sound of my voice, Aunt Za shrieked and clapped her hands.

"Darling! Quick, get inside before the bugs get away with us."

It was April, so the bugs were just beginning to bloom in full force. I turned off Old Blue who shuddered in gratitude. She was not made for long hours on the highway at top speed. But after leaving brunch with my dad in New York, I hadn't wanted to stop. Six hours later, and we were both at the end of our ropes.

I gave the dashboard and hula girl I inherited when I bought the thing a loving pat.

"You did good, Old Blue. I promise you an oil change and tire rotation before we get back on the road again. Pinky swear."

The hula girl had both her plastic hands raised, which made this easy.

Then I sprinted out of the truck, through the buggy night and into my aunt's waiting arms.

"Birdie," she sighed, squeezing me tight.

"Aunt Za," I squeezed her back just as hard.

Home, I thought again as we made our way to her trailer.

Inside, her trailer was even more beautiful. An old couch covered in quilts. Bookshelves full of books. A reading nook. A tiny little galley kitchen. There were three shut doors down a short hallway. A bathroom that was surprisingly spacious. Her bedroom, which was palatial. And a tiny little spare room with a single bed that she kept for me.

Aunt Za closed the door behind us.

"What do you need? Food? Wine? Coffee?"

I flinched at the word coffee. I might never drink another cup of the stuff for as long as I lived.

"I'm good," I said, and collapsed into the bench seat around the table.

"Well, you look slightly...terrifying."

I laughed and touched my hair. It was an absolute mess. My favorite One Direction t-shirt was covered in crumbs and coffee stains. "I've been on the road since New York."

Aunt Za hummed and put on her kettle. Then turned back to me.

She put her hand on my head and then my face.

"You're aura is all out of whack," she said. "You're usually pure blue, honey. Blue as the sky and now you're all yellow and orange." She pulled a face. "Brown."

"You saying my aura is shit?"

"I'm saying you're tired, but there's more going on than just tired."

She made an incredibly good living reading tarot and telling fortunes in Calico Cove, especially in the summer tourist season. A lot of people didn't believe her, which was fair enough. But I'd seen her be right more than she was wrong. Maybe that was just powerful intuition or the law of averages, but I liked to believe in her magic.

That she was successful in her unconventional life made my father absolutely crazy.

Thoughts of my dad sent an unwelcome shiver down my spine. The last of the adrenaline, anger and hurt that put me in Old Blue and sent me up the road to Aunt Za and her unconditional love, started to recede.

"Tell me what happened. Did you tell him?" she asked, putting two steaming mugs of what smelled like mint tea on the table. She scootched into the bench seat opposite me. My aunt was one of those women who could be thirty or seventy. She was ageless. Timeless.

"What do you think happened?"

"You told him you'd been invited to compete in the Masters vs. Apprentice Food Truck Competition in Portland next month and he told you how proud he was of you and what you've done with your talent."

"Okay, that. Only one hundred percent the opposite. Why did I think it was going to be different this time?" I asked, mostly myself. "Why did I think we could just sit down and be together like a normal father and daughter? Instead we went to this fancy brunch place where the chef fawned all over him, of course. I wasn't halfway through my omelet, gearing up the courage to tell him, when he started asking me when I was coming home for good. Which ended in this huge fight with me storming out of the restaurant."

"He really doesn't learn, does he?" Aunt Za sighed.

"He doesn't."

"Hmmm, so you just left?" she asked me.

"I couldn't stay. Nothing I do is ever going to be good enough for him. Nothing!"

"Hmmm," she murmured again, and I sensed there was something she was holding back but I was too tired to push. "So, what's the plan?"

"Can I stay with you until the competition? It's not for weeks, but it will give me a chance to try out my recipes with locals. People I know who will be honest with me."

"Of course you can stay. I love it when you come to Calico Cove. The whole town does. You're like a breath of fresh air with the additional benefit of some amazing cooking."

The relief I felt at her immediate acceptance was palpable.

"I just need to..." I was exhausted and the word didn't come to mind right away.

"Rest?" Aunt Za said.

"Yes."

"Hide?"

I laughed. "Sure."

"Heal?"

That sounded nice.

Finished with my tea and feeling half human again, I went back outside to Old Blue and grabbed my duffle bag. Aunt Za made up my cozy single little bed. I looked at it and remembered the first time I stayed with her.

When I was desperate and scared after another massive fight with my father. A nineteen year old, with no clue about what the future held.

Eight years older and nothing had really changed.

Something about that didn't feel right, but I was really too tired to dwell on it.

Suddenly choked up, I hugged her again. "Thank you," I whispered. "For everything Aunt Za."

"Of course, Birdie. You always have a place here," she said patting my back. "You know that."

The words were so exactly what I needed that I felt exhausted tears burn behind my eyes.

"Hey," I said. "You can't really hex someone, can you?"

She leaned back, her eyebrows lifted, and said in a deeper voice, "You don't want to know."

∽

Calico Cove

Spring
Antony

"That's some view," I said, staring out a wall of floor-to-ceiling windows into the hillside that ended abruptly at a cliff falling off into the water. All the trees were coming to life, vibrant green buds were bursting into existence. The arrival of spring.

A new start. Just like the one I needed.

"Private too," Mal Bettencourt said behind me. Mal was a tech genius billionaire who'd found himself in Calico Cove after recovering from a horrible helicopter crash. A good friend of mine, I'd done him a favor several months ago, spending time with his then housekeeper/now wife, teaching her a few cooking tricks.

Now he was doing me a favor in return by letting me stay here.

"Nothing but woods for an acre," he said pointing out the window. "The next house is three miles down the road."

"What made you buy it?" I asked him. Mal and Jolie already had their own very spacious property closer to the water with their very own lighthouse included.

"I didn't just buy this property. I bought all the available property I could in Calico Cove. Places that might be targets for developers and what not. This town is a slice of heaven and I plan to keep it that way."

"So you're taking being a control freak to city-wide levels?"

"Oh, you're one to talk, Chef."

I shook my head and chuckled. The feel of it rusty in the back of my throat.

"Jolie thought she lured you out of your lighthouse, but you just made your reclusive bubble a little bigger," I said to him.

"Something like that," he said. "Please don't tell my wife."

Yes, this house, this whole town was perfect for a man in hiding was what my old friend didn't say. Perfect for a man running from paparazzi and social media and think pieces putting him on blast.

Me. I was that man.

It had been a month and shit was not dying down as I'd been promised by my publicist and my agent and my friends. The story had morphed into a second life. Now, every newspaper and food magazine in the country was after me for a quote on the toxic nature of professional kitchens.

One bad day in the kitchen. One moment, that went viral.

I could hear the plate shatter against the wall. Feel the spittle falling on my chin as I'd shouted.

The silence afterward.

Quickly, I blocked out the memory.

"It's perfect, Mal. Thank you."

"My pleasure," Mal said.

"Come see the rest of it. Big kitchen with top end appliances too. I think you'll approve." Mal stepped away from the windows and through the beautiful living room.

He was leading me towards the kitchen.

I was not interested in the kitchen, so I didn't move from my spot.

When Mal realized I wasn't following him, he stopped and pulled the keys out of his pocket and handed them to me. "Two guest bedrooms upstairs on the second floor. The primary is on the first floor on the other side of the kitchen with a large ensuite. Shower, soaking tub. The works."

"I'm sure it's awesome." I took the keys and put them in my own pocket. "Thanks again for this."

How many times could a guy say thank you? I was going for a record.

"I'm glad you listened to me. Getting away from California and the craziness of the restaurant was a good choice for you."

"I just need to..." The right word didn't immediately come to mind.

"Rest?" Mal supplied.

"That," I agreed.

"Hide?"

"Definitely."

"Heal?"

That sounded nice.

"I think I was going to say...rebound." I offered.

"You can do all that here," Mal said. "But I don't want you to become a recluse like I did. Trust me, the locals will start talking about you and give you some stupid-ass nickname. You'll come to the house tomorrow and play poker with my crew, yes?"

Mal had told me about this monthly poker game, which had turned into a few times a month.

"I don't play cards." I shrugged.

I cooked. I created. I was a chef. That's all I was.

"Good, then we'll take all of your money," Mal said with a clap on my shoulder before he started towards the front door. "You're coming. You're playing. You're having fun. I'm not leaving you to sit up here all alone on this cliff. It's not good for your mental health. Take it from someone who knows."

I said nothing, other than offering a halfhearted wave as he closed the door behind him.

I wasn't worried about the locals forming opinions about me. I didn't plan to be here that long. This was just a temporary stop.

Until the news cycle died down. Until people forgot the events surrounding me. Until I got some tools to make sure that I never lost control again. Then I could go back to my regularly scheduled, completely under control life.

That's all I needed. Privacy. Tools. Time. Control.

2

Antony

At their heart, chefs were problem solvers. Most creative people were.

What's wrong with this?
How do I make this better?
What can I do to make this the best it can possibly be?

After a week in the beautiful house, in the beautiful setting, with the beautiful view – I had a problem I could not solve.

The dreams.

Every time I fell asleep it was the same thing over and over.

The man yelling at Jenny in the dining room. "What kind of server are you?"

The glass shattering.
My temper fraying.
The poorly plated dish.

The plate smashing against the wall. The plate I'd thrown.
I woke up in a cold sweat like four times a night.

I felt like a zombie. Zombies were not in control. Zombies did not get back on top of their mountain. It wasn't like I wasn't trying. I'd tried lots of things. Self-help books, meditation, yoga.

I'd even tried a mantra.

I will get my life back. I will get my life back.

None of it helped with the dreams.

I needed reinforcements. My agent had wanted me to see a therapist after the video of me throwing a plate at the wall...unfortunately very close to my sous chef's head...went viral. She thought it would look good that I was taking proactive measures to improve my mental health.

I wasn't doing anything just because it *looked good*.

However, here, out of the spotlight, I could admit that it wasn't the worst idea.

Unbelievably, Calico Cove had one therapist. I wasn't sure if I should feel lucky they had one, or surprised it was only one.

Dr. Benjamin Kowalski Clinical Social Work/Therapist, PHD, LCSW, LADC, CCS. I had no idea what the letters were behind his name, but on the day of my appointment, I wore a hat and sunglasses and drove the Land Rover down the mountain into Calico Cove. I'd been here a few times to visit Mal and the town's charm was undeniable. Especially on a spring day. Blue sky, blue ocean, green grass – it was a very alive kind of place. The people were friendly and hard-working.

I parked on the street. Checking the address on my phone, I went into the small office building that was built right on the waterfront just north of the main square. It was a new build and another sign that Calico Cove was growing. I wondered if Mal owned this building too.

I pushed open the door with Dr. Benjamin Kowalski's name on it and walked into a small waiting room, painted in bright primary colors.

"Hello?" A woman said from behind the reception desk. She looked at me over the top of her glasses and sighed. "Dr. Bernstein is two doors down."

"I'm not here for Dr. Bernstein," I said.

"It's nothing to be ashamed of," she sighed. "Really. Lots of men are getting plastic surgery these days."

"I don't need plastic surgery," I said. "I have an appointment."

"Here?" the woman asked, like she didn't believe me. "Where's your child?"

"I don't have a child."

"Then you shouldn't have an appointment with Dr. Kowalski."

"And yet I do. So, I guess wonders never cease." I pulled off my hat and my glasses. My plan had not been to reveal myself. I didn't imagine my infamy stretched to this tiny waiting room, but the second I took off my glasses and hat, the woman behind the desk gasped.

"You're..."

Shit.

"No?" I mean...it was worth a shot.

"Yes. You are. The blond hair and the eyes. I'd recognize your blue eyes anywhere." She looked down at her computer. "Tony Renard. You used a fake name."

"It's my name," I corrected her. "Just not the one I usually use."

"Okay, okay. Okay." The woman started flapping her

hands and I recognized what was happening. Stage 1 of a fan meltdown: The Hands.

"What's your name?" I asked carefully, with a smile, trying to keep her from progressing down all five stages.

The fifth stage was crying, and I just didn't have it in me today. I really didn't.

"Jessie," she said. "Josephine, but I go by Jessie. My dad's idea. People sometimes think I'm a boy. But I'm not a boy. I have a brother, and his name is Ryan but some people think he's a girl. It's like a whole thing."

Stage 2: Over-sharing.

"Sounds like it. Do you think-?"

"My mom, like, loves you. We get her your cookbooks every year and she rewatches your show all the time. She says it's your eyes. You really are... like... so handsome."

Stage 3: The Gush.

"Thank you and say hi to your mom for me. Do you think you could let the doctor know I'm here?"

Please, I thought, please let's stop here. Four was hugging. And I could hug all day. But if we got to four, five was inevitable. Though sometimes there was a strange detour between three and four where people liked to tell me:

"Your recipes are hard," she said, the gush over. "Really hard."

Alternate Stage 4: Things I Do Wrong.

"Every year we try that Beef Wellington, and it never works." Ah yes. The Beef Wellington from my second cookbook, Classics Reimagined.

"Well, you have to weigh the ingredients, not just measure, I try to make that clear-"

"We don't have a kitchen scale." She blinked at me, and I

wanted to offer her mine, just to make this moment go away. "The pastry is always mushy."

"You have to squeeze that spinach dry."

"Really?" She clearly couldn't believe spinach squeezing was such an important step.

"Really. Now, Jessie?" I said with my most charming, television smile. "Is there some paperwork I need to fill out or can we let the doctor know I'm here?"

Jessie shook herself out of the fan meltdown and I took a breath of relief. She was blushing bright red like she realized she might have over stepped. I smiled at her some more, letting her know it was all okay. Constant smiling. Endless smiling. It never used to feel like a lie. But these days it did.

"Yeah! Yes. Of course. For sure. Just...have a seat." She pointed to the waiting room with one adult-sized chair and seven kid-sized chairs.

There was a bin of toys and a bookcase full of board books. I sat in the grown-up chair and Jessie jumped up from behind the desk and knocked on a closed door on the other side. She gave me a bright smile before slipping inside and shutting the door behind her. There were muffled voices. Then the sound of the video.

My video.

The viral one. I heard the muffled sound of my voice swearing at my beloved and trusted team. I took a deep breath and tried my mantra again. I will get my life back. I will get my life back.

Jessie came out of the office and smiled at me with all her teeth. "The Doctor would love to see you," she said.

I stood and nodded at her graciously before stepping inside the office of Dr. Benjamin Kowalski.

"Hi," a very rumpled, friendly-looking man crossed the

room to shake my hand. He had a ring of curly hair around a mostly bald head. A graying beard. Glasses and a manner that put me immediately at ease. He was like Santa Claus and Mr. Rogers combined. "I'm Ben."

"Antony," I said.

"You are not a child," he said with a smile. "My clients are usually kids."

I looked around at his office. The window looking out at the harbor full of fancy sailboats side-by-side working lobster boats. Kids would like that view, I thought. There was a low table in the middle of the room covered with toys, crayons and pads of paper.

"Yeah," I said. "I'm beginning to see that.

"Jessie, my receptionist, says you're famous."

"She showed you the video." I said, cutting to the chase.

He nodded. "But you have a really full and creative and successful life outside that video," he said.

He sat back down in his big comfortable chair. The only other one in the room was a Thomas The Tank Engine chair.

"Sorry," Ben said. "Jessie can bring in the chair from the waiting room."

"It's fine," I said and sat in it. All six foot, two inches of me. My knees were at my chin. My butt practically on the floor. Ben was clearly making an effort not to laugh.

"You can laugh," I said, feeling ridiculous but not really caring.

"It's generally frowned upon in my profession to laugh at my patients."

"I can understand that."

"Look. I can recommend another therapist for you," Ben said. "There are several therapists in Portland that-"

"No," I said cutting him off. I didn't want to go to a bigger town. I wasn't interested in another therapist. I was here, and first impression, I liked this guy.

I liked his plaid shirt and the picture of his family on the wall behind his desk. Plus all the diplomas. Lots of them. I liked the view out the window.

"Perhaps if you told me what made you seek out a therapist."

"I need some tools," I said. "To handle stress better so I can sleep, stuff like that."

"You want a prescription?" Ben asked, his eyes narrowed.

"No." Beside me was a little maze table and I ran a big wooden bead through a painted hedge until I got to the end. Not so hard. "You saw that video. I had a temporary lapse in my control and I need some tools to put things back together."

"You feel out of control?"

"No, not currently." Well, maybe a little. The lack of sleep was really killing me. "I just don't ever want to feel... like that...again."

"Okay, maybe you can tell me why you think you lost control in the first place."

"No idea," I said.

"None?"

That seemed irrelevant to what I needed. "Why does it matter? I'm looking for some techniques to get it back."

Ben stared at me, mouth agape for a second, and then started chuckling.

"I thought you weren't supposed to laugh at your clients," I said.

"You're not my client. I only work with kids."

I sighed. Well, I'd tried. Maybe I could take up long distance running.

"Okay. I understand." Getting out of this chair was going to be a bitch, I thought.

"However," he said. "We could keep talking. On one condition though."

"I'm not cooking for anyone these days," I said, imagining what he might want. The miso Black Cod. The root vegetable tartlet.

"No, I don't want you to cook for me," Ben said, the laughter out of his eyes. He was serious. "Look, I can't take anything seriously with you in that chair. Let's get you out of there. Do you fish?"

"No."

"Are you willing to learn?"

"I guess?"

"Wonderful." Ben stood and helped me out of my chair and opened up the door to the main office. Jessie looked up, the brief appearance of the fan girl from earlier gone. She was all business in her blue cardigan and business casual pants.

"No need to make an appointment for him, Jessie," Ben said.

"Oh, do we need a referral?" she asked and started clacking away on her keyboard.

"No. He's going to join me on the dock."

"I am?" I asked him. "Because that doesn't sound like me."

"Your choice. I'm there every morning," Ben said. "Rain or shine at six am. It's a good time to...talk. And it sounds like you just need someone to listen."

"But I have to pay you. Like, isn't that how therapy works?"

"We'll settle up later. Get some fishing gear at Mervin's Sporting Goods," Ben said. "You can tell him I sent you and he'll give you the local price not the tourist price. I'll see you in the morning if you decide to come."

"Yeah. Sure."

Ben stepped back into his office and Jessie handed me the card with the phone number for Mervin's Sporting Goods and 6 AM, written in her precise handwriting.

"Where would I even go?" I asked.

"Right out front there," she said, pointing towards the ocean. I could see a dock jutting out into the water to the right of the building. "Every morning like clockwork. You won't be able to miss him. He wears a ridiculous hat."

"I heard that!" Ben yelled through the door.

Jessie made a face and I smiled at her.

"Oh," she said. "And since you do all those food shows, you might be interested. The Falafel Lady is back in town."

Ben's office door immediately opened. "Birdie is back?" he asked eyes wide, and Jessie nodded.

"Hot damn," Ben said. "Best sandwich I've ever had. You want one?" he asked Jessie, patting down his pants for his wallet.

"Sure. Extra sauce."

"It's ten am," I said as Ben started making his way to the door. "You're going now?"

"She sells out. Or she did when she was here a few years ago. You've got to line up early and it's worth it. Trust me."

Ben was out the door and Jessie went back to her business, which was my signal to leave. I put on my hat and sunglasses and got in my car.

I drove by the square and spotted the sporting goods store. Across from that I saw an old blue food truck with a bright yellow awning. Birdie's, it said along the side. With a very cute yellow bird painted below it. And there was indeed a line at ten AM in the morning.

Interesting, I thought, and kept on driving.

Four Hours Later

I DROVE up to the food truck, the afternoon being a far more appropriate time for a falafel sandwich. Only to find the place devoid of customers. The awning was closed and the chalk board next to the truck read *Sorry! Sold Out.*

The Next Day

I HAD JUST PARKED my Land Rover and could see a queue in front of the truck. Perfect. The Falafel Lady was still serving.

Only the second I stepped up behind the last person in line the yellow awning started to close.

"Sorry everyone! Sold out for the day," a feminine voice shouted from inside the truck. I was too far back to see her, she was just a shadow behind the awning.

Annoyed, I walked back to my truck.

What did it take to get a damn falafel in this town?

3

The Next Day
Antony

This was madness. In my life I'd never experienced anything as frustrating. Was it audacity or incompetence? I didn't know what to make of it. Nothing had ever gotten under my skin so quickly.

An irritant I couldn't scratch or smooth away.

Birdie's Falafel Truck.

"Sorry everyone," the woman called from under the hood of the food truck. "Sold out again today."

The line in front of me groaned.

"We'll just have to try again tomorrow," Ani Wong, who was standing in front of me in line, said with a deep shrug of her shoulders.

"This is unacceptable," I countered. "This is the third day in a row this has happened. There is a line around the block for this damn truck and she runs out. Again?"

"Wow. You're really hot for her balls aren't you?" Ani asked me, then snickered like a 6 year old.

I could feel the heat under my skin start to prickle, my cheeks flush.

I had a flawless diet, exercised regularly and only drank wine when paired exquisitely with a dish. My doctor in LA said the source of my high blood pressure came mostly from stress and an inability to deal with it properly.

Why was I letting a food truck stress me out?

I smiled at Ani, in on the joke, but what once came so easy to me, being charming and flirty, was suddenly hard. These days everything was under my skin or on my nerves. I'd been in control for over seventeen years. Now I felt like I was barely holding on. I wasn't getting better, I was getting worse.

Maybe it was time to take Ben up on his offer. I hadn't yet met him for fishing, because quite frankly I thought the whole idea was nonsense. All I needed were some damn techniques to handle my stress.

Stress that I now blamed on the Falafel Lady, a woman named Birdie, and her inability to plan. Also Ani... for making a bad balls joke.

I hated this feeling. Hated being irritated and annoyed. I hated that there was a problem I couldn't fix.

Or could I?

Maybe Birdie with the amazing sandwiches just needed some professional help. Some advice related to kitchen prep and planning.

Immediately I was calmer.

In control.

"Excuse me," I said as the line began to disperse, and I made my way closer to the open side of the truck.

I'd only seen glimpses of the woman working inside the

food truck because I'd never gotten close enough to the front of the line to actually order. I'd heard rumors of course.

Birdie, if the locals could be believed, was beautiful.

As I approached, I noticed her dark wavy hair that fell around her shoulders. She wore a bright pink kerchief on her head to keep it out of her face.

A face that was...okay, the locals were right.

Birdie was a goddamn knock-out. High cheekbones, a big wide mouth. She was young, in her twenties, which no doubt explained some of these novice mistakes she was making.

Her bright apron was tied around a trim waist. The apron had one of those script sayings splayed across her chest that read *Always Wear Protection*.

Wait. Was that a sex and food joke?

"Excuse me," I said as she wiped down the stainless-steel service counter where she served up the food and took everyone's money.

She looked at me and then did a double take. I assumed I'd been recognized, but then her expression went blank and she said, "Oh, hi, there. You're new in town."

So she didn't recognize me. That was good. Anonymity was preferred.

However, I was also simultaneously a little irritated. I had been a judge in season five of *Food Truck Wars*. One would think she would be a fan.

"You know everyone in town already?" I asked.

"I've been here before," she said with a smile. "And it's a small place."

"I could be a tourist."

She narrowed her eyes at me. "You don't look like you're here to relax."

Something hot ran over my scalp. I didn't exactly love that she saw me so clearly. "Well, I've heard so much about your sandwiches I've been excited to try one."

She offered me a sympathetic expression. "Oh, I'm sorry. Maybe you didn't hear from the back of the line, but I'm sold out."

"No, I heard you. Just like I have for the last few days. Why aren't you making more food?"

She seemed taken aback by my tone. Did I sound too harsh? I smiled. She frowned.

"I don't believe in food waste, so I'm careful to only make what I know I can sell."

"Yes, but you've turned away customers for three days in a row now. Which means you can sell more than you're making."

She blinked and I thought her eyes were pretty, too. The color of sugar as it caramelized, right before it burned.

Jeez, Antony, get it together. You're here for falafels not...eye metaphors.

"I'm happy people seem to be enjoying them, but I'm a one woman shop, so..." she shrugged like that was my cue to leave, to let her clean up and close the truck and go back to wherever Birdie's Falafel Food Truck took up residence each night.

Only I couldn't let it go.

I smiled harder. She frowned more.

"You had at least seven people in line who didn't get served. For three days in a row. At minimum that is twenty-one more sandwiches, which by your price point..." I did the quick math. Actually, she could be charging more. Maybe I'd tell her that later. "Is more money in your pocket. Buy more ingredients, make more falafel and sell it. It's simple economics. Running a business 101."

One side of her mouth kicked up and revealed a dimple. Fuck me. Beautiful and dimples?

"Oooohhhh. I see." She was wide-eyed and sarcastic. "Well, thank you for mansplaining how to run a business. Look mister, I make what I make. I make sure I sell out every day, and yes, maybe that creates a little buzz and interest that has people lining up the next day too. Which makes me profitable. I'm pretty sure that's what *running a business* is all about. See you tomorrow. Or not."

With that, she stepped back inside the body of the truck, hit a switch off to her right and the awning on the service side of the truck started to close. I bent down as it slowly descended so I could still see her.

"Yes, but you could be making *more* money," I said, as I tried to maintain eye contact with the very beautiful falafel lady. Like I wasn't quite ready to let go of the sight of her.

"My business, my choice, buddy."

The canopy fully closed and after several minutes of me just standing there looking at the bolted up truck, the engine started and Birdie's Falafel Food Truck drove away.

∼

Birdie

Oh. My. God!

That was Antony Renard! The *Antony Renard*.

I drove out of town to the turn off for Aunt Za's trailer, and stopped on the side of the road. My hands were shaking at little.

Because I didn't like confrontations with know-it-all men who happened to be extremely famous chefs?

Or because his eyes were actually as blue as they seemed on TV and book covers?

No, nope. I wasn't thinking about his ridiculously blue eyes. Or the scruff on his super chiseled jaw.

Or his wide shoulders. Had I known he was that tall? It was always hard to tell when watching someone on television.

Not that I watched him a lot.

Okay, maybe I'd seen him on everything he'd ever been on since watching him as a judge on *Food Truck Wars*.

No, no, no...no way I was indulging a TV crush.

He was a *chef*. Every chef I knew was cocky, arrogant and bossy. Clearly, he was not the exception. Forget the audacity of him telling me how to run my business after having met me for two seconds, I'd seen the video.

The very viral video of him throwing a plate at the wall as he yelled at his sous chef.

A complete and total chef meltdown that was now putting the spotlight on toxic kitchen culture run by misogynist bullies in professional restaurants.

What had been so disappointing to me was that Antony Renard had always seemed different than that. Better than that. He wasn't a chef who'd built his reputation by yelling and shouting like others had done.

Instead, he'd always come off as charming and easy going on television.

A guy you might want to have a beer with or share a bottle of fine wine.

Plus, the word around the foodie circles was that he was a great mentor. Usually very patient with new chefs who interned with him at The Robin's Egg.

So what had happened that day in the kitchen?

And what was he doing here in Calico Cove?

Was it possible he was the surprise judge for the Masters vs. Apprentice Food Truck competition?

M vs. A was a revered competition in all foodie circles because of the quality of the chefs who had competed and judged it over the years. A once every four-year event, it moved around the country. The amateurs who participated were invite only, which made it a huge honor.

It made sense that someone of Antony Renard's level might be the surprise judge.

Suddenly a new level of panic seized my insides.

He wanted my falafel sandwich!

What if it wasn't good enough? What if he found it lacking? What if he was the surprise judge and he cost me an opportunity to finally, finally prove to my father that I'd made something out of my life?

I needed a plan. Because the one thing I was sure of right now...

Antony Renard was never getting his fingers on my falafels.

∽

The Next Morning
Antony

"Hey, you made it!" Ben said as I approached with my brand-new fishing gear.

It was dawn and it was cool. Ben was indeed wearing a ridiculous hat, as promised, and an equally ridiculous vest, covered in pockets and lures and little things that looked like bugs.

I kind of wanted one.

"I don't really know what I'm doing here," I said. I only knew that I'd been irrationally mad about not getting a food truck sandwich and that didn't feel right.

"You're going to learn how to fish," Ben said with a smile.

Over the next thirty minutes, he walked me through the equipment, the purpose of each component of the fishing rod. He showed me how to cast a line and we sat on the edge of the public dock, facing a gently waving ocean.

The seagulls were not happy we were there if their squawking was to be believed.

"So, you've never fished before at all?" Ben said, like it was astounding.

"Never," I said.

"I always thought big deal chefs like you were all about the ingredients," he said.

"I am. I just don't personally feel the need to trick the ingredients to their death."

Ben laughed and recast.

"So," I said. "About those techniques I was asking about in your office. I was hoping you could give me-"

"Your dad didn't teach you to fish?" Ben asked, and I was brought up short by the question. I did not talk about my dad. Ever.

"No. He was not what you would call a fisherman."

"What would you call him?"

"An asshole."

Ben nodded. "Mine taught me to fish."

"Lucky you," I snapped, some of my frustration leaking out. Immediately, I caught myself. "I'm sorry."

"For what? Being frustrated with me? Seems reasonable. I'm a frustrating guy."

He reached into his bag and pulled out a sandwich. I recognized the wrapping from Pappas' Diner. One of the culinary mainstays in town. They did an excellent egg sandwich. My stomach growled.

"You want some?" he asked.

"No thanks."

"You'd be helping me out. I'm supposed to be cutting back. Wife has us on a diet so we can enjoy the grandkids we don't have yet."

He peeled open the sandwich and held out half. I was suddenly starving. I took it and demolished it in a few bites. Good crusty roll, fresh eggs. Plenty of butter, salty ham. Nothing wrong with that sandwich.

"You want the other half?" he asked, looking at me like I'd swallowed it whole.

"No. I'm good." I laughed.

"You not eating the way you usually eat?"

"I'm not cooking," I said, and then pulled in my empty line so I could recast. This all seemed rather pointless. Or maybe the fish off the coast of Calico Cove were just smarter than other fish.

"Why not?"

"I just don't feel like I should, you know?"

"Penance?"

"Something like that."

"You know, I dug around on you last night, and the guy who got hurt, he's made a lot of statements that he doesn't blame you. That it was just an accident."

"Nothing in a kitchen is an accident," I said, fervently. "It's in control or it's chaos and that's entirely on the chef's shoulders. I was out of control when I threw the plate. Didn't matter that I wasn't aiming at him."

Ben nodded and took a bite. A bit of egg got caught in his beard and he wiped it with a napkin.

"Why do you think you were out of control?"

"I was...stressed," I shrugged.

"Come on," Ben laughed. "I've read your bio. You've been in professional kitchens since you were seventeen. You've been under stress before. What was it about that day? That moment."

There was a man yelling in the dining room.

A glass shattered.

"Usual restaurant stuff," I said.

Ben laughed. "It's a good thing you're not an actual client," he said. "Or you'd be wasting your money and my time."

"What does that mean?"

"I think you know."

I hated his type of cryptic horseshit. This, I thought, this is why I'd never gone to therapy. But, instead of stomping off, which I was completely within my rights to do, I stayed there. And fished.

"Have you had a chance to try one of the falafels?" Ben asked after a while, like he was obviously changing the subject. "From Birdie's food truck?"

"Sore topic," I said. "She's been sold out every time I go."

"I told you," Ben said as he reeled in an empty line. "You have to go early."

"I did go early," I cried. "This is ridiculous. They can't be that good."

"They are transcendent."

I scoffed. "You know, if I want falafels, I can make falafels. I'm a Michelin starred chef."

"A Michelin starred chef who isn't cooking."

Low blow. I didn't think therapists were supposed to hit like that.

"If I paid you, would you actually treat me like a client?" I asked Ben and he laughed.

"You're not having fun?" he asked. "Because I am having the time of my life."

He started to pack up his gear.

"Wait. Where are you going?" I asked him. I didn't have a single fucking technique that I could use to help me sleep. This? Sitting here casting a fishing line was not going to help me.

"To work," Ben said. "I suggest you do the same."

"Fucking therapists," I muttered under my breath.

"I heard that!" Ben called over his shoulder, clearly not offended because he was laughing.

4

Antony

I didn't want to do it. Told myself there was no way I was going back to patronize a business that was woefully unprepared to be serving the people of Calico Cove.

My righteousness on behalf of that town, however, only lasted a few days before I caved and headed back into town.

I went early and ran into Jolie, Mal's wife and a former student, on her way to her own restaurant, eating one of Birdie's sandwiches.

"Hey!" she said, wiping her mouth. "You gonna get a falafel?"

"I don't know," I lied, looking over at the side of the square where the food truck was parked. "I've heard they're not bad."

"Not bad? They're amazing. Fresh. She uses local ingredients. She's got two absolutely killer sauces. One a tahini thing, and one a spicy zhoug. It's an inspiration, chef."

An inspiration? From another chef. High praise indeed.

Which is how I found myself in line again, already slightly annoyed based on my previous encounter with the woman I could only assume was Birdie.

A ridiculous name for a woman if there ever was one.

Except…it was kind of cute. The truck was cute too. A first-generation food truck. They'd gotten sleeker and more sophisticated since the food truck craze swept the country. But hers had a real vintage vibe. I wondered what made her decide on falafels. And if she went Egyptian or Israeli with her flavor profile.

One, two, three…eight.

There were eight people in front of me. It was twelve o'clock on the dot. There was no way she was going to run out before she got to me. I was finally going to have some damn life-changing falafels.

Which, at this point, had been built up so much they could only be disappointing, right? I'd had the best foods made by the finest chefs the world could offer. This little food truck seemed an unlikely life-changer.

However, I was keeping an open mind.

Bull shit, I heard Ben say in my head.

"Oh my gosh, everyone, I'm so sorry, but I can't serve these today." I couldn't see her from where I stood in line, but that was Birdie's voice from under her awning.

"Oh no, what's the matter Birdie?" This from a man up front wearing an orange construction vest.

"They're just not that good today, Bert. Something is off with the fryer and the oil is not getting hot enough. They're a smidge greasy and I won't be caught selling greasy falafels.

If everyone wants to come back around later, I'll see if I can fix the fryer and start a new batch."

What? I swear I could see black dots in front of my eyes. I'd been on this line for the last fifteen minutes. I was guaranteed, by volume of customers, falafels today and yet again, I was going to be refused.

I heard a lot of people in front of me saying, *that's okay* and *keep up your standards* and *we'll be back*.

No, no and no. It wasn't okay. The standard should be met from the door and I wasn't coming back.

I had many, many things to do today.

You literally have nothing to do today.

I squashed the sound of Ben's voice in my head. There was laundry folding. I needed more peanut butter from the market. There was...stuff.

By the time the crowd had dispersed, I was left fuming.

"Are you serious?" I asked as I approached the truck. Her long dark hair was pulled back in a ponytail and I watched as she tossed about ten falafels into a trash bin.

"You're back," she muttered.

"Yes, I'm back. Only to find, once again, you can't deliver the product!"

She leaned over, her elbows on the counter, chin in her hands. "Look, I'm sorry mister, they were greasy and mushy. Who wants that?"

"No one. Which is why you should test the heat of the oil with one ball. One! Did you consider how much product you just threw out Miss I-don't-like-to-waste-food? Or how many potential customers you lost by sending them away? You can't assume people will come back. In the food business, you often only get one chance to make an impression."

"Oh, here we go," she said, throwing up her hands. "I'm getting schooled again."

"I'm trying to help you!" I shouted. Why was I shouting? I shouldn't be shouting.

I smiled at her.

She frowned.

"Is everything okay here?" Bobby Tanner, the town's sheriff, strolled up to the truck with a congenial smile on his face. I didn't trust that smile. I'd played poker with him the other night at Mal's place and he'd bluffed me out of all my money.

"Hello, Bobby," I said.

"S'up Ant? What's going on Birdie?"

"Greasy falafels have disappointed this man gravely," she said with a tilt of her head in my direction.

"Oh, that sucks. But it makes sense her not wanting to serve you something that's not great," he said. "You know, with who you are and everything."

I grimaced. I had no idea if Birdie knew who I was or not. I wasn't clean-shaven and my dark blond hair was a lot messier than when I was on tv and being styled by professionals. She certainly yelled at me like she couldn't care less who I was.

Truthfully, I liked it.

It was oddly comforting.

"Who he is...is an annoying customer," she said, her lips twisted into a smirk. "Can I have him arrested for that?"

"Pretty sure there are no laws on the books for being annoying," Bobby said smiling. "But you should cut him some slack, Birdie. He's a foodie and is probably desperate to try your awesome falafels."

"Desperate seems like a reach," I muttered.

Bobby continued on; "Food is his whole life."

"Whole life?" she asked. "That sounds depressing."

"That's not true. I fish now," I said, which made no sense at all.

"Hmmm. You don't look famous," She lifted a single brow as if she was skeptical and suddenly I was annoyed all over again.

"Do famous people have a look?" I asked her.

"I don't think they're quite so... beach bummy. You know?"

"You're saying I look like a beach bum?" I asked her. I suppose I'd been called worse things.

"I'm saying you don't look famous."

"Well, I am," I said, because she'd tied me in knots. "I'm very food famous. I've had several shows on Food TV, any number of guest appearances on other shows. Not to mention, three award-winning bestselling cookbooks. Oh, and my restaurant is considered by many to be one of the best in the country."

She shrugged.

I almost laughed. Who was this woman? She taunted me into giving my resume and then dismissed it immediately. I'd be half in love, if I wasn't so infuriated with her.

"This is Antony Renard, Birdie," Bobby said. "He's like the best chef in the world."

"Country," I corrected Bobby. "Let's not get crazy. I was voted best chef in the country last year, not the world. There are so many others who are better..."

I stopped talking. My attempt at humility sounded weak to my own ears after my *I'm so famous* rant.

Besides, I had been the best. Not anymore. Now, I was a chef who wasn't cooking, yelling at a woman who was just trying to make a living.

"Hey Birdie, what was the problem with the falafels?" Bobby asked her. Then he turned to me. "Dude, these things are life changing. She's got this special sauce that takes them to the next level."

"I wouldn't know," I said obviously.

"My fryer might be on the fritz," she said, shifting a bit on her feet. "Oil's not getting hot enough."

"I suck at that kind of stuff, but I could get one of my dads to come over and look at it. They're always having to fix something at the coffee shop," Bobby said.

"It's a kitchen fryer, not a coffee maker. I'll take a look," I said grudgingly.

"Really, I don't need…" she started.

"Please," I said. "I'm a professional."

She rolled her eyes. "Oh. I didn't know I was dealing with a *professional* fryer mechanic."

"Thanks, Ant," Bobby said, slapping me on the back. "You'll get this town back in falafels in no time. See you around, Birdie."

"Later, Sheriff."

Once he left, it was just the two of us.

"You're called Ant?" she asked me.

"You're called Birdie?" I shot back.

"Fair."

"Are you going to open the back of the truck so I can look at your fryer?" I asked when she didn't move. She was staring at me with a suspicious expression which was entirely warranted given my recent behavior.

"Are you going to yell at me some more about everything *you* think I'm doing wrong?"

"I'm sorry," I said sincerely. "That was uncalled for. I've been…stressed."

I had no idea why I said that. Not the apology, that was totally warranted. But telling her I was stressed? I wanted to suck the words back into my mouth.

She pursed her lips. "You're not going to leave unless I let you inside my truck, are you?"

"Nope," I said honestly. "I'm on a mission for the town now."

"Fine."

She moved away from the canopy and then I heard the truck's back door opening.

I don't know why I hesitated. It was a food truck, not a kitchen. Still, it was the first time I'd been back inside one since I'd left The Robin's Egg. I'd avoided the one back at the house altogether.

I made peanut butter sandwiches in the living room.

Still, it was just a fryer.

It was okay. I could do this.

∾

Birdie

So. Again. Mistakes were made. I could see that. I let this little lie get away from me and now Antony Renard was on his knees in my food truck about to try and fix a fryer that wasn't even broken.

I'd made the whole thing up when I saw him standing on the line and panicked.

I couldn't risk Antony Renard eating my food, even if it was going to cost me my profit margins for the day and maybe some repeat customers.

Now he was in my truck. My tiny little truck. Taking up all the space and air.

What was wrong with me?

I've been...stressed.

Now, he was down on his stomach, the hatch on the side of the fryer open, so he could see the inner workings of my absolutely not broken fryer. Should I just come clean? Should I let him crawl around on my floor because he'd been rude?

I didn't mind the view. The guy had wide shoulders and big thighs, like in another life he was a rugby player.

"This fryer is old," he groaned. "When was the last time you replaced it?"

"That would be never," I told him, leaning against my prep counter. At least that was the truth. His legs practically hung out the truck door he was that tall.

He looked up at me. Those blue eyes were like a spear right through me.

"What?" I said, immediately defensive. "I bought the food truck four years ago, it came with a fryer. I change the oil. I say nice things to it every morning. It does the job."

"You say nice things to it?"

"Positive reinforcement. Never doubt it."

What I didn't say was that I spent way too much time alone and sometimes a girl just had to pretend an inanimate object was real so she didn't lose it all together.

"I can't do anything while the oil is still hot," he said. "Most likely if there's a problem, it's the heating coils. Replace those and you might get another few months out of it."

He got to his feet and dusted off his hands. He absolutely filled the back of this truck. Like it was suddenly crowded with the two of us and all my equipment.

"Well, thanks," I said. "I can take it from here."

"I'll wait. Just to make sure I'm right."

"Wait? Here? With me?"

"Sure." He said, like I'd invited him. He wore a pair of

black joggers, running shoes and a fleece sweatshirt. While I watched, he peeled the fleece off and tied it around his waist, revealing a grey tee shirt and that slice of stomach that I had no business seeing.

That was Antony Renard's stomach. I saw it. I couldn't unsee it. It was muscled. And a little furry. I wanted to lift the rest of his shirt up and see what else he was hiding under there.

"You've got a great set up," he said, looking around.

I suddenly wanted to throw myself across my truck like I could protect my tender little baby from his judgement.

"Thanks," I said, waiting for the criticism.

"Seriously," he smiled at me. "It's organized. Really clean."

He undid one of the latches holding a drawer shut. Pulled out the drawer revealing my knives in their sharpening slots. He grunted, shut the drawer and locked it back up.

"I ah...thanks."

"You do a sandwich and bowls, I take it?" He lifted the small little cardboard boat I used for people who didn't want a pita.

"Yes."

"Smart."

"I thought so."

He opened my fridge. All my containers holding my mise en place. He pulled out my tomatoes and sniffed them.

"All right," I said. "Okay. That's... you don't need to sniff everything. It's fresh."

"Yeah," he said. "It smells great in here."

"Why are you acting so strange?" I finally asked him.

"Am I?"

"Yeah. Like you haven't been in a kitchen in ages."

"I guess because I haven't been in a kitchen in ages."

"Why-?"

"Do you think the oil has cooled enough?"

"You know, I really do have it from here," I told him. "Thanks for the help."

"Why do I get the impression you're done with me?" his smile was stupidly charming.

Because I saw your stomach and you're so tall and you're Antony Renard and I'm lying to you.

"What are you even doing here?" I asked abruptly.

"In your truck or in this town?"

"I know what you're doing in my truck. You've got an irrational craving for falafels. What are you doing in Calico Cove?"

"My best friend lives here. What are *you* doing here?"

"Huh, so you're not here for the-"

"Helloooo Darling!" I heard my aunt calling to me from outside.

I leaned out over the counter where the canopy was still open. "Hi, Aunt Za."

"I had a premonition something awful was happening to you, so I had to race over from my table to check on you. Is everything okay?"

She had her Madame Za costume on. The scarves, the jewelry. The oddly unplaceable accent. She was half full of shit, half the real deal and I just loved her silly.

"You were right," I told her, looking over my shoulder at Antony. "Something horrible did happen."

"Are you referring to me?" he asked.

Aunt Za peeked inside the truck. "Who is that inside there with you... Oh! Chef Renard! I see you've heard about my niece's fabulous falafels. They're famous in these parts."

"I've *heard* about them," he muttered so only I could hear.

"And I'm sure she's told you about being invited to the Masters vs. Apprentice Food Truck Competition. She'll be competing in the vegetarian category!"

I winced.

"Masters vs. Apprentice?" he asked.

I could hear the surprise in his voice and I had no choice but to turn around. The jig was definitely going to be up.

"Yes, you have something to say about that?" My chin naturally lifted a few degrees.

"That's a huge honor. Amateur chefs are invite only."

I shrugged. "I guess I got lucky."

"That's not luck, that's talent," he said.

My needy little heart fluttered at the praise.

"Someone at that level..." his voice trailed off. Then his eyes narrowed on me. "Someone at that level...would know who I am."

"Of course she knows who you are," my Aunt Za said from the outside of the truck. "You're Antony Renard. Birdie knows everyone in the food industry, which only makes sense because she's-"

"A food truck person," I said, cutting my aunt off. Antony Renard didn't need to know everything about me. "Aunt Za, don't you have fortunes to tell?"

"Yes, I really must be getting back," she said, with a twinkle in her eyes. "Enjoy my niece's cooking, Chef. Everything she makes, she makes with love. Ta!"

He folded his arms over that ridiculously broad chest and I had to work not to think about his naked stomach.

"You knew who I was this whole time?" he demanded to know.

"Maybe?" I said with a shrug of my shoulders and a hint of a smirk. He really was full of himself.

"Beach bummy my ass. And your fryer?"

"Perfectly fine," I admitted. Then confessed to everything. "I thought you might be the surprise judge at the competition in a few weeks and I didn't want you judging my food in advance. I'm still working on some of the recipes. This might come as a surprise to you, but some of us, mainly me, have a more fragile ego than others."

"Fair enough," he snorted. Then he said, "I'm not judging Masters vs. Apprentice."

"Oh. I thought...maybe that's why you were here. It's in Portland, Maine, this year."

He nodded slowly as if that made sense, then looked away. When he looked back I could see something serious in his eyes. "You saw the video?"

I didn't want to lie again, so I nodded. "I guess that's what you're...stressed out about?"

"I'm here to lay low. Regroup. Get control of...things."

"Makes sense."

"I'm not..." he began, then stopped. "I'm not...that guy. In the video."

"Okay," I said.

"Okay," he sighed. Like that was that. Then he clapped his hands together. "So let's turn on that fryer and make me some falafels."

"Uh, hard no."

"Why not?" he asked, clearly exacerbated.

"Because it's like you said, I have to make a new batch, test the oil. I'm not giving *you* anything until I know it's my best."

"We are talking some seriously delayed falafel gratification," he grumbled.

"Sorry, Chef," I told him. "I refuse to compromise."

"Fine," he huffed and hopped out of the back of the truck. "I may, or may *not*, be back."

"Fine," I said, folding my arms over my chest, watching him leave. I told myself I hoped he didn't come back. My nerves couldn't handle any more run-ins with Antony Renard.

Still, weirdly, it felt like something was suddenly missing from the truck.

Like a tall, bossy chef with intense energy.

I flipped on my perfectly fine fryer.

5

Later That Night
Birdie

"So, Antony Renard," my aunt said as I passed her the bowl of peas across the tiny table in her trailer.

It was only a matter of time, I thought. My aunt was both mystical and hopelessly romantic. Antony Renard was too handsome by far for her to not comment.

"Don't even go there," I told her.

I'd made us dinner, Aunt Za's favorite: peas, mashed potatoes and pan-fried pork chops. Nothing fancy. It was pure comfort food and no doubt something Antony Renard would look down upon.

Not that I was thinking about Antony Renard. At all.

Aunt Za had traded in her scarves and rings for a pair of leggings and an old University of Maine sweatshirt.

"Of course I'm going there. He's handsome. He's single. And he's rich!"

"Aunt Za, you know me. Do you honestly think I care if a man has money or not?"

"Honey, I'm not saying you do or you should. I'm only saying it's just as easy to fall in love with a rich man as it is to fall in love with a poor man."

I smiled even as I rolled my eyes at her. "Says the woman who chose never to get married."

"Because I don't believe in the institution of marriage, but love is the real magic in this world. I want that for you."

"Well, it certainly isn't going to happen with *him*," I scoffed. "Let's forget he's a chef. *A chef*," I repeated for emphasis. "He's been yelling at me for days about how I run my business. I think he's a little unhinged."

"Well, honey, the chemistry between the two of you in that truck was visible. The truck was glowing with the power of your combined auras."

It's strange but I *felt* that. I felt that more than I'd felt anything with another man...ever.

"Also he looked very good in your truck. Good enough to eat." Her eyebrows were talking dirty about Antony Renard and I couldn't help but laugh.

He did look good. God, he was tall. And fit. With those blue eyes, it really wasn't fair.

"I'm sure that guy is drowning in interested women," I said. "He doesn't need anything from me."

"I'm worried about you," Aunt Za said, and it was so startling I put down my fork.

"Worried? About me?"

"You're in the prime of your life and you're... so alone. Out there on the road with no one."

"I'm not alone. I have you. And, not to get too personal, but there have been... dalliances."

"Hook ups," she snorted. "They don't count. Are you lonely?"

Sometimes. Okay...often.

But I didn't know how any of that was changeable considering the life I'd chosen for myself. The life I'd demanded for myself. So much so that I'd left home and my father to go get it.

"Listen, don't worry about me," I said. "Antony Renard is the last man in this town I would want to have anything to do with, so you can stop with your match-making."

"Hmmm. I had a premonition about you, you know?"

"Do tell."

"You're about to fall hopelessly in love with a stranger."

I rolled my eyes. "Maybe I'll adopt one of the stray cats in town."

"You'll see," Aunt Za said. "I'm never wrong. Well, mostly never wrong. Okay, fine. I'm only right sometimes, but this time I'm positive."

∽

The Next Day
Antony

"When are you coming back?"

I was sitting at my kitchen island, computer open, staring into the face of my restaurant manager, Venetia, on a Zoom call.

"I don't know that it's time," I said.

"Antony, you're the executive chef and owner of The Robin's Egg. This is where you belong. You've apologized, banished yourself for weeks. I think we can say your prison sentence is over."

"Actually, no one can say that because I wasn't charged with assault, so I received no actual punishment."

Only my own.

"Craig is completely fine. He's back on the line as your saucier. If he's over it you should be too."

"He's not the one who lost control. I'm not ready to go back," I told her honestly. Until I had things back under control. Which at the rate Ben and I were going with our morning meet ups...wasn't happening soon.

"I just don't know how much longer this can go on, Antony. Pretending like we're still the best restaurant in the country when you're not in the kitchen. You know those Michelin reviewers. They'll come back around like vultures once they hear you're not the one overseeing the execution of the menu."

"Vee," I said. "Come on. Between the book tours, and travel shows, and guest appearances on Food TV, I was out of the kitchen more than I was in it. You're doing a great job running things. Rinaldo is an amazing head chef. It's going to be fine. My presence back there now would only stir up trouble. I'm sure of it."

"Are you at least...?" her voice trailed off and she looked away from the camera.

"At least what?"

"Doing something to get better."

"I'm fishing," I told her.

She made a face. "Is that working?"

"Not really. But between fishing and poker, I'm learning a great deal about humility."

I hit the leave button on the screen and ended the call. Talking to my restaurant manager made me think of all the other loose ends that were out there. My half-finished cook book. The new food/travel show idea my agent, Melanie, was negotiating with Netflix.

All of it was still out there, but I didn't want to deal with any of it. Instead, I wanted to head into town and find a way to convince Birdie to give me one of her falafel sandwiches.

You're thinking about her too much.

That was certainly the truth. There was something about being driven crazy by her that I found...cathartic. I stayed away for three days. Three rainy, miserable days. Just to make a point.

I'd been denied falafels, lied to, told I looked like a bum...I should have absolutely nothing to do with her and her food truck.

Except...

I wanted to see Birdie. I wanted to argue with her. I wanted to be challenged by her. There was simply no stopping it.

I grabbed my keys and headed down the mountain to Calico Cove.

By the time I got to town it was almost one-thirty. Given the history, I knew I was risking her not having any inventory left.

I won't get in line. I'll just drive by. See if the place is still open.

I pulled my Range Rover into one of the diagonal parking spots around the town square which gave a person access to all the shops and stores downtown. Come summer, I was told this place would be packed, parking at a premium, but for now at least it was only the locals living their lives.

The truck was there. The side canopy still open. Two people appeared to be getting their food. Unless those were the last falafels of the day, I was finally going to get some. I got out of the Rover, hit the lock and jogged over to the truck, avoiding the giant puddles in the mud. I forced myself to slow down when I was a few feet away.

Running? For falafels? Come on, Antony.

"Oh, so glad you like them! Come again," Birdie was saying as she handed over a cardboard box. She really had an amazing smile.

"How long are you staying in town this time, Birdie?" One of the guys asked, looking at her like she was the sunrise.

"Just until the big competition," she told him. "You know me. Always have to be moving."

I stepped up behind the two departing men and as soon as she saw me that smile fell right off her face. Replaced by a frown. I felt a sizzle in the air when I was around her. All my senses woke up.

My smile in return could not have been more genuine.

"Do not tell me you sold your last remaining falafel," I warned her.

"I did not. In fact I've made sure to have a safety supply these last few days in case you showed up. Which you didn't, by the way."

"You missed me?"

"Like a toothache."

"No problems with your perfectly working fryer, I take it?"

"The oil is piping hot."

"How often do you change it?" I asked.

She lifted a brow.

"Shop talk," I held my hands up in surrender. "I can't help it. What do you want me to do? Talk about the lousy weather?"

"Do you walk into every place you eat around here and ask them questions like that?"

"As a matter of fact, yes. It's part of my charm."

She hummed, unimpressed.

"Tell me about your set up?" I said.

"You are not interested in food truck set up." Her skepticism was sharp as a knife.

"I'm curious by nature," I said. "Do you sleep in it?"

"Only when I have to."

"Do you do festivals as well as competitions?"

She nodded "State and county fairs too, if I remember to apply."

"The money?"

"Getting a little personal, aren't you chef?"

"Don't tell me you're just in it for the love of falafel."

"What would be wrong with that?" she asked, and instantly I knew I'd pushed a button. A Birdie Button.

"Am I rich? No. Am I loving this free lifestyle? Yes." she continued. "I love being my own boss. Low overhead, no employees I need to worry about. It's just me and what I can make and where I'm going next."

"You make it sound...romantic."

And a little lonely, I thought.

"Yes, it's very romantic!" Then she winced. "Well, until Old Blue breaks down on some dark road in the middle of Wisconsin."

"Old Blue?"

"Everyone deserves a loving nickname," she said, as if that made all the sense in the world.

"You talk to your truck too, don't you?" I asked.

"Doesn't everybody?" she asked, like I was the crazy one.

"Okay. Where's your favorite place?" I asked.

I'd travelled, but not like she had. My kind of traveling

barely gave me a chance to absorb anything. Learn anything. I was always in and out. There and gone. Back to The Robin's Egg before anyone could miss me.

This was my longest absence from the restaurant in, well…ever.

"It's hard to beat Calico Cove," she said with a sigh. "It's got all the things I like."

"Asshole chefs?"

"You are what I'm going to call a bonus. No. It's got the sea. Good people." She smiled at someone coming up behind me. "Handsome men who love my food."

"I do indeed," Levi O'Rourke was standing behind me.

Levi was undeniably handsome. He carried himself like a man who had been around the world a time or two and had some stories that would turn your hair grey. He was quiet and intense, and he, like Bobby, absolutely loved taking my money at poker. It was like my not knowing how to play poker was an affront to him.

"Birdie, your falafels make me feel like I'm back in Lebanon. But I'm here in an official capacity today." He held up his fancy camera. "Jonas down at the paper was hoping I could take a picture of Birdie's for the front page."

"Slow news week," Birdie joked.

Levi was a Pulitzer Prize winning journalist in town doing something out at the bird colony. In his spare time, he'd mentioned doing pro bono work for the paper and the Mayor's office.

"I think you're the most exciting thing that's happened to Calico Cove this week," he said. If I wasn't mistaken, he was flirting. Fucking Levi.

He lifted his camera. "Smile," he said. "The sun is hitting-"

"No, actually," Birdie said, her hand up. "No pictures please."

"Why?" Levi and I said at the same time.

"It's great publicity," I said.

"The light is really amazing right now," Levi told her. "Between your hair, the blue truck and yellow awning, it will frame really well. A compliment to your beauty."

Cool it, Casanova.

"Call me camera shy," she said.

"You sure?" Levi asked, and Birdie nodded. "All right. I guess I'll go find another cat to put on the front page." Levi walked off and I stared at Birdie.

"A business that doesn't want free press?"

"Word of mouth is giving me all the business I can handle," she said.

"Hell of a way to grow a business."

"I don't need to grow," she said, the steel back in her voice. I backed off. Even though she was clearly making a mistake.

"So, you're a falafel making gypsy. Is that why people call you Birdie? Because you like to fly away?"

She laughed, and the sound was rich and dark like chocolate. "People call me Birdie because my actual name is too much of a mouthful."

I raised an eyebrow, my question obvious.

"Genevieve," she said. "Named after my aunt, who, coincidently also doesn't go by that name. When I was little she told my mother she couldn't call me by *her* name. Something about the spirits not liking it. Hence, Birdie."

"Genevieve is beautiful," I said.

"I'm told my grandmother loved French romance novels." She smiled wistfully as if she was imagining an older woman tucked in a corner of a grand chateau with tea and a romance book. There was something there, in her expression.

Longing. I recognized it immediately because I felt it too sometimes.

But longing for what?

"Oh, and every other day," she said.

I blinked. "I'm sorry?"

"That's how often I change the oil. Every other day. Now do you want some of my falafels, or what?"

Or what? That was a question I could spend days thinking about.

"I want your falafels," I said carefully.

She took a breath as if she was summoning her courage. "Coming right up."

6

Birdie

I can do this. I do this every day for lots of people. This is my job, my livelihood and I am successful at it. I am not going to let some hot shot chef make me...or my falafels...feel inferior.

"Can I watch?" he asked, leaning further into the truck.

"No!" I shouted.

He frowned. "What's the big deal?"

"Can you just stand there like a normal customer?"

I dropped the balls into the fryer and watched them sizzle. In the meantime I cut open a pita, stuffed it with my home-made pickled onions, cabbage salad, Israeli salad and a healthy dose of my tahini dressing.

"Hot?" I asked him.

"Of course."

I gave him tons of zhoug, my spicy herby green sauce.

Taking the fryer bin out of the oil, I let the balls rest for a few seconds before stuffing three in the sandwich. I tucked in the bottom end, wrapped it in wax paper, twisting the bottom. I wrapped the whole thing in brown paper and with a couple of napkins, handed him my signature sandwich.

"My treat," I said, when he reached for his back pocket. "For the fryer help."

"You didn't need my help."

"Than an apology?"

"For lying about the fryer?"

"No, mostly for the names I've been calling you in my head."

He smiled at me. God, he really did use that thing like a weapon. A woman had to be careful around it. Then he took the sandwich and started to walk away.

Wait. What?

"Hey," I called after him. "Where are you going?"

"Well, I was going back to my car, but the sun is coming out and it's turning into a beautiful day so I think I'll go sit on that bench."

He pointed to a bench in the park that sat in the center of the town square. It was like fifty feet away. I wouldn't be able to see his expression or hear him react while he ate. Or know what he was thinking about my food.

Why do I even care?

Because he's Antony Renard and his eyes look right into your soul.

"So you're just going to eat my sandwich and not tell me what you think?" I asked, irrationally exasperated.

"I've been given the impression that's what you want from me. No opinion and silence."

Of course that's what I wanted.

What was I even thinking? I didn't want a rock star chef giving me critiques on my food. I was happy with my happy customers. But...I was so proud of that zhoug. I loved how it balanced the spice and the herbs. And the falafels were really out of this world. If he loved them, which – he would, of course he would – I would want to hear that. I would want that validation. Right?

But if he hated it? Or worse, thought it was... *fine,* or whatever. I would kind of die. It's just after all this build up, I thought there should be something. Some basic recognition that I was worth the wait.

I meant the falafels. *They* were worth the wait.

"I want your opinion only if it's good." That was honest if not a little ridiculous.

He laughed. "You know it doesn't work that way."

"Fine," I said. "Enjoy. Or don't. Whatever. Doesn't really matter to me."

"Okay then," he said and walked off to his bench.

I could see him as he sat down. Watched him lift the paper wrapper up to his nose, only to pull it away. What in the heck was he doing? If he waited too long to eat it, the falafels might cool down too much and then the sandwich wouldn't be as delicious.

"Hey there, Birdie. I'll take two sandwiches today. I'm meeting Mari for lunch."

The shock of someone standing at the truck startled me. Bobby was in his sheriff's uniform today and had a smile on his face.

"Sure, of course." I was watching Antony on that stupid bench. Still not eating the sandwich. "The bakery still busy?"

"Always, Steph and Mari are thinking of bringing on full time help."

"That's great," I said, but I wasn't really listening. I was waiting for that infuriating man to take a freaking bite.

"Everything okay, Birdie?"

"Yes. Actually no. Bobby, can you give me a second?"

"Sure. Need to make a pitstop?"

"Something like that," I said as I wiped my hands on the apron I had tied around my waist. I popped open the back of the truck and jogged over to the park.

"All your bitching and moaning about me selling out of food and now you won't even eat what I've made."

Antony looked up at me and his blue-eyed gaze almost stopped me in my tracks.

"I'm waiting until it reaches the perfect temperature," he said calmly.

"You have to eat it while it's hot," I insisted. "It tastes best when it's hot."

"Hot is not a taste," he said. "It is a temperature."

"Oh, for heaven's sake, just take a damn bite and tell me if you like it or not."

He pressed his lips together and I wasn't sure if he was frustrated with me or laughing at me. Neither option was appealing. "No. My mouth will not be compromised by your impatience."

"Fine!" I threw up my hands. "I don't even know why I care."

"Because I'm a professionally trained chef who is about to eat your food. Of course you care about my opinion. You can't help yourself."

I hated that he was right. I hated that after so many years of avoiding exactly this situation, here I was again letting a chef make me crazy. My instinct to never let him try my food had been right. I should not have wavered.

"You know what," I said, taking a stand. "I can. I can help myself. I don't have to care. Have a nice day and do us both a favor and please find another place to get your lunch."

"You know, you've got a line building up. You might not want to alienate everyone in town," he said dryly. "If you want to continue to make a living that is."

I turned and saw a few folks lined up behind Bobby, who was no doubt explaining to everyone where I'd run off to.

Shit. I had let this whole thing get out of hand.

"Are you going to take a damn bite now?"

He checked the wrapper, lifted the sandwich to his nose to inhale. "No. Another thirty seconds at least."

It was impulse. Pure unbridled impulse that made me do it. I snatched the wrapper out of his hand.

"Hey!" he shouted. "That's mine."

"No falafel for you!" I yelled back, channeling my inner Seinfeld Soup Nazi.

"You can't steal my sandwich," he said, getting to his feet.

"You didn't pay for it, so it was a gift and I'm taking it back."

"I earned that sandwich through labor," he insisted.

"You poked your head under my non-broken fryer, that doesn't count."

He took a step toward me and reached for the brown wrapper in my hand. "Give me back that sandwich."

I held my hand with the sandwich out to the side of my body and away from him. My intentions clear.

"You wouldn't," he hissed.

"Oh, wouldn't I?"

Then I did something I hated to do...waste food.

I dumped the sandwich into the grass and for good measure stepped on it with my hot pink Croc.

"I can't believe you did that," Antony said, looking down at the discarded now smashed sandwich.

I couldn't believe I'd done it either. Where had that anger come from?

A dog, who had been playing with a toddler nearby, raced over to get a sniff of what I'd destroyed.

"Tillie! Tillie! No doggy, no go." My attention switched from the angry man to the little girl who was running over after her dog. A dog who was scarfing up the smashed falafel.

"Nora, no running away from Mommy!" A very beautiful, pregnant woman waddled after the little girl, a leash dangling from her hand.

Antony scowled at her. "You shouldn't be running in your condition, Vanessa. Roy would have a fit."

She beamed. "Then let's keep this our secret. Oh no, did you drop your sandwich?" She tried to pull the dog away from what was left of the food. I hoped that spicy sauce didn't upset his stomach. The last thing this pregnant woman needed was a sick dog.

"Tillie! Bad dog," Vanessa said, leashing up the dog and giving it a tug.

Once the dog was away from the sandwich, I grabbed what was left and wrapped it up for the garbage.

"Hi, I'm Vanessa Barnes," the pregnant woman introduced herself and held out her hand. "You're Madame Za's niece, right?"

"Birdie," I said and shook her hand.

"Your name is Genevieve," Antony grumbled. "It's a perfectly good name. You should use it."

"I've heard a lot about your falafels. I'd be all over them but fried food is not agreeing with me these days." She put her hand on her stomach.

The little girl clapped her hands. "Mommy, go home?"

"Yes, we're going home. I can't risk any more dropped falafels. Tillie seems to have a taste for them."

"Well, there you have it," Antony said. "Your food is a hit. With *dogs*."

I wanted to strangle him. Instead, clamping my teeth together, I gave Vanessa a big smile and said, "I have to get back to my *paying* customers. If you'll excuse me."

By the time I made it back to the truck there were now five people in line.

Bobby gave me what I imagined to be, his concerned sheriff face. "Everything all right, Birdie?"

Tossing more balls into the fryer, I relished in the sound of them hitting the hot oil. Listening to them hiss and pop.

"Everything is brilliant, Bobby," I said, even as I was still seething inside. Mad at Antony and myself. Embarrassed. Why in the world would I let that guy get so deep under my skin? "In fact, how about a free cookie with every sandwich for making you all wait?"

Using Aunt Za's oven, I'd added some homemade chocolate chip cookies to the menu.

"No complaints from me," I heard someone behind Bobby mutter.

"I'll pass on the cookie," Bobby said, when I finally handed him his sandwich. "Mari gets jealous if I eat someone else's cookies."

I laughed and spent the rest of the afternoon decidedly not thinking about one pissed off Antony Renard. Or the way his eyes practically sparked when he hissed at me.

Nope, not thinking about that at all.

7

Later That Night
Mal's House
Antony

"I have an announcement," I said to the group assembled around Mal's fancy poker table, in his beautiful wood-paneled games room. There was a billiards table behind me. And dart boards on the wall. But no, we never played those games. It was poker and only poker. And it was time for my bi-monthly shakedown. But things were going to be different tonight.

"You're going to just hand us your money instead of pretending to play poker?" Levi asked.

"Hilarious. No. Tonight my luck is changing. I can feel it."

"Your luck won't change if you still don't know how to play poker," Mal said.

With all this free time on my hands, you'd think maybe

I'd spend less time not catching fish and more time learning the rules of poker. But no. Tonight I'd only brought two hundred dollars so I couldn't lose that much money to the group. It wasn't really about the money, more about my pride.

"Hey, Ant," Bobby said. "I was just telling the gang about your feud with Birdie."

"I do not have a feud with Genevieve."

"Who is Genevieve?" Fiona asked, not looking up from her cards.

"Birdie," I said.

"You know, Birdie," Bobby said. "She sells the falafels out of the food truck in town. I didn't know her name was Genevieve. Fancy."

Fiona looked blankly at Bobby.

"She's literally parked right outside your shop," Bobby said.

"It's wedding dress season," she said with a shake of her head. "I don't have time to look outside my shop."

Around the poker table tonight was Mal, Bobby, Fiona, who owned the dress shop in town, Matthew, the park ranger and ferry captain for the bird preserve on the small island just off the coast of Calico Cove, and Levi.

Roy, one of the local lobstermen who sometimes played, was home with his pregnant wife, Vanessa.

I sat down and handed Mal a hundred-dollar bill. He passed me back a series of chips and I walked myself through what each color was worth.

"Why would anyone want to piss off Birdie?" Matt asked as he dealt out the cards. "I'm addicted to those sandwiches."

I still would not know.

"Well, Ant did something big to piss her off because she

snatched back her sandwich and fed it to a dog. No falafel for you!" Bobby repeated, laughing.

I raised an eyebrow. "Heard that, did you?"

"The whole town heard it," Bobby chortled.

When Matt dealt out the second card, I checked them both.

Shit. Pocket eights. This meant I actually had to play the hand. I preferred it when I could just fold and watch everyone else play.

The truth was, I didn't care much for gambling. There were too many elements that were out of my control in a game of cards. Not knowing what cards people were holding, but also the people themselves. If they were feeling lucky? Reckless? I didn't know their tells or their habits. There were just too many variables I couldn't manage.

There was no way for me to predict an outcome.

"I call," I said, limping into the pot.

"Her sandwiches are great. And she's pretty terrific." Levi tossed his chips into the pot with a flick of his wrist that annoyed me. "Funny, smart. Easy on the eyes."

"Interesting," Mal said, still looking at his cards behind his hands. "Thinking of pursuing something there, Levi?"

"Don't bother," Matt said. "Birdie comes and goes as she pleases, but she never stays for long."

"Well maybe Levi is looking for something short term," Bobby said.

"I'm pretty sure she's not," I stated.

Matt dealt the flop, three more cards in the center of the table, and I checked it. A jack of diamonds, a six of hearts and a two of spades.

I squirmed in my seat and was grateful someone else had to act first.

"All I said was that Birdie is great," Levi said.

And that she was funny and smart and easy on the eyes. You're not fooling me, Levi.

"Really, as adults, shouldn't we be using her actual name?" I said.

"Bet's to you, Ant," Bobby said. "Two bucks."

I put my chips in without thinking.

Matt turned to me. "She told you her name, huh? Are you feuding or flirting?"

"You're the expert Matt," Mal drawled. "You and Carrie Piedmont have taken feuding to all new levels."

Matt snorted. "Carrie and I aren't feuding. We mutually loathe one another. That's entirely different."

"Why do you loathe each other?" I asked, and the whole room turned to stare at me. The temperature dropped a few degrees. I looked around from person to person. Mal was waving his hand across his neck, telling me to drop it.

"Speaking of," Fiona said, smoothly changing the subject. "Did they find a new lead to play the romantic hero opposite of Carrie? It would be a shame if the whole film fell apart because of one asshole actor."

"Last I heard, it's been recast. No official announcement," Bobby said. "But they're calling the cast and crew back, which is great news for Calico Cove."

"Is that true?" Matt asked. "Carrie's...I mean...the entire cast is coming back?"

Bobby nodded.

Matt dealt the turn card. The eight of spades.

Shit. That meant I had trips. Which meant I was probably in the lead. Which meant I had to raise.

"Let's get back to Levi's love interest," Mal said dryly. "There is a beautiful single woman in town, and if I'm not mistaken, you Levi are also single-"

"No," he said.

"You're not single?" Mal asked.

"I'm not really looking for...anything."

I swallowed down that knot of anger that had been sitting in the back of my throat. I did not want to think too hard about why I didn't like Levi being interested in Genevieve.

"What about you Matt? Someone should pull you out of your hardcore bachelor ways," Mal said. "You're practically feral on that ferry."

"My life is exactly how I like it," Matt said, and he left it at that.

"Raise," Fiona announced and pushed in five dollars.

It was a bluff. It had to be a bluff. If she had something she would have bet after the flop. There is no way the turn helped her.

"I call," I said, and pushed five dollars' worth of chips into the pot.

"Besides, I've seen Antony and Birdie in action, and if I was a betting man," Levi said. "I'd say what's going on between the two of them is definitely more flirting than feuding."

"Well," I said. "You'd be wrong."

But would he? Flirting in my experience was long looks, quiet conversation, glancing touches. I don't recall flirting ever involving smashed sandwiches and yelling.

Matt dealt the river. A three of hearts.

Wait? Was I actually going to win this hand?

It would be my first.

"Who is to say she'd have any of you?" Fiona said.

"Fair enough," Levi said.

Levi and I were in agreement about that. I was in absolutely no place to even think about dating anyone.

I was trying to pull the threads of my life back together.

But I could not argue that there was something about Genevieve. Arguing with her made me feel more alive than I'd felt in ages. She reminded me that there was something more than work.

Was all this energy between us actually flirting?

Fiona raised five dollars again. This was it. The moment of truth. It was time to put to the test what I'd been learning this past month.

"All in," I announced boldly. With a hefty shove, I pushed my chips into the center of the table.

"Call," Fiona said, and immediately turned over a pair of pocket Jacks making her trip Jacks more significant than my lowly Eights.

"Someone tell me why I play this game again?" I asked.

"Because you need a life outside of cooking," Mal said. "Now give me your other hundred-dollar bill and you can keep playing."

I think I preferred fishing.

∽

It was hours later and everyone had gone home. I'd lost my next hundred dollars too, but fortunately much more slowly. Jolie had gone to bed an hour ago, but Mal and I were having one last nightcap before I headed back to my rental.

The truth was, I didn't like it there very much. Yes, it was beautiful, spacious, luxurious but...I don't know...pretty isolating.

Mal's home just felt warmer. Homier.

"All teasing aside," Mal said. "Are you really fighting with Birdie?"

"I don't know," I said honestly. "I don't know if we're fighting or flirting."

When I looked up from my glass of expensive whiskey, I could see Mal's concern.

"That feels like something a man should know."

"I've just never met a woman like her," I said. "She's infuriating."

"Has the great Antony Renard met his match?"

"Everyone in town is talking about her damn falafels, but every time I've tried to get one of those sandwiches, something happens."

"Hmm."

"She instigated everything that happened today. All I wanted to do was wait until the damn balls cooled down before I took a bite, and she went berserk on me."

"Well, it sounds like an easy situation to resolve," Mal said. "Just stay away from her."

Yeah. That was not an option.

"Actually, I have a plan and I need your help."

Mal raised an eyebrow that made the scar on his face more prominent. "*I* have to *do* something?"

"Yes, you're my friend and that's what friends do." At least I was fairly sure that's what friends did.

I was going to eat those falafels, or die trying.

∽

The Next Day
Birdie

"Hello Ms. Birdie," the handsome man with the dramatic scar across his face said in a deep and smooth voice. "I would like two falafel sandwiches. One is for me and the other is for my lovely wife, Jolie, whom you've met."

I knew who Mal Bettencourt was. By reputation of course.

The Beast of Calico Cove.

When he'd first moved to town Aunt Za had talked about the reclusive stranger with the disfiguring scar. She'd desperately wanted to tell his future, but he hadn't been interested in mingling with the rest of the town.

That was, until he got involved with Jolie Petit. Now they were married and living together on the property connected to the lighthouse.

I also happened to know Mal was friends with one Antony Renard.

There was no reason to be suspicious of his order. No reason to think it unusual that he should show up at my truck for the first time, after yesterday's kerfuffle with his friend.

Except for one thing.

"You said the second sandwich was for your wife?"

"Yes. She is a fan of your falafels."

"Yeah, I know that. Especially since she was here fifteen minutes ago ordering a sandwich for herself. Watched her scarf it down right in front of me too, she was that hungry."

His cheeks blushed. I knew it. The dirty bastard was lying.

"Ah. I see. Well then, I guess I'll just be getting one."

"I am very sorry to report, but we are all out today," I lied.

"Why don't I believe you?" he asked, a mischievous smile playing around his lips.

"I don't know. Why do I think I'm getting Cyrano de Bergerac'd right now?"

He considered my question. "Are you suggesting falafel by proxy?"

"That's exactly what I'm suggesting, and you can tell your *friend* the answer is definitively... no."

He tucked his hands into his jean pockets and had the decency to drop his head in shame. "Please accept my sincerest apology. This was not my idea."

"Oh, I know whose idea it was," I said. "And of course, *you* are welcome back any time. Just not with him."

"Understood."

He walked away, and since there was no line of people waiting for food, I spent the next few minutes tidying up the counter space where I assembled the sandwiches.

"Are you serious?!"

I easily recognized the voice of the man shouting outside my truck. It made my whole body tingle.

"Well, hello Chef Renard," I said, with what I could feel was a very smug smile.

He was wearing jeans and a heather gray Henley that made his eyes particularly piercing. Like White-Walker-Game-of-Thrones blue.

Should the residents of Calico Cove be worried about a zombie invasion?

"You wouldn't even have to see me eat it. Mal could have given it to me and you could have just looked the other way."

"I don't like being tricked," I said defensively.

"You were the one who went crazy on me yesterday just because I wanted to let it cool down."

I winced. That had been a slightly psycho food truck lady moment.

"You're a chef! You're going to judge my food. You can't not judge my food. All I was doing was making sure you had the best possible experience. Don't make this out to be all my fault."

"What if I just ate it and said nothing?" he offered.

I shook my head. "That would make it worse."

"Fine, I'll just eat it and say that it's delicious, no matter what."

I shook my head again. "Nope. We both agreed that's not the way it works. I'm not a charity case. It's either good or it's not, but I won't be pandered to."

He sighed and stuffed his hands in his pockets. "You're impossible."

"Some people think I'm delightful," I countered.

"Oh, trust me, you are impossible and delightful."

That was...well, it was nice. And a little confusing. I didn't want him to think I was delightful, did I? That felt...dangerous.

"How old are you?"

"Rude!" I said, taken aback by the question. "How old are you?"

"Thirty-five," he offered. "You can't be what...twenty-five, twenty-six?"

"Twenty-seven, what of it?"

He muttered something under his breath about being driven crazy by a child. That brought joy to my heart.

"Look. Let's be reasonable. You are an invitee to the M vs. A competition. That automatically means you're good. You should be confident enough in your food that anyone could eat it."

He was right. I should be that confident. Only the sad reality was, I wasn't. It was part of why I was competing in the first place. To finally prove I was worthy. To show my dad a ribbon and say, *look what I did!*

I could just cave to Antony. Only, where was the fun in that?

"That is true. But as the owner and operator of this food truck, I decide who I serve and the truth is, I don't like you very much. You're very shouty."

That shocked him into silence. Something like shame washed over his face and he nodded.

"Right," he said. "This is still about the video. I'll... ah... I'll leave you alone. Sorry to bother you."

He walked away and I didn't want him thinking that I was influenced by a story on social media. I popped out the back of the truck and jogged over to where he was crossing through the park.

"Wait!"

He turned around and stopped walking.

"I wasn't talking about the video. I know that's not your style."

"You don't know me."

"I know enough. What did happen that day?"

He looked off over my shoulder like he was replaying a song in his head.

"I lost my temper. Something I hadn't done since I was seventeen years old. It was unforgivable, but Craig, my sous chef, well, he...he was loyal. He brushed it off like it was nothing."

"If that was the case, why did you leave?" I asked him, curious despite myself.

He tucked his hands in his pockets. Watched one of the town's stray cats sun itself on the sun-warmed stone of the gazebo in the middle of the square.

"I had to suffer some kind of punishment."

"Says who? If Craig doesn't want you punished, who says you should be?"

"I do."

I crossed my arms over my chest. I was wearing my *May the Forks Be With You* apron, over a plain white t-shirt, jeans and my pink Crocs. As someone who lived on the road, I didn't invest a lot in my wardrobe, so I felt a little exposed standing in the middle of town, in my cooking gear. What I should do was go back to my truck and forget this whole conversation, except I couldn't.

Punishment. I wasn't sure why, but that resonated with me.

Immediately, I thought of my dad and then shut those thoughts down. They only ever made me sad.

"So living here in Calico Cove is your punishment?" I said. "Let me guess. You're allergic to cats."

"No. I'm in Calico Cove hiding from the press and trying to get control of myself. Not cooking is my punishment."

He was looking at me when he said it and I could see all the pain and loss in his expression.

It *was* a punishment for him. Like cutting off a hand or a foot. I was overwhelmed with a sense of sadness that made me want to touch him. Comfort him. To stop myself I clasped my hands behind my back.

"When are you going back to the restaurant?" I asked him. "When is your punishment over?"

He shook his head. "I don't know. Maybe when I can forgive myself."

Oh god. That just broke my heart.

"Antony, it was one bad day."

"That's what they say, but I know different," he said.

"You should cut yourself some slack," I said.

"Why do you care?" he asked. "You don't like me, remember?"

"Well," I said, as I started walking backwards. I did have a business to run after all. "True. But I don't *not* like you."

"Really?" He laughed. "Is that anything like, liking me?"

"I don't know," I told him, with more honesty than I'd planned.

"You know," he said with a crooked smile. "I was starting to think this thing between us was flirting."

"Flirting?" I hooted. "You and me?"

He shrugged and my stomach did a little squeeze.

"I've done plenty of flirting in my life and this, my friend, is not flirting."

"That's what I thought," he said.

"Are you going to keep trying to get your hands on my falafels?" I asked him, and maybe I was smiling, because if I was honest with myself, this was all sort of fun. Was it flirting? Battle flirting? Competitive flirting?

"Absolutely, yes."

"You're going to have to be pretty sneaky," I told him.

"Oh, I understand I have a worthy opponent."

"Good." I turned around then and jogged back to my truck.

I stopped when I saw a kid, maybe fifteen, maybe sixteen, poking his head in the back of the opened truck.

"Can I help you?"

He immediately startled and pulled away. He was in a faded maroon t-shirt that was frayed around the collar, jeans that had also seen better days and sneakers that looked tight on his feet. Like he'd outgrown them.

"No, sorry, I was just looking," he said, his eyes pinned to his feet.

"Never seen a kitchen in a truck?"

"Nope. I was just looking."

"It's okay. I'm Birdie," I said, pointing at the sign painted on the side of the truck.

"Yeah, I figured."

"Want to try a falafel?" I offered, because instinctively I knew this kid was hungry.

"What's that?"

"Basically, mashed up chickpeas with some seasoning, deep fried to make them crispy."

"Sounds gross," he said.

I shrugged. "Your loss. Can I get back to work?"

He stepped to the side and his face flushed red. "I was just looking at your truck, lady. No big deal."

"Yeah, I get it. We're cool."

I hoped we were cool. There was cash inside the truck. A broken register I stuffed cash into casually, without thinking. I brought it inside with me every night to Aunt Za's, so I could settle my receipts for the day, but I hadn't even thought about leaving the truck open while I ran after Antony.

Yes, this kid was younger than me, but he was also taller and despite how lanky he was, he was probably stronger too.

"You from around here?" I asked him.

"Just moved with my mom."

He was lying. I didn't know how I knew, but I was sure of it.

"Well, if you change your mind about wanting to try something new, stop by and I'll give you a free sample."

"Yeah, thanks."

"Hey, Birdie! Guess what time it is?"

I turned my head at the greeting and saw Mrs. Wong heading towards the truck and waved to her. We had a new game we were playing.

"Hi, Mrs. Wong! I'm guessing it's falafel time."

"You got that right," she cackled, rubbing her hands together.

When I looked back, the kid was already walking off in the direction of the park.

"Hey, you didn't tell me your name."

"Nick," he said, then stuffed his hands in his jeans.

It was strange, but he reminded me of another man who had done the same thing. Like he didn't know what to do with his hands if they weren't busy.

"See you around, Nick."

"Maybe," he grunted.

Hmm. I was going to ask my aunt if she'd heard anybody talking about a possible runaway in town. It took one to know one.

I'd been nineteen once, on my own, and so furious with my father that leaving had been my only option.

Or at least I'd thought so at the time.

I'd been alone and scared, living off beef jerky and crackers for weeks before I made my way here to Calico Cove. To Aunt Za.

Who had shown me that there was a different way to live than what my father had planned for me. I didn't have to be what he wanted me to be, what he was forcing me to be.

For the first time, I was free to explore who I was and what *I* wanted to do.

I shook off the memories and focused instead on my customers.

There was nothing gained by looking backward.

8

Later That Day
Birdie

I stepped into Pappas' Diner and smiled. This place never changed. Georgie was in the back working the grill, and Lola was running around in a t-shirt and jeans chatting with customers and filling coffee cups. The place smelled like cooked burgers and french fries and suddenly it made me feel like I was...home.

Which was strange because Calico Cove wasn't home. This was just the place I came to when I needed...Aunt Za. And people who knew me. And cats. Lots and lots of cats.

"Hey, Lola," I called out.

"Oh hey, Birdie," she said, lifting her coffee pot in a salute. "Heard you were back in town."

Lola and I didn't stay in touch when I wasn't in Calico Cove, but I liked to consider her a friend. One of those people who I might not talk to for months or years, but when I was back it was like I never left.

I saw my aunt sitting at the counter, as she preferred, and joined her there. "Hey Aunt Za, what's for dinner?"

"The meatloaf special with mashed potatoes. Don't miss it."

"Sounds awesome," I said, sitting down on the round stool next to hers.

The bell above the door announced another customer and I turned to see who it was. My jaw dropped.

"Oh my gosh," I whispered to my aunt. "Is that Carrie Piedmont?"

I didn't do much social media, but I wasn't oblivious to one of the world's more popular actresses.

"Oh yes, she's supposed to be filming a holiday romance in town, but everything was halted until they found a new lead actor. They just recast and now everyone is back."

She was followed by a local I recognized. Matt, a local parks official, who oversaw the bird reserve on Piedmont Island. He didn't look happy.

"Are you following me?" Carrie asked him as they both stepped inside the diner.

"Yeah, I've taken up stalking as a new hobby, but instead of finding someone I like, I picked the person I'm least interested in in the world to follow."

"Someday you'll drop dead and I'll come to your funeral in a red dress."

"*Moonstruck*," Matthew spat. "If you're going to insult me, can you please come up with your own lines?"

"Well, the script writers have some free time, maybe I'll see if they can put something original together."

"You do that, in the meantime, I'd like to eat in peace," he said, stepping around her.

"No one is stopping you!" she shouted at his back, then must have realized the eyes of every customer was on her.

I would have been mortified. Carrie just bowed gracefully; her dark red hair nearly as dramatic as she was.

"You're welcome everyone, for the dinner show," she proclaimed.

Then she found an empty booth and tucked inside.

"Wow, animosity much?" I said.

My aunt wiggled her eyebrows. "Well, you know what they say. Where there is heat, there is fire. Speaking of, word around town is that you and Chef Renard are setting off fireworks."

I was starting to think this thing between us was flirting.

"You know Birdie, I did see that video of him. Where he threw the plate." She put her hand on my arm, her brow wrinkled with concern. "I know I was encouraging your interest in him, but the man does seem to have a temper."

Why didn't I think that was really true?

"He's not dangerous. I'm certain of it. I think whatever happened that day goes deeper than just a pissed off chef. I mean, I've worked in enough kitchens to see how they can be. A tossed plate is nothing in that world. But I don't know, it's like he's lost his way entirely. He's not cooking. For a man like that..."

Aunt Za was looking at me strangely.

"What?"

"That's an awful lot of insight into a man to whom you're denying falafel."

I shook it off. "Not really, he's just around a lot. It doesn't matter. Hey, I want to ask you about something else. There was a kid hanging around the truck earlier today. Said he just moved here with his mom, but something feels off.

Have you seen a teenager around? Super tall and really skinny. Said his name was Nick."

She shook her head slowly. "No, but I'll keep an eye open. If he is a runaway, I'll spot him in town eventually."

"Yeah, just let me know."

I got another look from my aunt. "You can't save all the homeless teenagers, Genevieve."

"No," I sighed. "Not all of them. But if one walks across my path, then I'm going to help. Just like you helped me."

"All I did was give you a little nudge. You were ready to fly."

It hadn't felt that way at the time. It felt like for the first time someone was actually seeing me, listening to me. Helping me make decisions, instead of just handing them to me already decided.

"I don't know how many times I've thanked you over the years, but whatever it was, it wasn't enough. Being able to come back here, to this place, it's special to me Aunt Za."

She smiled and reached out to grab my hand. "You know I adore having you with me. I just wish you would finally decide this is your place and these are your people and stay."

Stay? The concept was entirely foreign to me. I needed to keep moving. Standing still just wasn't an option. There were people to meet, places to stay, experiences to have.

Staying was what my father had done. One city, New York, his whole entire life.

It was part of what made him so intractable.

"Darling, sooner or later you're going to have to stop running away from your father."

I got used to Aunt Za seemingly reading my mind a long time ago.

"I don't want to talk about dad," I said sullenly.

"And you don't think *that's* a problem?"

I rolled my eyes. "Let me know if you see a tall skinny kid around. Sandy colored hair. Sullen expression."

"I'll be on the lookout," my aunt assured me.

The bell over the door rang and my aunt turned in her stool to see who it was. It was like she personally needed to greet all visiting customers on Lola's behalf.

Meanwhile, I was studying the menu just in case there was something else besides the meatloaf special that caught my eye.

"Oh, look who it is, Chef Renard," Aunt Za said. "I guess that means Lola doesn't have an issue with feeding the man."

Instantly, my stomach did that little happy, excited curling thing it did.

Damn it. Were we flirting?

He sat down on the stool next to me. "Genevieve," he said, and I could hear the smile in his voice.

"Antony," I said back, trying to keep the smile out of mine.

"Hello, Madame Za," he said around me. "I hope it's okay I'm sitting next to you both."

"Why Chef Renard, of course, it's an open counter. Tell me, how are you feeling these days? You know a good chakra cleanse can do wonders for your spirits. Improves sleep, digestion. Temper."

He smiled politely, his cheeks flushing red. "If fishing doesn't work, I'll come see you."

"Yes, that's right. I've heard you've been fishing with Dr. Kowalski," Aunt Za said. "Have you caught anything?"

"Not even a nibble."

"He's a lovely man. A wonderful doctor. But a terrible fisherman," Aunt Za said and they both laughed.

"What kind of doctor is he?" I asked.

"Child psychiatrist," Antony said. "I didn't realize he didn't see adults until I'd made an appointment."

"Oh. So, he's your therapist?" I couldn't keep the surprise out of my voice. He really was tied in knots about what happened in that video.

"Sort of?" He smiled. "He's a friend, that's for sure."

"Hey, Antony," Lola said, as she popped back around the counter. "What can I get you?"

"Whatever your favorite is tonight," he said.

"Meatloaf special," she told him and he nodded.

"I'll have that too, Lola," I told her.

If it was good enough for a Michelin starred chef, it was good enough for me.

"Two specials coming up," she said.

Aunt Za was busy eating her dinner and all I could do was fiddle with my silverware. But I was aware of him. Physically. Where his knee was in relation to mine. Where his shoulder was. Of course we weren't touching, but I bet if I took out a ruler, he was no more than two, maybe three inches away?

So close I could smell him. No cologne. Just soap, and maybe the sea. Had he been walking along the beach?

Had he been thinking about sneaky ways he was going devise to get his hands on me... ?

I meant my falafels. Of course, that's what I meant.

"I didn't have you pegged as a fan of diner meatloaf," I said.

"What? You think I'm a food snob?"

"I know you're a food snob. You made a television show called The Food Snob."

"I hated that title. But the other one they wanted to use was The Finnicky Chef."

"Oh, that's worse."

"I know. It made me sound like a prick. Which maybe was why the whole idea was wrong. The show got cancelled after one season."

"Did you like it? Being on a show?"

"I thought it was a chance to travel and eat excellent food, and it was. I met some lovely people. But it wasn't very...romantic."

Oh. Like the way I travelled.

He smiled at me and I felt myself blushing a little. It's not every day you realize you made an impression on a world-famous chef.

"Well, get yourself a food truck," I told him. "You'll find plenty of romance."

"I like the romance right here, actually," he said. There was no mistaking his tone or the twinkle in his eyes. That was pure flirtation.

"Ha," I scoffed. "I'm sure you have all the romance you could want."

Were we speaking in code? I felt like a teenager. It was awful and wonderful all at the same time.

"Well, you'd think. But somehow I am being denied romance."

"I think you're doing it to yourself."

"Far too much these days."

I choked on my iced tea and Antony laughed and patted me on the shoulder.

"Two specials," Lola announced, saving me from some kind of awful self-combustion. She slid the plates in front of both of us.

Happy to have something to take my mind off the man sitting next to me, I unfurled my silverware from the paper napkin and took a healthy bite.

It was steaming hot and I had to keep my mouth open to let the heat out before I could swallow.

Meanwhile Antony sat still, patiently waiting for his food to cool. He'd also unraveled his silverware, napkin in his lap, fork in his right hand, knife in his left, in preparation.

Eventually, he bent down and sniffed it.

"Oh my god, you and sniffing," I muttered, because of course it annoyed me for absolutely no reason. "It's meatloaf covered in gravy. You know what it's going to smell like."

He looked at me like a professor might a student who asked a really dumb question.

"Eighty percent of what we taste is what we smell. Without smell we would only taste sweet, salt, bitter, sour and umami. With smell comes everything else. For instance, I can smell the rosemary Lola simmered in the gravy. I can smell the garlic coming off the mashed potatoes. Perfectly cooked, so as not to burn. The soy sauce, to add depth to the flavor of the meatloaf. Browned onions in butter. Now, the steam has abated, so unlike you I won't burn my mouth when I take the first bite."

He broke off a piece with his fork, brought it to his mouth, hesitated as if to savor the experience and then pushed it into his mouth and chewed.

I told myself there was absolutely nothing erotic about a man eating.

He continued to chew thoughtfully, his lips closed but still in motion, then swallowed.

"Delicious," he said.

He took another bite, this time with the mashed potatoes, and tilted his head back and closed his eyes. As if he truly was savoring, not just the food, but the experience of eating it.

This was a man in tune with his senses.

"I bet you know what you're doing in bed."

I heard the words in my head. Surely, that's where they had stayed. I wouldn't say anything like that out loud. And definitely not to *him*!

Only he was smiling smugly and my Aunt Za was chortling.

"I thought we weren't flirting?" he said, in a low voice that felt like a hand down my spine. My nipples were hard under my t-shirt. Damn the man, now his voice gave me hard nipples?

"She gets that from me, Chef Renard," Aunt Za, laughed. "The two Genevieves. We like to say things how they are and never hold back. Now I'm done my dinner and ready for my night cap. I'll see you back at the trailer, darling."

Aunt Za kissed my cheek as I nodded, still utterly mortified. Once she was gone and it was just the two of us at the counter, I had to say something.

"I...uh...I don't...I'm sorry," I sputtered. "I have no idea why I said that. Forget it. Please."

"Forgotten," he said and then went back to his meatloaf.

What in the heck was it with this guy? He was under my skin. In my head. Making me do and say crazy things.

I wasn't some silly little girl to get flustered by a dude. No matter how handsome or charming or...interesting he was.

"Why aren't you married?" I asked.

He carefully set his fork down on his plate. "I'm trying to put your question into context. Are you asking me because you've decided I am good in bed so you're surprised I'm not off somewhere making my wife very happy?"

I frowned. "No. Hate to burst your bubble buddy, but mostly I'm asking because you're old. Like you know, most-guys-are-married-at-your-age old."

"Well, that's disappointing," he said, as he wiped his hands and placed the napkin on his plate, the knife and fork perfectly situated on top. "I'm not married because I've spent my life dedicated to being the best chef I can be. That doesn't leave a lot of room for healthy relationships."

That made sense. "Do you regret that?"

He looked at me, completely serious. "I only have one regret."

I nodded, not having to ask what that was.

"What about you?" he asked. "Why aren't you married?"

"My life doesn't really work for relationships."

He nodded like he understood. "No, I imagine not. It can be lonely, chasing a dream."

I was breathless for just a moment. The way he said that. The way he understood my decisions. Even Aunt Za didn't understand me that well. It shook me.

"Let me pay for your dinner," he said as he stood and reached for the wallet in the back pocket of his jeans. "A gesture of goodwill."

"Absolutely not," I said lifting my chin. "There shall be no goodwill between enemies in battle."

He laughed. "So we're battling, are we?"

"About what I said earlier," I pushed the mashed potatoes around my plate. "It really was...uncalled for. If you had said something like that about me, it would have been really inappropriate, and I would have called you out hard for it."

"Yes, well I'm done losing my temper these days and certainly not over something that, whether you meant it as such, felt complimentary," he said with a soft smile. "Oh, and Genevieve, I want to be clear. I really like the way we battle."

∽

The Dock
6:00 am
Antony

"So," Ben said. "The whole town is talking."

We sat in our usual spot. In our usual way – not looking at each other. He'd handed me some zinc to put on my nose because the sun was coming up earlier and he was worried I was going to get a sunburn.

I dutifully put on the sunscreen. The sun was milky and the breeze was cool. A beautiful spring morning. He poured me some coffee from his thermos and I took a sip.

I was about as happy as I'd been in weeks.

"About the movie coming back?" I asked. "I heard."

"No," Ben chuckled. "About Birdie not giving you her falafels."

"Which reminds me," I said. "Could you pretend you were buying sandwiches for the office and get one for me?"

"I do not practice deception."

"Yeah," I sighed. Ben was about as straight and narrow as they got. Incorruptible. It was annoying. "I figured."

He pulled a pair of binoculars out of one of the many pouches in his chair and looked out at the ocean.

"Looking for fish we won't catch?"

"Thought I saw a whale breeching," he put the binoculars back in that pouch and picked up his reel. "It must be frustrating. Not getting what you want."

"As frustrating as fishing with you."

"I've heard about some rather heated arguments between you and the lovely Birdie," Ben said.

"The woman is a menace."

"Hum. So I frustrate you, but you haven't lost your temper with me. She frustrates you too, but you haven't lost your temper with her either. Not really."

Again, a wash of shame ran through my body. "Look, I may have raised my voice but you have to know I would never... I mean, never, do anything to hurt her. Or you. To hurt any-"

Ben lifted his hand. "That is obvious to everyone who has met you, Antony. I'm just saying, you seem to have control in other frustrating situations. So you must have some insight as to why you weren't able to control yourself that night at the restaurant."

A man yelling in the dining room.

A glass breaking.

It all seemed too ephemeral. I shook my head, recast and sipped my coffee.

"God, you are stubborn," Ben muttered. "Okay, if we're not going to talk about that night, let's talk about how you got into cooking. And don't give me that glossy shit in the bio on the website. Give me the real deal."

"The real deal?" I snorted. "I ran away from home when I was seventeen."

"Why?"

"My dad was a drunk. Mom left a few years before me and without her to kick around I became my dad's favorite punching bag."

Ben hummed the way he did sometimes, like I'd said something interesting, and we would get back to that.

"I stopped going to school. I'd never had very many friends, but the few I did have, had had enough of me sleeping on their couches and stealing their food, so after a few months I was on the street. I'd started dumpster diving at night in the alley behind this restaurant. One night the chef – Francois – caught me."

I laughed at the memory. At the time it had been terrifying. Francois was built like a boxer with giant muscled ham hands and a face only a mother could love.

"He grabbed me by the back of the shirt and I swung a fist hard enough to connect to something that hurt him. He let me go and I took off, thinking no way that guy was coming after me. But fuck if he didn't."

"He caught you?"

"Caught me and dragged me into his kitchen. I thought he was going to cut off my hand or something. Instead, he fed me. Hosed me off. Let me sleep in his office. The next morning, he woke me up with coffee and a hot homemade baguette and told me if I wanted I could have a job."

"You took it."

"Washing dishes to start and then I worked my way up to bussing tables. He started to show me stuff in the kitchen and I became his prep cook. Cutting onions, carrots, that kind of stuff. Then one morning he showed me how he made his pasta. The flour, the well for the eggs. I'd never seen eggs that yellow. He said he got them from some farm and it blew my mind."

"He sounds like a special man."

"He saved my life," I said without any hyperbole. "He gave me a future. Taught me to cook, and after the cruel chaos of my father, the controlled order of the kitchen was like heaven to me. After a few years Francois wrote me a recommendation and paid for my first year of culinary school. Told me I had to go or he'd fire me."

"It must have been hard to leave."

"Harder to leave that kitchen than it had been to run away from my dad."

"Did you ever see your father again?"

I shook my head. "No. An old neighbor knew who I was though. Reached out a couple of months ago to let me know he died."

Ben hummed again. "Do you have any feelings about that?"

"That the asshole died?" I shrugged. "Not at all."

"Do you really believe that?"

"Honestly, I haven't thought about him in years."

"But you got this news, about his death, before the whole plate throwing incident?"

"Like a month before. Look, Ben, I know you want to connect the dots," I told him. "I get that. All my unresolved feelings about my father bursting through upon learning of his death. But I had no unresolved feelings for the man. He was a drunk. He was nothing to me. I didn't give a shit about him dying."

"Okay."

We both recast.

"Hey," I said. "You mind if I borrow those binoculars for a day?"

"You going bird watching?"

"Sort of."

9

Antony

This wasn't creepy.

I had to tell myself that multiple times. Genevieve was the one who had proclaimed me an enemy on the battlefield, so I was just living up to that proclamation. A good combatant had to study their opponent. Learn about any weaknesses, so I could exploit them.

There she was, with her hair down, held back by a red plaid kerchief today. She must have an entire drawer of them.

She was smiling and greeting every customer by name, and quite frankly she took my breath away.

Except I wasn't using these binoculars to confirm she was beautiful. I already knew that. I was using these binoculars to get a better sense of how I would engage in the next battle without her knowing that's exactly what I was doing.

Yeah, okay, this was creepy.

I was about to set the binoculars down when I spotted something unnerving. Apparently, I wasn't the only one watching the food truck. A kid, a teenager, really, was standing behind a tree and was watching the truck too.

Had he also been denied falafel?

Or more likely, was he experiencing his very first crush on the beautiful food truck lady?

Hmm. A teenager might be a better proxy than Mal. She knew I was friends with Mal. She knew Mal wasn't the type to frequent crowded food trucks. Too many people for him. Yes, he'd been a terrible choice now that I thought about it.

But this kid?

I tossed the binoculars into the back seat of the car and got out. Then I carefully made my way over to where the kid was standing.

It was April, but there was still a bit of a chill in the air. However, the first thing I noticed about the kid was that he wasn't wearing any kind of coat. Just a faded maroon t-shirt. His eyes were still pinned on the truck, so he didn't see me come up from behind him.

"Hey," I said and watched his whole body flinch.

He turned around, his expression completely guilty, and I realized he was younger than I thought.

"What the fuck?" he said, once he'd recovered.

"I saw you watching the food truck," I said.

"So, it's not a fucking crime."

Hmm. The kid went right to crime.

I took another approach.

"You want to make some easy money?"

"Fuck you, asshole. I don't do that shit for money."

Another red flag. Because I knew exactly what he meant by *that shit*.

This kid was alone and he'd been propositioned by someone while living on the streets. I knew it like I knew the smell of Francois's kitchen.

"Relax, kid. I'm talking about walking over to that food truck and ordering two sandwiches."

He looked back at the truck, then at me suspiciously.

"Why?"

"See the woman in the truck?" I told him.

"Yeah."

"She won't serve me."

"Why not?"

"It's complicated, we're kind of battle flirting."

"That's not a thing."

It was, but I wasn't getting into it with the kid. "She won't serve me a falafel."

"So eat somewhere else," he said, like that was the obvious answer.

"But I want what she has," I explained.

"Why?"

I sighed. "You're full of questions, aren't you? I want what she has because everyone around me says it's awesome and I don't want to miss out."

"FOMO much?" he quipped.

"Yeah, pretty much. So how about I give you twenty bucks to go over there and get us a couple falafel sandwiches? You get to keep the change."

He was tempted. The twenty bucks meant something to him. I could see it in his eyes.

Is that what I looked like? To Francois when I was rummaging his dumpster for food?

Wary, suspicious, but also totally on edge.

"I don't think it will work," he finally said. "I told her the other day I thought falafel sounded gross."

"Falafels," I corrected him. "Everything is gross if it's not done properly."

"Not pizza."

"Fair point."

"Or tacos."

God. I could practically hear the kid's stomach growling. "Just tell her you changed your mind and you want to try them."

Again, he seemed skeptical. "Show me the cash first."

Smart businessman. I took out my wallet. "Twenty for the delivery service, another twenty for the sandwiches."

"Ten bucks a pop?" he squeaked. "For something that's not a burger?"

"Plus tip," I told him. "A stranger takes the time to make you something to eat, you tip them."

"Okay. Whatever. Twenty bucks is twenty bucks."

I put the cash in his palm and hid behind the tree as I watched him make his way toward the truck. There was no line, and I could see her lean over on the counter to chat with him.

They chatted well beyond whatever time it took the kid to order, but eventually he handed her one of the bills and she handed him a cardboard box.

Success!

I expected him to make his way back to me, but instead he tore into the box and immediately started inhaling the sandwich. He was barely chewing. The whole thing was gone in five bites.

The kid turned back to her and said something. She smiled at him and waved.

That smile. Big and wide. There was no artifice in that smile. She didn't use it to take selfies and show the world she was living her best life. That smile was a gift she gave freely.

I bet the kid's heart skipped a beat when he saw it.

Mine did.

Eventually he trotted back to where I was standing behind the tree.

He pushed the box in my direction and I took it.

"You were right about them being awesome," the kid said. "Like who even knew chickpeas could be so good? Did you know that's what they're made from? It's like a vegetable."

"A legume."

"A what?"

"A bean," I said.

The kid nodded, like he was absorbing it all.

I opened the box and peeled away the wrapper, only to find nothing. "What the fuck?"

The kid had the audacity to laugh.

"Sorry, man. She made me do it. Look at the wrapper. She said to tell you to read it."

I pulled out the brown paper wrapper and sure enough there was writing in thin black marker.

Dear Tony,

Reduced to paying off teenagers now? You're going to have to do better than that. At least something more original.

Birdie

P.S. Give Nick another twenty for doing your dirty work. I think he needs it.

I pulled out my wallet and handed the kid another twenty.

"She says you earned it," I said.

"I just told her the truth, man. That some creepy guy in the park paid me to order two sandwiches. She knew exactly who you were by the way."

I closed my eyes. Clearly, I was off my game.

"Was it that good?" I asked the kid.

"Yeah, man. It was. She said I could come back for

samples and stuff," he turned back and looked at the truck. Already there was a line of about four people waiting for her food. "And people are just handing her cash. Lots of it. No credit card machine or anything. That's so retro."

"You have a home around here, Nick?" I asked, using the name Genevieve had written in her note.

"Yeah. Sure."

"Because it's a Thursday and you're not in school."

"Just moved here," he said, shoving his hands in his jean pockets. "Mom is at the school today doing all the paperwork and shit."

I nodded. Not believing a word of it.

"Yeah, well thanks for nothing," I told him.

"That's what you get for being sneaky. You should try just being nicer to her."

I hated that he was right.

But when you were engaged in battle, being nice to your adversary wasn't exactly an option.

No, the only thing left for me to do was to pull out the big guns.

It was time to go to war.

∽

The Next Day
Birdie

IT WAS ALMOST noon and I was waiting for my typical Friday crowd of customers. Friday was a treat lunch day for the folks at town hall. At least that's what they told me last week. They called themselves the Friday Lunch Bunch, which was basically the entire administration staff. On a beautiful spring day like today, they would all take their sandwiches and drinks to the park. Maybe take a slightly longer lunch than the normal hour.

I was looking forward to their arrival when I heard a truck pull up next to mine. But not one of the local's pick-up trucks. No, another food truck.

It was shiny and silver and outclassed Old Blue by a mile. Damnit! No doubt another competitor in the M vs. A competition trying to work out their recipes.

Calico Cove was a literal cash cow, but only for one truck. No way this town could support two.

"Oh no. No, no, no," I said, even as I hopped out of my truck to assess the competition.

The truck parked and immediately the driver got out. I was about to ask him for his permit, because you needed one to set up shop in the town square, when I froze.

"No. Way."

"Yes. Way," Antony said with a smile.

"You didn't," I protested.

"I did. I borrowed it from a friend in Boston," he patted the hood of the top of the line truck. "Got here this morning. She's nice, isn't she?"

I opened my mouth, but no words came out.

"You said you weren't cooking. You said you needed to punish yourself," I reminded him.

His smile, in the middle of this suddenly smoking battlefield, was sweet. Grateful. A white flag that totally disarmed me.

"Well, I have you to thank. You got me back in the kitchen,"

"How was it?"

He looked down at his hands, spread his fingers wide. "It

was so good, Genevieve. It was like it used to be. When cooking was fun."

"I'm glad, Antony. But this is taking things a bit far, isn't it?"

"You wanted war. You got war. Food truck war."

I huffed. "All this trouble just to prove a point?"

"Well, the choice is yours, you can make me a falafel sandwich and I will get back in this beauty and drive away."

I crossed my arms over my chest. "And if I don't?"

His smile was pure evil. "Tacos. Not just any tacos. I'm doing a Maine riff on Chef Roy Choi's world famous Korean fusion tacos."

"This is not fair!" I sputtered. I stomped my foot. I had a posse of town hall staffers on their way any minute for lunch. That group alone would pay for my day.

"You said war, Genevieve. This is war."

"That's Birdie to you, buddy!"

"Time is ticking. Do I need to fire up the flat top?"

I clenched my teeth. The easy thing to do here was to cave. To recognize this whole feud we were having was ridiculous and give him a stupid sandwich and make him go away.

That's what a rational sane person would have done.

But I was my father's daughter and I was nothing if not stubborn as hell.

"You don't scare me, Renard," I said boldly. "Do your worst."

"That's Chef Renard to you, and fine. You asked for it."

I stomped my way back into my truck.

While I waited for my customers to arrive, the most delicious smells I could imagine started emanating from his truck. Garlic, ginger, sesame.

Ugh!

I watched as he put the chalk board up next to the truck listing three types of tacos. Lobster, beef and sweet potato with black beans.

That last one was particularly a low blow.

"Vegan!" I shouted at him, to where he was kneeling by the chalk board. "Seriously?! You're going to try and steal the vegans away from me too?!"

"All is fair in love and food truck war," he said, and walked the few steps between our two trucks. "You could have avoided this, Genevieve."

"You could… you could…drop dead and I'll come to your funeral in a red dress," I stole Carrie's line from the diner the other night.

"I'm sure you would look smashing in red," he said casually. "Oh look, here come all the people. Let the games begin."

I seethed inside. I wanted to break something over his stupid head. If I had plates I would be winging them at his food truck and I didn't care if anyone caught a video of it.

"Game on, Renard!"

"May the best taco win!" he shouted back. "Oh sorry, I meant best dish."

"You're going to rot in hell for this," I shouted.

"Nope. Today I'm going to rot behind this grill kicking your ass."

10

Antony

It wasn't exactly a fair fight. I was a James Beard Award Winner many times over. A Michelin starred chef. I was basically serving my version of what had become in Los Angeles the most famous tacos on the planet.

And did I mention the price?

Three tacos for five bucks. Because I wasn't in this game to make money like she was, I was here to win a battle.

The price might have been a low blow.

"Wow! Two trucks," Bobby said. "It's like Christmas all over again."

"Sheriff," Genevieve called, from behind her yellow awning. "Are you here to check his permit? Because I'm pretty sure he couldn't have gotten one in such a short amount of time."

"Tell her, Bobby."

He winced, knowing she wasn't going to like the answer. "Sorry, Birdie. He fast tracked one last night. I was staying at the station late, so I went ahead and cleared the paperwork. Guy knows what he's doing to validate a safe kitchen."

"Of course, I do," I said. "So Bobby, what is it going to be? Falafels for the fourth time this week or a trio of tacos?"

"Sorry again, Birdie. I can't pass up tacos, but Mari is taking a break to come meet me. I'll make sure she evens us out. Wouldn't want to make any enemies."

"What am I evening out?" Mari joined the melee that was the throng of people in front of the two trucks. It felt like the entire town had been alerted to the food truck scene in the square.

"Hey Babe," Bobby said and kissed Mari's cheek. "Ant's selling tacos and it's eating into Birdie's falafel business."

"Why is one of the top chefs in the country selling tacos out of a food truck?" Mari asked me.

"To piss her off," I said, pointing over at Genevieve, who was giving me a death glare I feared might actually work. She was wearing a different apron today that read *No Bitchin' in the Kitchen*. Appropriate for a day like today.

"Oh, well, in that case I'm totally team Birdie."

It continued along those lines. Men lining up for tacos and women lining up for tacos until they found out that my taco truck was really a grudge match against Genevieve. In which case they became team falafel.

Mrs. Wong being the only exception.

"Mrs. Wong! What happened to falafel time?" Genevieve called as the older woman moved to stand on my line.

"I'm sorry, Birdie, but tacos are my comfort food."

After a couple of hours though, even the women started to cave.

Because it really wasn't a fair fight. My product was new and cheap.

Plus, once the first person tried my tacos, word got out about how good they were. Everyone came out of their shops, their offices. The entire town hall administration staff wanted my tacos and I delivered.

Last night having a knife back in my hand had felt like growing back a limb.

The guilt was still there. The sickness and dread too. It had taken me about double the time to do all this prep, but I powered through it.

Because my cause was worthy.

Defeat Genevieve. Demand her submission.

The truth was, I had absolutely no idea what I would have done with all the food I'd prepped, if she had given me one of her sandwiches.

I suppose I would have had to drive out of town. Maybe as far as the state capital to sell out the product.

But she was the one who declared war, so I knew she wouldn't cave. That woman was as stubborn and fierce as they came. So, I'd bought plenty of food to make sure there would be no problem with supply and demand. However, as two o'clock in the afternoon rolled around, I was out of both lobster and beef.

"It's kind of a dick move."

I looked up and saw Nick standing by my truck. Same faded maroon t-shirt, same jeans from yesterday, I was sure.

He'd told me to be nicer. "I chose a different strategy from the one you suggested."

"Yeah, to be a dick. You know, she's over there crying."

"What?" No.

There was no crying in food truck wars.

Except...I was Tiger Woods calling out the local golf pro to play a round of eighteen holes. LeBron James playing in a pick-up basketball game down the block and choosing to dunk. I had nothing but money to burn and ego to stroke and…Birdie was trying to make a living while she prepared for the upcoming competition.

Nick was right. I'd been a dick.

But it had all been in good fun, hadn't it?

She challenged me! She was in on the joke. On the over-the-top fun of it.

Wasn't she?

I hopped out of the back of the truck and walked over to hers. She wasn't inside, I could see that quickly enough. I looked around. She couldn't have gone far. Then I saw her, walking towards the park, shoulders curled forward.

"Shit."

I jogged after her.

"Genevieve. Wait. Please stop!"

~

Birdie

See? All chefs were bullies. They couldn't help themselves. That constant drive to prove they were the best. It was the only thing that mattered to them. They'd burn down the world to feed their egos.

Of course, Antony didn't know who my father was. I purposefully hadn't told him.

He couldn't know what his obvious win today did to me.

Couldn't know how I'd always been judged against my father's food, his cooking, and been found lacking.

No, Antony couldn't know that setting up a truck beside me, watching all my customers flock to his tacos, knowing his food was *better,* was gut wrenching. Like my own worst nightmare come to life.

Sure, he knew it had to hurt in some way. My bank account at the very least. Except he didn't care because he was proving a point.

I wasn't even crying because Antony was a jerk. No, I was crying about all the shit he brought to the surface.

My dad.

Bad memories from our failed brunch a few weeks ago, to bad memories from my last year at home. From every time my dad found me on the road. This afternoon made fresh the pain of knowing I was never going to be good enough to be respected by the man with whom I shared DNA.

Who should have just loved me.

At some point after my mom died, I became a failed project to my father. Not a daughter.

The kicker – the absolute kicker was that I really missed my dad.

Knowing I had to leave had never once stopped me from loving him. Needing him.

But Dad was proud and stubborn and I was proud and stubborn, so we barely spoke. Every time we did get together and he asked me when I was going to give up this food truck business was usually my cue to storm off in a huff.

No, Antony couldn't know any of that, but he made me *feel* it. He brought it all back like a punch in the gut.

"Genevieve, wait!"

"It's Birdie," I snarled over my shoulder, even as I used

the back of my hand to wipe the tears from my cheek. My apron to clear away the snot under my nose. I was done for the day anyway.

"Fine, Birdie. Slow down."

"Go. Away!"

I could feel him coming up behind me. His hands were on my shoulders. I wanted to shrug him off, but the truth was, the weight of his big hands felt steadying.

"I'm sorry. I'm so sorry. I thought we were playing a game. That it was a joke."

I turned around and pressed my finger into his ridiculously wide, hard chest.

"A joke? My livelihood is a joke to you? The money I didn't make today because you got cute with your price point-"

"I'm sorry. You're right. I swear I didn't...I mean yes, I knew it was going to piss you off, but I didn't think it would make you cry."

I shook my head and took another pass under my eyes with my apron.

He didn't know about my hang ups. He thought we were playing at some made up feud. Which we were, but he couldn't possibly know how often I'd been beaten up in exactly this way.

He was better. Or I wasn't good enough. I wasn't sure which.

"You're a jerk!" Because really, it was all I had.

He sighed and nodded. "I am. I didn't think it through. How it might seem like I was trying to show you up. I promise, I swear down to my soul I didn't think I would make you cry."

I swallowed hard.

My feelings weren't his fault. He'd just been the trigger. Intellectually, I knew that, but I still wasn't ready to let him off the hook.

"I need to get back," I told him. "I have to clean up and close out."

"Yeah."

"You're donating any profit you made to the 7th Street Food Bank," I told him.

"Yes. Of course. I will do that."

Silently, we walked back to the trucks.

I ignored him as I stepped back into my truck and instantly knew something was off. Like my brain registered the difference even before my eyes caught up. Someone had been in my truck and something was missing.

Shit. I looked at the register. The one that never properly closed. It was empty. My entire day's earnings wiped out.

"Genevieve!" I heard Antony calling my name, but I couldn't look away from the empty register. This town seemed so safe. We were both only gone for a few minutes. It was still the middle of the afternoon.

He hopped into my truck. "Are you okay? Was someone in here?"

I turned around and saw the concern on his face.

"You too?" I asked him.

He saw me standing by the empty register and nodded. "They cleaned me out. Every dollar and a bag of tortillas, which seems odd."

"I've never had this happen before," I said lamely. Then I realized how lucky I'd really been. I was basically an open truck traveling around with tons of cash on hand. I should have had a sign painted on the side of the business that said *rob me*.

"Pretty bold too, considering the police department is across the street in town hall."

"Who do you think could have done this?"

His handsome face creased in concern.

"Unfortunately, I think I know. But instead of calling the cops on him, I just want to shake him real hard and then help him."

"Nick?"

He nodded, each of us turning and looking out at the park and the shops around the square.

"He was here today. Watching from the park," I said.

"I saw him, too."

"I figured maybe he was waiting for the line to die down so he could ask for the free samples I'd offered him the other day." I looked at Antony's face. "You don't think he just moved to town with his mother, do you?"

Antony shook his head. "No, I think he's a runaway."

We looked at each other then. Like we were sharing a secret without saying it out loud.

"Do we get Bobby?" he asked.

Every part of me rejected that idea and I thought he felt the same way too.

"No," I said. "I think we should find him. See if we can help. We get Bobby involved, he's required by law to do something that we know might not be for the best."

"Fair. Where do you think he would go?"

"Someplace where he can hunker down and eat some tortillas with cold falafels," I said grimly, looking at my empty fryer on the counter. Inspiration struck. "Hideaway Beach."

"What's that?"

"It's where all the kids go to make out in the summer. Lots of places to hide behind rocks and stuff. Walking distance if you're motivated. It's where I'd go to get away from everyone in town."

"My truck or yours?"

"Mine. I don't want to smell your stupid tacos."

"My food was delicious," Antony said, and I practically growled at him. "Fine. Your truck."

11

Birdie

"So, can I ask you a question?" he asked me. I could feel his attention like a heat lamp. I felt vulnerable, not just from the crying, but from thinking about my father. The one-two punch of it had me completely tenderized and if he went full jerk on me now, I'd probably kick him out of my truck

"You can ask, doesn't mean I'll answer," I told him.

We were heading down Beach Road toward Hideaway Beach. I wouldn't be able to get the truck that close to the water and we'd probably be stealthier on foot anyway.

"Why were you really upset about losing customers to me today? Surely, you're not the only food truck wherever you go."

"Of course not. I've been in food truck wars for the last two years. Dayton, Ohio... bloodbath. Montpelier, Vermont...like cage match fighting. Heck, I'm going to be competing against some of the best in a few weeks. Professionals and amateurs."

"Okay, then why today? What upset you so much I made you cry?"

"Because you're a jerk."

"Already established."

I lifted a shoulder. "You reminded me of my...father a little bit."

I thought about telling him who my father was, but I knew if I said his name Antony would get a little star struck. Maybe his loyalties would shift. His attention, strange as it was, would become about my father. It happened all the time.

Instead, I tried to describe what my dad was.

"He's a bit of a...bully. Always thinks he's right. Always knows better than I do. He likes to prove that every once in a while, too. Let's just say we don't have the easiest father daughter relationship."

"What about your mom? How does she fit in?"

I sighed as the sadness hit, like it always did when I thought of my mom. "We lost her when I was twelve. Cancer."

"I'm so sorry, Genevieve."

"Thank you." Because it was all anyone could say.

"I honestly thought we had the same attitude about our feud."

"We did, until we didn't. And that's on me. You didn't know. Also, I talked a lot of trash," I said, looking at him. "You were a trigger and not responsible for my feelings."

"I don't ever want to hurt your feelings," he said, and I knew that was true. I could feel it.

"I guess for a jerk, you're not a bad guy."

He grunted his reply and I pulled the truck over to the side of the road.

"We'll have to walk from here," I said.

We got out and stepped onto the beach. I pointed north where you could see the rock formations that had been worn down by the sea and wind for years.

"It's just a hunch," I pointed out. For all we knew, Nick could have stolen a car after taking our cash and was already on the highway headed out of state.

"Yeah, but a good one."

Antony walked ahead of me and picked up a piece of plastic bag that was drifting along the sand. He showed it to me. It was an empty tortilla shell bag.

I tsked. "You didn't even make your own tortillas. So lame."

"Didn't have time," he grimaced. "Still, I was good enough to beat your ass."

"Too soon!" I cried.

"I'm sorry. I can't help myself."

He winked at me and I wanted to believe it was cheesy, but somehow it wasn't. Somehow it was kind of sexy.

Just so he didn't get any ideas I rolled my eyes at him and he smiled.

The crashing of the waves against the sand was hiding any sound we might make.

"We should have a plan," I said. "What if he runs?"

"I think I can outrun a teenage runaway stuffed with carbs."

"What if he doesn't have the money on him?"

"We tell him to take us to the money." Antony shrugged, like it was all so simple.

"You do this a lot?"

He shrugged. "The kid is exhausted and terrified. He's not a criminal mastermind. Trust me, I know."

There it was again. That secret we were sort of sharing.

"I left home when I was nineteen," I offered. This time out loud. "No money. No real clue what I was going to do. Had a terrifying night at a rest stop in Connecticut until I made it up here to Aunt Za."

He nodded. Didn't say anything for a few steps, but then he stopped walking. "I was seventeen," he said. His voice a little rusty. "My dad wasn't a bully. That's too nice a term. He was just a mean drunk."

"I'm sorry," I said. I reached out to grab Antony's hand. Instantly, large fingers wrapped around my smaller hand. His palm was thick with callouses and old burns and scars. A working man's hand. I squeezed and he squeezed back.

Then suddenly it was too much. We were standing on the beach having this moment together and it was important. I knew that deep in my soul. Only we were supposed to be focusing on Nick. I pulled my hand back and he let go, turning to head down toward the water.

"Wait," I whispered, jogging to catch up with him. "Do you think he could be dangerous? He could have taken any one of our knives with the money."

"Don't worry. I'll protect you," Antony said over his shoulder.

"Okay, seriously? Like that's not even cool to say anymore. How about I was thinking I'll protect-"

Antony stopped and I ran into his back. He smelled vaguely of sweat and tacos. It was a good smell. He turned and pointed. There, in front of us, was a jean-covered leg sticking out from behind a large boulder.

Antony pointed to me to take one side, while he came around the other. That way if he ran, he couldn't get far.

My heart was beating out of my chest, but I did as instructed and came around the opposite side of the boulder. I had no idea why I did it, but I locked my fingers together, two fingers pointed straight out like I was holding a gun.

"Nick?" Antony asked, coming around the rock as I jumped out the other side.

In the end, Nick didn't even try to get up. He just sat there, with a stack of tortillas in his lap, his cheeks stuffed with falafel.

"Are you holding a finger gun on me?" Nick asked.

"Seriously, Genevieve?" Antony said, shaking his head.

"What? It was instinct. Be glad I didn't say, *Drop it, punk!*"

Nick leaned his head back on the boulder. "I'm so stupid. I should have just bolted."

Antony crouched down next to him. "But you didn't."

"Figured I would eat first," he said.

"Or maybe you thought we would come and find you," Antony suggested.

Nick looked at him. "Are you going to take me to the cops?"

"Are you going to give back the money?"

"I guess. I buried it over there," he said, pointing to a smaller rock further away from the water.

Antony looked up at me and nodded. My cue to go dig up our stolen money while the two men had a chat.

∽

Antony

"You know you could have asked for help."

Nick snorted. "Yeah, right."

"Yeah, right," I repeated.

I hadn't asked Francois for help. I'd decked him and he'd broken my nose in retaliation. I sat down on the beach and leaned back against the rock next to Nick.

Nick was shaking his head, his expression perplexed "You practically invited me to take the cash. Both of you. Left the trucks open. Just sitting there."

"Yeah, it's our fault you stole our money."

He finally made a move to get up, but I stopped him with an arm across his chest.

"Look, I don't want some fucking speech about right or wrong, okay? I took the money because I needed it and fuck you. You want to take me to the cops, fine. It won't be my first time in juvie."

I could feel the anger rolling off him. I remembered that anger so well. Mad at the world for what felt like years of bad luck and zero breaks. The anger of a kid forced to be a man without any tools to succeed. It sucked. It flat out sucked.

"How old are you?"

"Eighteen," he spat.

"How old are you?" I repeated my question.

He rolled his head around the rock. "Sixteen."

"Parents?"

"No clue."

"What are the cops going to tell me when they get your name?"

He sighed. "That I ran away from a foster home in Portland, where I was placed after being released from juvie."

"For..."

"Shoplifting."

"Bullshit." You didn't go to juvie for shop lifting.

"Shoplifting a car."

I tried not to laugh, but the kid was funny.

"The fosters?"

"What about them?"

"Were they bad?"

He shrugged. "There were too many of us. I was sharing a room with three other kids. I...I just wanted out."

So not abusive. That was some relief. However, they would need to be notified that Nick was at least safe. The system would be in motion trying to find him. But the system was also bogged down and slow moving. So, I had that on my side.

I was going to need to talk to Bobby. Find out some way around what I'm sure would be a legal mess.

"Do you trust me?" I asked him.

"Fuck no," he answered. "You lied the first time I met you."

Fair enough. "Do you trust her?"

I looked over at where Genevieve was pulling together the money and stuffing it in her jean pockets. When they were stuffed to capacity, Nick and I both watched her stuffing it down her shirt into her bra.

"Yeah, she's cool."

"Cool?" I questioned his judgement. "She pointed a finger gun at you."

He half laughed, half snorted.

"Come on, let's go," I said getting up.

"Where are we going?"

"My place. Genevieve is staying with her aunt. You go there and she'll want to read your aura or your future and cleanse your chakras and shit. My place, you'll get a decent meal and a bed to sleep in. Genevieve will come with us because you trust her."

"I thought her name was Birdie," Nick finally said.

"That's her nickname. Genevieve is her real name. Is Nick your name?"

"Sure?" he shrugged.

"Are you lying?"

"Of course I'm lying. I don't trust you, remember?"

"Well, I hope you will at some point." I called to Genevieve over the wind. "Do you have all our money?"

She offered an exaggerated confusing expression, even as her shirt was bursting at the seams with dollar bills.

"I know I got all my money back. Not sure how much of this was yours though."

"Dude, burn," Nick said, coming to stand beside me. "That's what you get for being a dick to her."

Yeah. That's what I got.

"What's going to happen when we get to your house?" Nick asked me, clearly still wary of me and my motivations.

"We're going to make dinner. Together."

"I don't know how to cook."

I remembered saying the exact same thing to Francois. So I said the same thing he said to me.

"Well, then. You're going to learn."

12

Birdie

It didn't take long for us all to come to an agreement. The plan was to go to Antony's place, a house he was apparently renting, for the time being.

Together, we'd piled into my truck to take Antony back into town to get his food truck. Then, because Nick felt more comfortable with me, he got in the passenger seat of Old Blue with me and together we followed Antony back to his place.

"He lives in a big house on the mountain behind town. It's a little isolated," I said, once Antony had given me the address. Everyone in Calico Cove was familiar with the house. It was designed by some fancy architect. "Are you cool with that?"

"Are you staying?"

"Do you want me to?" I asked him.

Nick shrugged. "Whatever."

"Well, I'm definitely staying for dinner. But you're safe with him. He's going to feed you some good food and you're going to stay in probably the nicest bed you've ever slept in."

I could see the kid was tired. It was in his eyes and the curve of his neck. I had the urge to put my hand on his shoulder and tell him everything was going to be fine, but I didn't know if that was the truth. The kid didn't need false hope.

He needed food and sleep.

And a shower. Badly.

"What's the deal with you two anyway?" Nick asked after we cleared the town square. I rolled down my window because that boy was *ripe*.

"What do you mean?"

"He was a dick to you today but now you're working together?"

"Yeah, he was."

"Did he apologize?"

"Yeah, he did."

"It looked like you guys were about to kiss. In the park earlier. When he caught up to you."

He was probably looking at us the entire time he was stealing our money. I didn't say anything about it.

"Getting a little personal here, Nick," I said, and he shrugged with a smile in the corner of his lips.

"He likes you," he said. "The guy can't play it cool around you to save his life."

I barely, just barely, stopped myself from asking Nick to elaborate on that idea. However, I was a grown ass woman and wasn't going to talk about my love life with a teenage runaway.

"It's a little complicated," I said.

Nick laughed. "Yeah, that's what he said too."

I glanced over at him. "Shut up!"

We made the turn up the mountain and Old Blue immediately started huffing and puffing.

"Lean forward," I said. It was a trick I learned riding horses in Montana.

"What?"

"Just do it."

Old Blue's engine made some alarming sounds.

"Oh, you sweet thing. You're just the best truck that ever lived," I said, rubbing her dash and patting the hula doll on the head.

"What are you doing?" Nick asked, his face all kind of horrified.

"Say nice things to her," I told him.

"No."

"Fine. When she breaks down out here in the middle of nowhere and we get eaten by bears, it's on you," I told him.

There was a loud grumble from under her hood and the truck lurched forward.

"Hey..." Nick said awkwardly, patting the glove box. "You can do it. You can totally get up this hill you...truck."

The hill evened out, the engine stopped making noise, and I grinned at my scowling travel companion. "Great job."

"Lady, you might be crazy."

I sighed and nodded. "You might be right."

The dirt road opened into a clearing where the modern glass house sat overlooking the bluff. In the parking area was the silver food truck and his Range Rover.

"Holy shit," Nick said. "He lives here?"

The house was more than impressive. Floor length glass windows. Views of the forest behind and the ocean in front. With the lights on, it glowed like a jewel.

"It's just a rental," I said.

A good reminder for me, I thought. All of this was temporary. Eventually, he had to go back to California and I had to move on with my life, too. We got out of the truck.

"The air smells different up here," Nick said.

"Less ocean," I said. "More trees." It was more than that, too. It was old forest. Ancient pine trees and granite mountains. A real wilderness smell. Nick took a deep breath and then another.

"Where are you from?" I asked him, and Nick immediately shut down.

"I'm from New York City," I said. "First time I came here I understood what nature smelled like. I liked it."

"Yeah."

"Hey!" Antony said, smiling as he opened the door. "Welcome."

He went back inside and Nick took that as our cue to follow him. Stepping inside the luxurious home it was easy to see it was just as impressive on the inside as it was on the outside. Large open foyer, a sunken living room with a beautiful fireplace and a big television on the wall. Tons of luxurious seating.

All the comforts of the country, completely modernized.

"I've never seen a house like this," Nick said, his eyes wide. "Except in movies."

It did look like a set. Immaculate and empty. It made me a little sad for Antony.

Maybe I should have taken us all back to the trailer. At least that space looked like a home. Like people lived their messy beautiful lives in it.

"All right, Nick," Antony said, coming back into the living room. "I have some sweats you can borrow and we'll throw your clothes in the laundry. I'll leave a hamper outside by the bathroom. Make sure everything goes in it. I'm not picking up your underwear off the bathroom floor."

He turned to me. "You want anything to change into?" he asked.

"What's wrong with what I'm wearing?" I looked down at my Birdie's t-shirt and jeans. My hot pink Crocs.

"Not a thing. I just didn't know if you wanted something more comfortable. Or that didn't smell like falafel," he said.

Suddenly, I had that image of putting on one of his button down dress shirts and nothing else. Standing in the doorway, striking a pose.

He'd like that.

I'd like that.

Nick would die seven million deaths.

"I'm good for now," I said. "But I wouldn't mind cleaning up a little."

"You can use the guest bath upstairs," he told Nick. To me he said, "You can use the ensuite off my bedroom. It's at the end of the hallway. Chop, chop, everyone," he said. "I'll start dinner prep, but I'll need both my sous chefs."

"That means he's going to bark at us and tell us what to do," I told Nick.

Only Nick wasn't really paying attention. Instead, his eyes were bouncing all over the place. From the television to the art. To the wallet Antony was taking out of his pocket and putting on the mantle.

Eventually, he made his way upstairs.

Twenty minutes later, the kid came out wearing a pair of Antony's sweatpants and a t-shirt that hung off his thin frame, making him look even younger. A knot of emotion filled the back of my throat and I saw Antony's throat bob too.

This was big, what he was doing, trying to help Nick like this. I admired him for it.

More importantly, I *liked* him for it.

"You hungry?" Antony asked Nick as we made our way into the kitchen.

"I could eat." Nick said, like it was no big deal.

"We're having pasta aglio e olio," Antony said.

"What's that?"

"Pasta with cheese," I answered.

"Wait, like Kraft Mac & Cheese?" the kid asked, clearly delighted. I swear I could see Antony's soul shudder.

"Something like that," I said, smiling smugly.

"Better than that," Antony protested.

"The only thing better than the Kraft, is the Kraft with hot dogs," Nick proclaimed.

"Blasphemy," Antony said and immediately put him to work, carefully and patiently explaining how to fill the pot with water and properly salt it. When and how to test the pasta to know when it was done.

I thinly sliced the garlic and Antony threw it in the pan and showed Nick how to keep it moving so it never burned.

He's done this before.

It's what I thought as I watched him walk Nick through all the steps. Careful, exact directions all given with calm patience. A couple of jokes.

He was a good teacher, a patient one.

Unlike my father.

"Voila! Dinner is served," Antony said, and even Nick had a smile on his face.

That was the power of learning something new and being told you had done a good job. It was a big deal.

We ate at the giant kitchen island. Antony and I had barely sat down before the kid was halfway through his giant bowl. We shared a look and I jumped up to fill a pot with more water for a second round.

"So?" Antony asked. "Is it better than, gulp, the Kraft?"

Nick, his mouth full, nodded enthusiastically.

After a mountain of pasta and nearly a carton of milk, the kid was asleep on his feet and Antony showed him to his room on the second floor while I started in on the dishes.

"You don't have to do those," he said quietly when he was done saying good night to Nick.

"You cooked, it's the least I can do." Frankly, it was easy with his gigantic state of the art dishwasher.

"You want a glass of wine?" he asked.

"I shouldn't," I said. But it was one of those talk me into it moments. Which was sort of unfair to him really. I was a grown woman and I should know exactly what I wanted. Which was to have nothing to do with Antony Renard, but that just wasn't the case, obviously.

"Stay, Genevieve," he said softly in the quiet light of the kitchen. "Stay for Nick. Stay for me."

"Tony," I whispered, and wasn't sure where the name came from. It felt right though. It felt intimate.

"Not to…I promise I won't take advantage. That's not why I want you to stay. We had a day today. Let's just talk about it. I think my therapist/not therapist would say it was a good idea."

I nodded then. "Okay. But if I'm staying, I'm going to need something else to wear. Now I smell like falafels and garlic."

He smiled. "I pulled out another pair of clean sweats. Just in case. You can shower in my bathroom. I left the clothes on my bed."

"Just in case," I repeated with a suspicious eye, but he shrugged and looked so freaking harmless.

I left him to finish up the dishes. I took a quick shower, tried not to think about what it meant to stand naked in a shower he'd only recently stood naked in himself.

I remembered that slice of his stomach from that day in my truck.

Dear God. What would Antony Renard look like naked? And wet?

Bad Birdie. Bad Birdie!

Quickly, I finished the shower, dried myself off on one of his big fluffy towels and got dressed in a pair of oversize sweats that were so soft I wanted to live in them.

Barefoot, I made my way back into the kitchen. I sat on a stool at the quartz island with the waterfall finish, while he perused a full wall-sized wine rack and slid out a bottle of wine. There was a wine glass rack mounted over part of the island and he expertly pulled out two glasses by the stem.

"It's a full bodied Shiraz with hints of-"

"I don't need the sommelier's notes," I said, cutting him off. "Stop being a chef for five minutes."

He snorted. "I don't know if that's possible, but I'll spare you the description."

He poured my glass and handed it to me. My bare feet, perched on the bottom rung of the stool, must have caught his attention because he stared at them and grunted.

"Wait here."

He left the kitchen and strode off down a connecting hallway leading along the back of the house. There was a way he walked, I thought. Always with purpose and direction. Maybe a little bit like a soldier. As if I'd spent any time around soldiers.

Although sometimes people referred to my dad as *The General*.

A minute later he returned with a pair of men's sweat socks rolled together, with one stuffed into the other.

"Fresh from the laundry," he announced.

Even as I held out my hand for the socks, he tugged at my ankle. Like I was a little girl, he pushed the sock on my foot and tugged it up. I was so surprised, I didn't stop him when he did the other foot.

"There," he grunted, clearly satisfied in some way.

"So I guess we've got a kid now." I took a sip of the wine.

He was right, of course. It was full-bodied and delicious.

"Hardly," he said, then sighed. He took a seat on the stool next to me and I could see the crinkles around the corners of his eyes. The pull of skin around his mouth. A reminder he was older, not that mid-thirties was old. But this moment he felt *older*, like somehow he'd lived more.

"I think I'll start with Mal tomorrow."

"Mal Bettencourt? He's a software engineer," I said. "What's he going to know about a runaway?"

"He's a *billionaire*," Antony said, with emphasis on the word. "He'll have contacts, people who he can reach out to. Ways to move the system in a way us millionaires can't understand."

I huffed. "I wouldn't know. I'm only a thousander."

Antony smirked. "I wasn't bragging. I just know how this works. You try to work in the system and there are all these hurdles. You go outside the system and you get to pull levers we mere mortals can't see."

"What levers do you want to pull? If you send him back to the foster home, he's just going to run away again," I said.

"You can't be sure of that."

I shook my head. "You want my prediction?"

"Are you channeling your aunt right now?"

"Don't mock the magic," I told him. "But this is just good

old-fashioned intuition. In a few hours, Nick is going to wake up and realize where he is. Think that this is all too good to be true, and my guess is he's going to run again. Not before taking your wallet you left on the mantel over the fireplace in the living room."

Now, Tony was shaking his head. "No, he already stole once. He's not going to do it again."

"Okay," I humored him. "So, what are you thinking? That you might apply to be some kind of foster parent?"

"No. No way. I'm not qualified *at all* to watch over a teenager. Besides, I don't know how long I'm staying in town. Eventually, I have to go back to my restaurant."

That made me sadder than it should, so I tried to brush it off.

"Yeah, me too. After the M vs. A, I'll probably head out to the Midwest for the summer. It's cooler than the south."

His expression closed down too.

"Does your very hard to please father know you've been invited into a major food competition? You know past winners include Wolfgang Puck, Bobby Flay, Edouard Manet, Ina Garten, just to name a few."

I shrugged. "I haven't had a chance to tell him yet, but I will."

"Well, then let me say...congratulations, Genevieve."

He tipped his wine glass to mine until the rims clinked.

"Thanks, Tony," I whispered, something shifting in my chest.

"I haven't been called Tony in a long time," he said thoughtfully.

"I'll stop if you don't like it."

He gave a small shake of his head. "I like it too much. Done with your wine? Come, I'll walk you to your room."

I set the empty wine glass down on the island and

followed him through the living room to the other side of the house, where the stairs led up to the second floor and guest rooms.

We stood at the bottom of the stairs in awkward silence, not really knowing what happened next, but also knowing exactly what was going to happen next.

He stepped closer.

"You are so freaking beautiful, Genevieve. Can I say that?"

I didn't need his compliments. We were in something real here. More real than anything I'd had in a while. Maybe ever. He saw me and I saw him and that mattered to me. Scared me a little too, if I was being honest.

Made me feel alive.

"Shut up, Tony," I said, and I put us out of our misery and kissed him. I felt the startled gust of his breath and there was a second of stillness. Surprise. Then he pulled me into his arms, his hand at the back of my head, deep in my hair, holding me still. Close.

I don't know what I expected. Instant heat, sure. The ignition of some massive chemical reaction in my body. All the gooey deliciousness that goes with a first kiss.

It was all of that and so much more.

I loved how big he was. How broad. The way our bodies fit together. His chest, my breasts. I felt him take another breath, his stomach pressing against mine. I moaned against his lips and his tongue swept deep into my mouth.

It occurred to me in the small bit of functioning brain I had left that I was being savored.

Savored.

He was kissing me like I knew he would. But the step after being savored was being devoured, and from that I wouldn't be able to walk away.

I managed to take a step back. Wobbly at first, brain fuzzy, lips swollen and tender. But I did it.

He kept his hand on my waist, his fingers clenching my shirt, like he didn't want to let me go. Like he wanted more of me. More contact. More heat. But then he released me.

"We're not fooling around with Nick upstairs," I told him.

"I know. I just like knowing you're here."

Those words had the unmistakable vulnerability of the truth in them. He wanted me close and that was nice. Dangerous and foolish. But nice, too.

"I'm going upstairs now. Nick is going to be up soon and robbing you," I told him, but he didn't laugh.

"He ate a box of pasta. That kid's not waking up for a week."

"We will see about that. Thanks for the meal," I said.

"Thanks for the kiss."

I made my way upstairs and snuggled into the second guest bedroom, where I knew I wasn't going to sleep. An hour later, I made my way back downstairs and hoped Tony was actually getting some sleep.

I slipped my Crocs on over the socks Tony had given me and made my way outside in the chilly night air to sit and wait in Old Blue. I opened my phone, sent a text to Aunt Za to let her know I wasn't coming home tonight, then put on an audio book.

It was probably only going to be another hour or two.

13

Birdie

It had almost been a close call. I'd started to drift off. The food, the wine, Tony's congratulations...the kiss. All of it lulling me into a sense of cozy deliciousness. I couldn't remember the last time I felt this good about...life.

There was a low-level excitement to everything now.

I'd gone from Antony Renard being a mortal enemy to kissing him, all in the space of twenty-four hours.

Thankfully the rush of that, plus leaving the driver's side window open a crack, so the cold air would keep me somewhat alert, worked to keep me awake.

When the front porch light flickered on, I checked my phone and saw the time was just after three AM.

Nick was closing the front door behind him. He took three steps down the walkway and the flood lights came on.

I heard his muttered *fuck* when he realized he'd triggered the motion-detector light.

Hopping out of the truck, I waited for him to see me in the dark.

"Fuck!" he said, this time more loudly.

"Yeah, you're caught kid." I approached him and held out my hand.

"What is your freaking deal anyway?" he said in a half shout half whisper. Clearly, he didn't want to wake up Tony.

"My freaking deal is that running away isn't going to solve a single one of your problems."

And wow! This from the person who had spent the last eight years doing exactly that. However, I had no plans to inform Nick of my great and horrible hypocrisy.

He huffed and there was a second where we were at a standoff. He was taller than me. Stronger than me. Definitely faster than me. If he wanted to, he could get around me and take off running down the road. I wouldn't be able to catch him.

"There are bears," I said. "They eat people."

"Bullshit."

I shrugged, like his being mauled by a bear meant nothing to me. "I'll just go inside and get Antony. You won't make it a mile before we catch up to you," I said logically.

Another sigh. And in that sound I heard how exhausted he still was.

"Or you can give me the wallet you took, go back inside, get a bunch more sleep and when Antony wakes up he'll probably make you a sick breakfast."

Because clearly he was cooking again.

The front door behind Nick suddenly opened.

"What the fuck?" Tony said, sleep rumpled and discombobulated. His hair, sticking up at every angle. I hated how cute he looked.

"How did you know we were out here?" I asked him.

"I get an alert on the damn phone if there is movement by any of the doors." He glared at me. "Get back inside. It's too cold out here for you. And you, too," he said to Nick.

Head down, Nick knew he'd been beat. He headed inside, but Tony stopped him.

"My wallet?"

Nick pulled it out of his back jeans pocket and put it in Tony's hand.

Then with a gentle shove on his back, Tony pushed Nick inside the house and I followed.

"You're not going to say *I told you so*," Tony told me, as he closed the door behind us and then set the alarm by the door.

No one was getting in or out without him knowing it.

"Too obvious," I told him, even as I patted his cheek. "Also, don't freak out when I'm not here in the morning."

He followed me to the stairs. "Why won't you be here?"

"I need to prep for tomorrow."

That seemed to mollify him. He understood what it meant to be ready for the day before service began. Mise en place didn't just happen.

"Is he going to do that again?" he asked me as we both listened to the sound of Nick slamming his bedroom door shut.

I sighed. "Not tonight."

We were all too tired now.

∼

THE NEXT MORNING
Antony

. . .

I WAS GRUMPY. I could acknowledge that.

I spent the rest of the night absolutely not sleeping.

When the kid woke up at one in the afternoon, stumbling into the kitchen like a bear coming out of hibernation, he took one look at me.

"You look like shit," he muttered.

"Thanks. Do you know how to drive?"

"Yes," he said quickly.

Right. He shoplifted cars. Stupid question. "Do you have your driver's license?"

"Not exactly."

That meant no. Which meant everything about today was going to be a challenge.

I'd already placed the call to Mal and he immediately got me connected to a family lawyer that worked at the same firm that managed his business. We had a call scheduled for later this afternoon.

But now, I needed to get the food truck back to Portland, where my friend would send his guys to pick it up.

"You feel like helping me out a little today?"

"What does that involve?"

"First, we're going downtown to meet Genevieve. She's demanding to see your face."

"Why?"

"I don't know," I said. "Maybe she likes it. Or a better guess is, she wants to make sure you're still here."

The kid stammered and blushed and had the decency to look a little guilty. I took some pity on him.

"Go get changed and we'll head down there."

Seconds later we were out in the driveway, standing in front of the giant silver food truck and my Range Rover.

"You can drive the food truck or you can drive my car."

He looked at my sleek, beautiful, very expensive car. "Are you shitting me?"

"I shit you not."

"Your car."

I tossed Nick the keys to the Rover. "Don't try and steal it or I will have to call the cops."

He was back in his clothes from yesterday, now freshly laundered, but still threadbare. He needed new shit. I added it to my list of stuff to do.

"Town is literally two miles down this hill. I'll go first so you can follow me. You've got one stop sign. One stop light and a parking situation."

"I can do that," he said. He got behind the wheel and I watched him through the driver's side window. He adjusted the seat, the rear-view mirror, used the controls on the door to adjust the other side view mirror then adjusted his seat again.

"You want me to take your measurements to make sure the car perfectly fits you?"

He jerked a little and I thought the kid wasn't ready for sarcasm yet. Sarcasm wasn't something you were afforded when you didn't have parents or money. You need to be comfortable to appreciate sarcasm.

"I was kidding," I said more seriously. "Take your time. Get comfortable."

"I'm fine," he nodded. I jumped in the food truck and led us down the hill towards town. At the bottom of the hill at the stop sign, the kid could have turned left instead of right and headed for the highway, but he put on his right blinker and followed me right into town.

He hadn't lied. He could drive.

It was Saturday, so town was busier and we parked a few

blocks away from where Birdie would be working and both hopped out.

"Great job!" I told him as we took off down the sidewalk towards the square. It was a cool day and the kid shoved his hands in his pockets. "Someone taught you."

"There was a class at juvie. They wanted to keep us active so they had driving classes, mechanic classes, all kinds of shit. It was like everybody just assumes you're stupid in there. Well, I mean I guess because you got caught and you're there in the first place. But whatever. They had all these classes so I just took everything I could."

Which meant the kid was curious.

"Anything in particular you liked?"

"I liked working with my hands. They think they're helping you to get job skills so you can be some kind of a scrub. But if you can fix things? Make things? That's the shit."

"Yeah," I said. "It is the shit."

We turned a corner and we were back in the center of town.

"Oh man, you're not going to do the truck war thing again?"

I laughed. "No, that was, how did you say it? A dick move? I've got to return the truck today."

He nodded like he approved of my life decisions.

We made it into the town square and I was annoyed to see Levi standing outside of Genevieve's truck. I glanced at my watch. It was after the lunch rush.

If I wanted to chat up the beautiful food truck lady, I'd come after the lunch rush too.

Levi was talking and leaning forward into the truck and I could see her nodding as she made his sandwich. Her head tilted back, that gorgeous hair falling down her back. My hand clenched as I remembered how silky that hair was, how warm her skin.

How hot her mouth was.

She laughed at something Levi said.

Geezus, save me from those dimples.

What was so freaking funny anyway?

"Come on, kid," I said, my voice slightly gruffer than it should be, considering the circumstances.

We jogged over to Genevieve's truck.

"Hey, Levi," I called.

He turned at the sound of his name.

"Hey, Chef. Please tell me you haven't come here to feud with our local falafel food truck phenomena."

"That's some alliteration." I said. "A little obvious, isn't it?"

"More obvious than a Michelin chef wowing the crowd with tacos?" Levi returned with a lazy smile.

"Touché," I acknowledged. "But the residents of Calico Cove seemed to enjoy it."

"Those of us passing through liked it too," Levi said. "Don't tell Birdie, but I had her falafel and your tacos. Both amazing."

"Your secret is safe with me."

"I notice you don't talk about when you're going back to the restaurant much when we're playing poker."

"That's because I'm too busy giving you all my money."

"This is true."

I thought of Venetia asking me when I was coming back to The Robin's Egg. If she knew I was messing around with food truck ladies, tacos and runaway foster kids she would have my head.

But this was my prison, I held the key and I wasn't letting myself out until I was satisfied I was...

What? What was I waiting for?

Until I was normal again? Until I was happy again?

Did I even know what happy felt like?

Genevieve handed Levi his sandwich, then she was popping out of the back of the truck, grabbing onto Nick's shoulders.

"You survived the night!" she cried. Today her apron read *I Like Pig Butts and I Cannot Lie.*

I hated that I was amused by that.

"Yeah, it wasn't hard," Nick said with a smile. I noticed she got all his smiles. "That bed was seriously comfortable."

"So, are you hitting the road today or sticking around?" she asked him. She looked at me and then back at Nick. Nick looked at me and then back at Genevieve, and I held my breath until Nick finally shrugged.

"We have to return this food truck." Nick said, like it was top of his to-do list.

"Yeah?" she asked, putting her hands on her hips. I'd had my hands on those hips last night. All too briefly. She'd been in my arms one second then backing away from me the next.

I wanted to touch her again. I needed to touch her again.

"Where you going?" she asked us.

"There's a place I can drop it off in Portland," I said, tearing my attention from her hips. "I'll take the truck and he'll follow in my car."

"Do you have a license?" she asked Nick, and he, who clearly had no problem robbing me blind – twice - couldn't even lie to her. He shook his head no.

She glared daggers at me. "That's not safe."

"He just drove down from the mountain." I told her.

"The mountain road is not a highway."

"Driving is about overcoming your fear of things," I bullshitted her. We weren't going on the highway, I was planning on back roads, but it was fun winding her up. "A highway is just another road. It will be okay."

She slapped her cheeks with her palms as if I'd surprised her.

"What? A highway is just a road? That's so crazy. I've been driving for years across this entire country. East coast to west coast, north to south, only to finally be mansplained by you *again* that a highway is just a road. However did I live this long without your manly guidance?"

"Now you're just being dramatic," I said.

"Drive the truck and Uber back," she offered.

"Do you know how far that is?"

"You're the million-er, remember?" she asked, her eyebrows up.

Then Nick stepped in between us. "Hey, no fighting. Not over me. Please."

He was agitated and I got it. He must have had some experiencing with arguing adults, maybe his parents. And it's what Genevieve and I sounded like, even though we didn't mean anything by it. I locked eyes with Genevieve and we both nodded. Cease fire.

"We'll Uber back here," I agreed.

"Great," she said. "Wait here."

She jumped back into the truck and emerged again counting some dollar bills.

"If you're going to Portland, you should pick him up some clothes. Turns out I had a little leftover cash based on my receipts from yesterday."

"Funny how that just happened." I smirked at her. She smirked right back. She was a thieving liar and we both knew it. That was all my taco money.

Damn, I wanted to kiss her again. Kiss her, throw her

over my shoulder, take her from behind in her own damn food truck.

"I don't need anything," Nick said quickly.

Which was painfully not true.

"I can get him some stuff," I said, and tried pushing the money right back at her.

"Hey," she said to Nick. "Go make yourself a sandwich for the road. Only one. And grab a cookie too!"

She didn't have to ask Nick twice.

"I don't have the money that gets big levers pulled," she said to me, her voice low so Nick couldn't hear. "But I have the money to get him some new clothes. I was going to make you give it to the food bank. Let's give it to him instead so he can walk around with some dignity. Please."

I nodded and took the money.

"Anything in particular I should get?"

"A pair of jeans, a long-sleeved shirt because it still gets cold in spring. A light weight jacket. Sneakers that fit. A pack of socks, underwear and white t-shirts. Anything that comes in multiples." She'd been thinking about this and I was oddly moved.

"Got it."

"A toothbrush."

I started to walk away when she grabbed my hand.

My hand, which was callused and scarred by a hundred cuts and burns over the years. My hand that could grab a hot pot off the stove and not even feel it, felt the touch of her delicate fingers so acutely it sent chills across my body.

"And deodorant. Everyone wants their own deodorant."

I nodded but said nothing, just looked down to where she was holding my hand. I squeezed. She squeezed back.

I liked how much we could say to each other with that simple action.

"You know, you could have dinner waiting for us when we get back," I told her. "Give me your phone number and I'll text you the code to the door."

She shook her head but was smiling. "You'll do anything to taste my food, won't you?"

I was pretty sure I would do anything to have her waiting for us at my house at the end of the day.

I bent down closer to her. Kissing her now seemed like too much of a privilege. Like I didn't quite yet have that permission to be so bold. So instead I got a breath away from her ear and simply said:

"Yes, Genevieve. I'll do anything to taste…your cooking."

14

Birdie

"What's the matter, darling? You seem distracted."

I blinked once I realized Aunt Za was asking me a question. I'd closed up shop for the afternoon and grabbed a cup of coffee. I was enjoying some end of the day sunshine beside Aunt Za's table. So far I'd watched her tell the fortune of a little girl, carrying a thick book under her arm, and read Tarot for two teenagers who were trying to pretend they weren't crazy for each other.

"Earth to Birdie," Aunt Za said.

"I'm sorry, I guess I am distracted."

"Is it the man or the boy you're thinking about?"

"Both," I admitted. I hung my head backwards, letting the sun hit my neck and face. I'd told her about everything that had happened yesterday, over coffee this morning.

Well, not everything. I hadn't told her about the kiss.

Mostly because I just wanted to hold it inside a little bit longer.

"Antony wants me to go back up to his place and have dinner ready for him."

"You're still going on about him eating your food, are you?"

"No. I mean...yes. Probably. But that's not what's giving me anxiety right now. It's just... you know, I was up there last night."

"And it was awful? His house is unfit for habitation?"

"No," I laughed. "No. You know the house is beautiful. The rest of it, us, it's just messy."

"Messy how?" Aunt Za asked. "Messy because you like them? Because you have feelings for them?"

"Yeah," I said. "Exactly."

"That's not messy, honey. That's life." Aunt Za shook her head. "You think you're such a rolling stone, except, do I have to point out that you keep rolling back here? To Calico Cove," she stopped and looked at me like there was some point I was supposed to get.

"What?"

"You're looking for a home," she finally cried. Aunt Za reached across the table and patted my hand. "Your father called me. He had a suspicion you came here after your last fight."

"What? You didn't tell him where I was, did you?"

"No, I told him if you wanted him to know where you were, you would tell him. However, talk about you running away from messy emotions." Aunt Za shuffled through her tarot deck. I hadn't touched them, so they weren't for me. "I believe in letting an adult determine what her life is going to be for herself. However, I also know that life is short and regret is a curse. As you move into this next phase of your life, you're going to want your father around. That's just a fact."

"Next phase of my life?"

"I can see it. Your aura, it's changing. It signals a significant life change."

"I love you Aunt Za," I said as I stood up. "At least that's not messy. I'm leaving right now, but that does not mean I'm running."

She blinked at me in her costume. The scarves and the rings and the dark eyeliner. The truest person I've ever known in my life. "Where are you going?"

To make a bigger mess of things, I thought, but wasn't about to say.

"To Antony's. Don't wait up."

～

I RAN to the grocery store and then texted Antony.

> Genevieve: Send me your door code.
>
> Antony: You're coming over?
>
> Genevieve: On my way.
>
> Antony: We might beat you there.
>
> Genevieve: Then you don't need dinner?
>
> Antony: Are you honestly going to cook for me?
>
> Genevieve: That was the plan.
>
> Antony: Then get yourself up here. Nick wants to show off what he got.

I was... inappropriately excited. With some groceries and a bottle of wine, Old Blue and I made our way up the mountain to see what the men had bought with my money, aka Tony's Taco money.

Antony met me at the front door. He looked tired but satisfied. A man who'd been running errands with a teenager for a few hours. He wore jeans and a flannel shirt over a t-shirt. Thick socks. He was so handsome and so real I wanted to throw my arms around him.

"Hello, Genevieve. I'm glad you're here." The way he said it, the words sunk right into me. A hook through my chest.

"Are you?"

"Shouldn't I be?"

"I don't know? You were trying to ruin my business yesterday."

"I wasn't trying to ruin your business. I was trying to win an argument that you started."

That was a fair assessment. "So? How did it go today?" I asked, holding onto the grocery bag like it was the only thing keeping me afloat in suddenly turbulent waters.

"Come and see for yourself," he said.

I followed him and when I turned a corner from the foyer into the main living space, I could see Bullseye bags on every surface.

Nick was sitting on the sectional couch in the sunken living room, wearing fresh socks, unwashed jeans and a new t-shirt, with a gaming console in his hand and eyes locked on the tv mounted on the wall.

"No man, not that way, it's a trap!" Nick shouted at the screen.

Antony stood beside me, smelling good and feeling solid.

"Did you buy out the entire store?" I asked him.

"Not the entire store, but have you ever been in one of those places? They have everything. We grocery shopped, clothes shopped, and man-toy shopped all at the same time. Don't worry, you didn't pay for the game. Then he talked me into some junk food."

"The guy hasn't been to a McDonald's in fifteen years, can you believe that Birdie?" Nick said, glancing at me and then back at the screen.

"The egg McMuffin is a classic and no one hates fountain soda," Antony said with a shrug.

"Then I guess you're not hungry?" I asked, shifting my bag of groceries, suddenly feeling ridiculous.

"I could eat," Nick called out.

"That," Antony said, "is code for, I can eat more than a large family. So yeah, if you're cooking, we'll eat."

Antony waggled his eyebrows at me like my cooking was code for something dirtier.

"It's not my falafels," I said.

"I don't care. I want whatever you'll give me."

Oh my god! The mouth on this guy, and in front of a teenager. I scowled at him and he just smiled. Interesting, but a few days ago I was sure that smile of his was a smokescreen he hid behind. Now he just looked…happy.

"I'll cook. But you're not allowed in the kitchen. I don't need a sous chef."

"That's all right, I'm having fun learning another thing I'm not good at and getting my ass handed to me in this game." Antony sat back down next to Nick.

I walked into the kitchen where it was quieter, but I could still hear them laughing and arguing. It was nice, I thought. I was so used to silence. To being alone.

I unloaded my groceries, keeping everything tucked away where no one could see what I was making. It took no time at all, so I opened my cheap and cheerful wine and poured myself a glass. One. Because I was absolutely driving home tonight.

When everything was ready I set the counter island with three plates, napkins and utensils. I put the dutch oven I was using to keep it all hot on a trivet, and had to smile imagining Antony's face when he saw what I'd made them.

"Come on in boys," I said, and refused to dwell on how nice it was to call the boys to the table.

My boys.

No, I thought. Not my boys at all.

This was all just temporary. I had to remind myself of that.

There was a scuffle, a dropped controller, and then the tv was turned off and the two of them came into the kitchen. They wore socks and goofy grins and something between my stomach and my throat went tight. Nick had a serious giddiness about him. Full stomach, some sleep, some fun. He was a new kid.

Antony had his own swagger, and he lifted an eyebrow when he saw my wine glass.

"Would you like some?" I asked.

"Does it pair with what we're eating?"

"Yes or no, buddy," I was not giving in to his food snobbery.

"Yes," he said. "I'd love some."

They sat at the island and Nick looked at me and then at Antony. "Go ahead," I told Nick and he lifted the lid on the dutch oven.

"Yes!" He hissed with an excited fist pump. "Kraft and dogs."

"You're joking," Antony said, looking into the pot. Nick stirred the bright orange macaroni with the cut up hot dogs

I'd put in it. I didn't even get the gourmet organic hot dogs. Just some Hebrew Nationals.

I expected any number of things.

He would refuse it. He would push it around on his plate without eating it. Or he would make something else. Something fancy, with foam, shaved truffles and extraordinary plating so he could prove to me that I was a fool and he was an artist.

What I didn't expect was for him to tip back his head and laugh.

"Do you want some?" Nick asked, his own plate fully covered in chemical orange noodles.

"Of course I do," Antony said. Nick scooped a bunch on Tony's plate while Antony was setting his napkin in his lap like he was sitting down to a three-course meal. "Genevieve thinks I'm a food snob. I am not."

"Again," I pointed out. "You starred in a show called the Food Snob."

He made a face at me, but nothing after that. Just ate what Nick had put on his plate while I did the same. It was companionable and felt comfortable. Maybe a little too comfortable.

So it was a good thing Nick ate like an insane person and had gone through almost a box and a half and probably four hot dogs when he finally declared he was done. Which was only twenty minutes after the time we'd started eating.

"Hey, can I go back to my game?" Nick asked when his plate was clean.

"Rinse the dish and put it in the dishwasher," I said. Nick hopped up and did as I asked and shuffled off to the living room.

"He's a good kid," Antony said in low tones. "Whatever

happened to him growing up, didn't break him. I'm certain of it."

"He didn't try to run again?"

Tony shook his head. "He stuck by my side the whole day. Maybe we built some trust? He's got new clothes, he's got a full stomach. He's completely entertained. He's not stupid and he knows this is the best of a bad situation for him."

"What about the lawyer?"

"We have an in-person meeting on Monday. She'll walk us through what needs to happen." Tony reached for the bottle of wine and filled my glass.

"No, thank you. I already had one. I have to get back to the trailer tonight."

"You work Sundays too?"

"No," I said. That wasn't why I needed to go home. I needed to go home because Tony was every temptation there could ever be and then some.

I was weakening.

Like really weakening when one of the country's top chefs ate Kraft and dogs like it was fine dining. My dad never would have done that.

"Or you could stay over," he said. "You know you have a room."

"Nick's fine. You said it yourself. There is some trust now."

"He is. Stay over anyway."

I swallowed like there was something stuck in my throat. "Why?"

He shook his head. "I just like knowing you're here. Under my roof. Is that too caveman for you? Are you worried I'll come to your room, knock on your door, maybe ask you for sex?"

"Worried?" I whispered. "No. I'm not worried about that."

He bent down closer to me, so close I felt frozen by his stare. "Do you want me to? Do you want me to come to your room and say, Genevieve, I want...no, I *need* to fuck you. Desperately. That I think it would give me some peace."

That word. Need, fuck or peace. I wasn't sure which one did it, I only knew it went right between my legs and pulsed. I couldn't pretend this wasn't happening with him and I couldn't pretend I didn't want it.

I wrapped my hand around the back of his head, my fingers sliding into hair that was getting too long, and brought his forehead to rest gently against mine.

"I don't think peace is the best reason for fucking."

For a second we just breathed together.

"I know that. But I want you so badly," he whispered, almost like he surprised himself. I felt the soft whisper ripple all through my body.

I raked my nails gently down his scalp to his neck and he made a low groaning sound.

"Whoa, get a room."

We jumped away from each other like Nick had shot off a gun entering the kitchen.

"We were just talking," I said quickly, patting down my hair.

Nick snorted. "Sure, talking. I just came in for a soda. Don't let me cock block."

"Hey, language in front of the lady," Antony admonished him.

"I was leaving anyway," I said and got up off my stool. I put my dishes in the dishwasher. Antony walked me through the house to the front door.

"If I come to the truck on Monday, am I going to get your falafels?" His voice was low and rich and it made me shiver.

"No," My voice sounded raspy in my throat.

"Genevieve, I really want your...falafels."

"Tony," I leaned into him. "Get used to disappointment."

Then I took a few steps back and shouted loud enough so Nick would hear me.

"See you around, Nick."

"See ya, Birdie!" Nick shouted back.

"Goodnight," I called over my shoulder.

With a little skip in my step, I made my way back to my truck, absolutely looking forward to Monday.

15

The Dock
Sunday 6:00 am
Antony

I don't know if I was surprised to see Ben down at the dock on a Sunday or not. I guess when he said every day, he meant it.

"Hey Ben," I said, standing beside him.

"Antony!" He said, with delight. "Glad you could join me on this fine Sunday morning."

It was grey, overcast and drizzling. Completely miserable.

"Doesn't your wife ever get upset that you spend so much time out here fishing?"

"Nope," he said. "She likes her mornings to herself and I like to give her what she likes."

"That's…nice."

"That, my friend, is thirty years of marriage. You didn't bring your gear today."

I shoved my hands in my jean pockets and shook my head. "I didn't really come down here to fish. I guess I have to tell you about this thing I did."

I explained all of it. Nick. Genevieve. Our similar histories. Why we were both so in sync with helping the kid instead of shuffling him off to some social worker and being done with it.

Ben nodded along and didn't say anything until I was done.

"Okay," he said slowly. "So what does this mean? Are you thinking about staying in Calico Cove?"

"No. Why would you think I might?" I said it a little defensively, probably because I couldn't possibly be thinking about staying in Calico Cove. Could I? My life was back in California. At The Robin's Egg. Hell, my chef's roll of knives was back there. If that didn't mean anything, nothing did.

"Got it. You're just taking on the problems of a troubled kid for now, and spending time with a woman who is also leaving in a few weeks."

"Everyone knows this isn't permanent."

"Does Nick?"

"I'll talk to him."

Ben snorted. "The way you talk to me?"

"You're implying I don't?"

"No, I'm not *implying* anything."

The water lapped against the old wooden pier in front of us. The big granite rocks that made the storm break beside us. Everything was so permanent here. Like this pier had been here for hundreds of years before me and it would be here hundreds of years after me.

Everything in Maine had legacy. Maybe that was why I liked it.

"I was hoping you could see him. Nick." I finally said. "Talk to him. In a professional capacity. He's a teenager. He can be your client, right?"

"Of course." Ben pulled a piece of gum out of one of the million pockets in his vest. Offered it to me first, then popped it in his mouth when I shook him off.

"Okay, then. I guess that's all I needed."

"No," Ben said in that way he did. "You need more. A lot more. But until you're willing to acknowledge the trauma you have not dealt with, you'll just keep running on the same mouse wheel."

"Anyone ever tell you you're annoying?"

"Everyone does," he agreed. "This thing with you and Nick though, it could be good. Maybe it will help both of you see your way to the other side of things."

I shrugged.

"Because it's all about getting back on top for you, right? Getting control, figuring it all out so you can be the best again."

I was silent. Those things I wanted so clearly a few weeks ago...they seemed distant now. Hazy. Like a horizon I would never reach.

"Bring the kid here after you've talked to the lawyer," he said, when I had no comment to offer in return.

"Thanks, Ben."

~

The Next Day

"So walk me through it again, if you like her, which you clearly do, why did you do the dick move with the food truck?"

Nick was showing me his skill at parallel parking. We were back in town and not far from Genevieve's food truck.

It was Monday and I had a meeting with Mal and Sheila Tran, the family lawyer Mal found for me. I didn't want to bring the kid with me in case the news was bad. Nick would take off so fast I would never be able to catch him. I wanted to hear everything unvarnished, and then whatever that was, I could let the kid know the good and the bad of it.

"What do you mean *like* her?" I said, like a middle-school aged boy.

"Like you wanted to suck off her face the other night."

"Okay, so that's *not* what I wanted to do and don't you worry about it. It's adult stuff."

"Yeah, I'm sixteen. Like I don't know shit about sex. You know what, adults are assholes," Nick said smoothly, backing into the spot carefully to leave enough room in between the two cars, front and back. "Present company excluded because you made a kick ass breakfast this morning. Birdie is also an exception, because she's cool."

I stopped before I opened the car door. "Nick, I'd like to introduce you to someone so you can talk about stuff."

"Stuff like what?"

"I don't know. Personal shit. Feelings. What's in your gut," I said awkwardly.

"What's in my gut is some...what did you call it? Eggs what?"

"Eggs Benedict," I supplied. "And you know what I'm talking about."

He shrugged. "Yeah, I know what you mean. I don't need that shit. I'm fine."

Francois had never asked me if I needed to talk about my feelings. Instead he'd put a peeler in my hand and let me peel a thousand potatoes until my hands cramped up into bird claws. It had worked for me.

Had it? Had it really worked?

"His name is Ben," I said. "He's a really great guy. Terrible fisherman. But I think if you talked to him, you'd feel better."

"About what?"

"Life."

"I already feel better," Nick said, smacking me on the shoulder. "Let's go see Birdie."

He got out of the car and I followed. It was eleven and Genevieve had already opened the truck for business. I could smell the hot oil as we crossed the park.

"Wait here," I told Nick.

"Why?"

"Because I said?" I tried, and he laughed.

"You want to suck her face off."

"Kid. You are disgusting."

I had no real clue what I was supposed to say to her, but I was so excited to see her.

"Hey," I said, as I approached the truck's open side.

"Hi," she replied and was that... was she blushing? Was she maybe just as discombobulated as I was? That was a good thing, right?

The reality of my life, I wasn't as smooth with women as I liked to think. Cameras loved me. And maybe it was easy for me to put on a show, but when it came to real life relationships...well, there hadn't been many of those, had there?

Casual affairs. One night stands. Women I knew who were more interested in the version of me I presented to the world, rather than me.

Fan girls.

Genevieve was so not one of those women.

"I have a favor to ask," I began.

"No, I'm not giving you my falafels," she crossed her arms over her chest. "I thought about you a lot yesterday, you know after the other night and-"

"You thought about me?" I asked her, cutting her off.

She lifted a shoulder. "Maybe. A little."

I smiled. "Yeah, well, maybe I thought about you too."

She tucked her hair behind her ear and blushed even harder.

"But that's not why I'm here," I said quickly. "For your falafels, I mean. I need to talk to the lawyer and I thought it would be better if Nick hung back. Could he work in the truck with you today? Give him something to do. I really think we're past the stealing part of our relationship."

She nodded. "For sure. He can take orders for me. It will help."

"Nick," I called to him and waved him over. "You're working the truck today. You do what she says, you give her zero attitude, understood?"

"Yeah. Of course."

She smiled at the kid and now I was pretty sure Nick was blushing too.

God, what a mess the three of us were. Smitten I think was the appropriate word.

I left them and walked past the square, down Harbor Road to Pappas' diner where I was meeting Mal and Sheila.

Mal was already there, seated in a big, wide, bright blue booth with a woman in a suit and dark hair in a bob so sharp it could cut glass. Suddenly I wished I'd worn something more than a pair of dark jeans and a long-sleeved red shirt.

"Hiya, Chef," Lola greeted me from behind the counter. "Black coffee?"

I nodded. "Whenever you get a chance, Lola."

Genevieve didn't call me chef. No, she called me Tony.

I hadn't been Tony since high school. Which maybe meant I shouldn't like it, but it connected me somehow to the kid I'd been before I'd burned all those connections to the ground, once I started making a name for myself as Antony.

It made me feel like I was so far beyond just Chef Antony Renard to her.

I liked it.

I sat down next to Mal and across from Sheila, who I had spoken to briefly on the phone. An attractive woman whose age I could not begin to guess. She exuded competency and I couldn't help but feel we were in excellent hands.

"Chef Renard," she reached across the table and I shook her red nailed hand. "I've had the privilege of eating at The Robin's Egg once. The finest meal I ever had."

"I'm glad," I said. Right. The Robin's Egg. My restaurant that I wasn't rushing back to. Because instead I was here getting invested in Nick's life. "So did you have a chance to look into Nick's story?"

I'd given her all the information Nick had given me that first night, including the name of the juvenile detention center where he'd served time and the name of the public defender who was involved in his case.

"I have," she said, and her face told the entire story. A story she'd no doubt heard a few times in her life as a family lawyer. "Nick Steffens comes from Portland, Maine. It appears his mother left his abusive father several years ago. The father has had a few stints in rehab and multiple DUIs on his record. Nick has had several trips to the hospital with cuts and broken bones, unfortunately nothing severe enough that triggered any intervention by the state. Last year Nick was charged with car theft and sentenced to detention. At that point CPS got involved. It was determined he shouldn't be placed back with the father upon his release and instead should be placed in foster care. Where he'd been until he ran away. CPS knows he's safe, and they've let the family know."

"Did he break some kind of probation by running away?" I asked. "Is he in any legal trouble?"

Despite our similar upbringings, I had no experience with the *system*. I left home and hit the streets until I was found by Francois.

"No," she said, then stopped as Lola quietly set a cup of coffee next to me and moved on. I glanced around and noticed people watching us.

A town the size of Calico Cove, it wouldn't surprise me if folks were already hearing about Nick's story. Za knew everything from Genevieve, and she was better at getting news out than the town paper. Mal's wife Jolie and Lola were tight, so Lola likely knew what this meeting was all about too.

"No legal trouble. He wasn't under any kind of probation, and as a minor his record will be expunged when he turns eighteen. That said, he has to be placed in a CPS approved foster home. I've filed the paperwork to get his case transferred to this county." She pressed her finger to the table. "I've been talking to a social worker named Ellen Hughes. That paperwork will be filed today."

"Sheila," I shook my head in amazement. "You work fast. All that over the weekend?"

"Well, the process slows down now. A lot. Are you interested in being a foster parent?"

I shifted in my seat. I lived in California. Not here. But I could stay, for a while. Couldn't I?

"How long does that process take?"

She looked grim. "There are interviews, several inspections, reference checking. I just don't see it happening before the beginning of summer even if you were interested in taking on the responsibility of a teenage boy. However, if we could find a qualified foster home in the area..."

Sheila's voice trailed off as she realized someone had approached the table.

I looked up expecting to find Lola ready to take our order, but Roy Barnes stood there in his yellow rain coat and a grim expression on his face. Any time I saw Roy around town or at poker, he always had the same expression – like someone had stolen his car. The only time it ever changed... when he was looking at his beautiful wife.

"Hey, Roy," I said, not sure why he'd approached us.

"Roy Barnes," he said, as a way of introduction to Shelia. "Jolie talked to Lola who talked to Ness. Ness talked to me. Kid needs a place? I'm an approved foster parent. We'll move Nora in with me and Ness, give the kid the spare, but this only works until the baby comes in a few months."

I blinked as I unpacked the most words Roy Barnes had ever said to me in one sitting. "Are you serious?"

"You vouching for the kid?" he asked.

"I...I just met him a couple of days ago...but yeah. He's not dangerous or anything. Just a little desperate."

Roy grunted. "Got to meet him. Not letting someone I don't trust around my family."

"We can arrange a meeting. We'll need CPS to be part of that as well," Sheila said.

"I know Ellen. Ellen knows our family. She'll approve."

Sheila looked both impressed and happy. Which made me happy.

"There's one more thing," Sheila said. "He is required to go to therapy weekly with a licensed therapist. It's paid for by the state as part of a program to decrease the rate of recidivism, but it is mandatory."

"Already on it," I said.

"Okay," Sheila said. "We'll make this happen. Given this outcome, I think there's no problem with the boy staying with Chef Renard for the next few days while we arrange for the meeting with Mr. Barnes and his family. And you can schedule the therapist."

"Later," Roy said with a chin lift and left us, like a grumpy foster father guardian angel. Man, sometimes the world was strange.

"I feel good about this," Mal said. "This is a good community for a kid to get his head straight. A good place to heal. You and I would know, Antony."

I hummed an agreement as my brain raced. This had all moved so fast.

"Okay, if that's all you need me for, I think I'll head back to Boston," Sheila said.

"Wait," I said, as I made a quick and possibly life changing decision. "I want to get the paperwork started."

Sheila blinked. "You mean you want to apply as an approved foster parent in Maine?"

"Yeah," I said.

"Antony, you live in California," Mal said.

"I know, but I think it...feels right?"

I didn't operate by feel. I was a perfectionist, a precisionist. I wrote recipes, I refined them and then I executed them. It was why I loved my job so much. Everything could be accomplished with controlled execution.

This felt sloppy. Haphazard. Which should have been another red flag in a series of red flags in my life. My temper tantrum with a sous chef. My obsession with falafels. My sudden and unchecked desire for a woman I'd let under my skin .

And now this? Involving myself in a troubled kid's life. What was happening to me?

"I want to do this. I'm certain of it."

If it meant being in Maine, I could be in Maine. The Robin's Egg was practically self-sustaining. Plenty of executive chefs never stepped foot in their restaurants. I could go back a few times a year, take zoom meetings with my staff.

It could work.

Sheila nodded. "Well, we can certainly get the process started. To be fair, it might be harder for a single man to get approval, but you also have means to hire help, and that will all be taken into account."

What wouldn't help was a viral video of me smashing a plate and hurting an employee.

Maybe I wasn't the one who should be applying to be a foster parent. Maybe there was a better fit.

16

Antony

I walked back over to the food truck after our meeting broke up. I'd given Sheila all the necessary information she needed to get the process started, but I couldn't avoid the reality of my recent viral past.

Inside the truck I could see the tall kid working with Genevieve. He was moving behind her seamlessly like some coordinated dance they'd already perfected. She was stuffing pitas, he was taking cash.

She said something to him, poking him with her elbow and he laughed. She handed out a sandwich and smiled with her big wide mouth. That surge of desire came over me again like a wave.

I wanted to end my day with her again. I wanted to sit in my kitchen and have a glass of wine with her. I wanted to kick Nick out of that food truck and fuck her up against that service counter. Her fingernails down my back, her screams in my mouth.

A fantasy I was experiencing almost daily.

Fuck. Now I was hard.

Despite the insanity of trying this one more time, I got in her line. Two people before me were served, and thankfully there was no one behind me to witness the potential fireworks. Swear to god, after everything we'd been through the last few days, if she didn't give me a damn falafel…

She saw me and her lips twisted.

"How did it go?"

"Good," I told her, and behind her the kid saw me and took out the ear buds we'd picked up yesterday and pulled his new phone out of his pocket.

"What's going on?" he asked, trying and failing not to look nervous.

"You okay sticking around Calico Cove for a while, Nick?"

He nodded quickly. "They're going to let me stay with you?"

"For a few days, but there's a family in town who is approved to foster. You'll want to meet them and they'll want to meet you, but that will give us all time to figure out what's next."

I didn't say anything about applying to be a foster parent because I didn't want to get anyone's hopes up. I also didn't want to answer complicated questions about me possibly moving to Calico Cove permanently. I'd acted on impulse and I didn't regret it, but I just needed a second to figure out how to rearrange my life.

"What about school?" Genevieve asked. "Don't we need to get him signed up?"

"It's almost summer!" Nick cried.

"Not yet it's not," Genevieve said, sounding like a stern but loving mom.

Should she be the one doing this? Was she better suited? I felt like all I had was money and loose ends.

"That thing we talked about this morning. About you seeing my guy? That has to happen. State mandated." I told Nick.

That caused a more extreme reaction. "Fine. Whatever."

"I like him. You'll like him."

"Wait? You see a shrink?" Nick asked me.

"You're not supposed to call them shrinks," Genevieve said. "You're trivializing the profession which, now more than ever, is needed to help people work through their mental health issues. Therapy is a positive thing for everyone. Especially for people with maybe untapped anger issues? Hmm?"

Nick looked properly chastised and again I thought she'd be such a good mom figure.

"Spoken like a woman who has seen a therapist."

She bit her bottom lip. "Heck no. They scare me. I just let Aunt Za read my aura."

"I'm not sure your aunt would be state approved. But what do you say, Nick? You cool with going to go see my friend Ben?"

"I guess," Nick said with a shrug. If nothing else worked out I could feel good about introducing Nick to Ben. That was a good thing. "So, Birdie? You going to feed me or what?"

"Didn't you eat at Lola's?"

I shook my head slowly.

She sighed and looked at Nick.

"He's done me a solid," Nick said. "You should feed him."

She stared at the ceiling as if the answers were in the

steel. "Fine," she finally said. "But I'm only doing this for Nick."

"If that's what you need to tell yourself," I smirked. Nick grinned and put his earbuds back in and continued his cabbage chopping which she had him doing between orders.

She pulled out a pita, split it and put in heaps of her two different salads. When she was ready she pulled the fried balls from the fryer, stuffed the sandwiches and drizzled the whole thing with a tahini dressing and then her spicy green sauce.

"Consistency of product looks good," I muttered.

"I decided I don't want a review," she insisted. "Just go somewhere else and eat it and we'll never speak of this again."

"That's not possible," I said.

She handed the wrapped sandwich through the open side of the truck and I took it with both hands. I watched the steam rise and took the opportunity to sniff.

"Gimme a break," Genevieve muttered. I did it again just to annoy her.

I poked at one of the balls with my finger, excellent crust. The vegetables looked fresh. I touched my finger to the zhoug and tasted it. Herbaceous and spicy with some warm notes from cumin and coriander.

"What's that sound mean?" she asked.

"What sound?"

"The sound you just made. Like you were growling at it."

"The zhoug is excellent," I said.

"Oh." She flipped her hair off her shoulder. "Glad you like it."

The heat was just right, so I finally, *finally* took a bite. Fresh flavors exploded on my tongue. The sauces, yes, that punch of zhoug followed by the smooth, creamy, garlicy tahini. The falafel broke open with a crunch. Perfect texture.

The pita was excellent. Chewy but thin. Excellent ratios. The cabbage and the pickled turnip were zingy and added another dimension of texture and flavor. My brain loved this food. My mouth loved this food. Everything was in perfect combination. And it was manageable, not too sloppy. Another bite and I might need a napkin, but the pita was keeping everything in one place and nothing was going to go dripping down my hand.

I was sad when the sandwich came to an end. I took my last bite, chewed, swallowed and looked up at the truck where she was pretending not to watch me.

"So?" she finally asked.

"It's good."

"Good?" Her dimple appeared, and then she made it go away like she didn't want to show me too much joy. I was suddenly obsessed with the idea of stripping that impulse from her. Making her feel so good she had nothing to hide behind. Laying her bare before me and making her come and come and come again. She wouldn't be able to pretend she didn't care because she'd be screaming for me.

Shit. I was hard *again*.

"Yes. Very good."

"Well," she nodded. "That takes care of that, I guess."

"If I was going to make a suggestion-"

"I don't want your suggestion," she cut me off. "It will only make me doubt everything. You said you liked my food and you liked my falafels. That's enough for me."

"It needs more salt."

Her arms flew out to her sides. "I told you I didn't want your suggestion!"

"I'm incapable of not giving it to another chef."

"I'm not a chef," she corrected me. "I'm a cook and it's salted perfectly."

"We can agree to disagree, but I'm right."

She frowned. "I hate you. You know that, right?"

"You're feeling something for me. But it's not hate." Her eyes met mine and neither one of us could hide how we felt. How impossibly drawn to each other we were. Even this falafel feud was just a way for us to manage how under each other's skin we were.

She leaned over the counter and I stepped closer to her.

"What are we doing?" she whispered to me. Even though with the buds in his ears Nick wouldn't hear a thing.

"I told you. Flirting."

"This doesn't feel like flirting. It's never felt like flirting."

We were in the middle of town, surrounded by people. Nick was in that food truck with her. This was not the time or place for this conversation.

"Nick," I said, and Birdie tapped him on the shoulder until he took the ear bud out. "You want to go home? We can play Call of Duty."

"Actually, Birdie said she would pay me if I worked the full day."

Money over virtual war. Fair enough. Birdie over me. Another sign maybe I was the wrong person for this job?

"You'll bring him back to the house after his shift?" I asked her.

She nodded.

I shoved my hands in the front pocket of my jeans and set about getting what I wanted, which was her, in my home at the end of the day.

"Drop him off and I'll make dinner."

She crossed her arms over her chest. "Show-off chef food or real food?"

"Real food," I offered.

"Well, I'll have to see what it is. I'm very picky."

"You made Kraft and hot dogs, Genevieve. You're picky like a seagull."

She hooted with laughter, her dimples flashing, which made me smile in return.

"Thank you for the sandwich," I said, tossing the wrapper away.

"Uh, where do you think you're going?" she said. "You need to pay me for that. That will be twenty dollars, please."

My eyes popped wide. "Twenty dollars? You charge everyone else seven bucks!"

She shrugged. "No one else comments on the lack of salt."

I fished a twenty out of my wallet and slapped it on the counter.

"It was worth it," I said. "To have a bite of your...cooking."

"Dude," Nick said, shaking his head, his eyes lowered. "Not even remotely cool."

Genevieve was smiling though. So I didn't care.

∽

Birdie

"This place is lit," Nick said from the passenger seat next to me as I brought the food truck to a stop in front of the house, next to Tony's Rover. We shut the truck down around five. By the time we got through cleanup, which went much faster with two of us, it was just after six and the sun was starting to set. Antony's house was beautiful in the twilight, glowing and warm.

"I wish I could just stay here," Nick said.

"It's not how the system works," I told him.

"Yeah, well, two years and I'm done with it."

I looked over at him. "That's when you turn eighteen?"

He nodded. Chin out, eyes hard. I remembered when turning eighteen sounded so great. The freedom to finally be out from under my father's rules. To be seen in the world as an adult with my own mind, making my own decisions.

But freedom was hard. Rent, food, jobs. None of it was easy at that age.

"What's your plan Nick?"

He blew out a breath and it was comforting to know he felt the weight of it. He wasn't taking it lightly, adulthood, and that was a start.

"I can do a lot with my hands. I'm good with cars, too. Maybe find a job with a mechanic. If I have to pick up a couple of gigs, I can do that too. I don't mind work. I had fun with you today."

"You did a good job," I said. He'd been a good listener, a quick study. "I would hire you, if I could afford you, but I'm a one woman show. But, don't you want to think about college?"

He laughed. "Take on massive debt so I can get some nine to five I hate just so I can pay off the debt? No thank you. I would rather get a dog, teach it a cool trick, put it on Tik Tok, become an influencer and make a million dollars."

I frowned. "Is that a thing?"

"It's totally a thing. Aren't you on TikTok?"

"I stay away from social media," I said, and he stared at me like I was an alien.

"You know, you could make an Instagram account for Birdie's and you'd get a lot more business."

"That's what people keep saying, but I like my business

just the way it is." I hopped down and together Nick and I made our way to the front door.

"Yeah, but if you made more money," he said. "Then I could work for you."

I stopped in the gravel drive.

"After school or whatever. During the summer. I could help with the truck. Food prep. Clean up."

He was serious. I'd been joking before about hiring him and now I was going to hurt him.

"I could start an Instagram account for you. Be like your social media coordinator."

"Nick-"

"I would totally earn my keep."

"I don't live here," I said. "I'm just in Calico Cove for a few more weeks. There's a big competition I've been invited to over in Portland, but after that...I'm hitting the road again."

"You're leaving?" he asked, and he made it sound so personal it broke my heart. How did I tell a sixteen-year-old that leaving was what I did.

"Yeah...eventually."

"Oh." He looked so young. So disappointed. "Where are you going?"

"I'm not sure yet."

"Is it better than here?"

"No. It's just different."

"Whatever," he finally said, and shook off the disappointment like it was nothing. Only I could tell it wasn't nothing. "Worth a shot."

"Nick," I touched his shoulder and pulled my hand back when he flinched. He didn't like being touched. "I'm sorry. You know it has nothing to do with you."

"Sure. You just met me. I get it."

He walked past me, shoving open the front door to Antony's house, kicking off his shoes in the foyer, like he belonged there.

I felt like I'd been hollowed out.

"Hey! Antony! We're here," Nick called out over the sunken living room.

"Oh good, you're just in time," Antony said as he walked into the living room. He was wearing a chef's apron I knew by brand cost hundreds of dollars. A cloth towel was perfectly folded in the front pocket.

The apron was immaculate, like he hadn't cooked a thing while wearing it. My aprons were never like that. They were always splattered with sauces and grease. I caught the whiff of something delicious coming from the kitchen and my stomach rumbled.

"I'm hungry," Nick said, but I could tell some of the light he'd had in him all day had been diminished and it hurt that I had done that. "How long until we eat?"

"You practically ate your weight in falafels today," I reminded him.

"Yeah, but those were just like snacks."

For him that made sense. He was tall and lanky and completely too thin for his frame. My guess was, he was always hungry.

"Go get cleaned up and then head back to the kitchen," Antony told him. "I need the potatoes peeled. I'll show you how I want it done."

"Sure thing," he said with a salute. The kid had no problem earning his keep.

We watched him head up the stairs to his bedroom and I followed Tony to the kitchen.

"He turns eighteen in two years," I said, biting my bottom lip. "He thinks he can make it on his own."

"He can if he gets the right kind of help," Tony said, filling a pot with water over the stove.

I took my familiar seat on the island. "He asked me if he could have a job. I guess he thought I was here all the time. I had to tell him I'm leaving."

"Shit. How did that go?"

"Awful," I breathed out. "I mean, he pretended not to care but..."

"You care."

"I do."

He came over and wrapped his big arms around me. My face was pressed up against the expensive apron and his white shirt. He smelled like clean clothes and herbs and it was becoming my favorite smell, and this hug was becoming my favorite hug and it was all too much.

"We need to just have sex and get this over with," I said into what was practically his armpit.

"What?" He put his hands on my shoulders and pushed me back. "Did you just say-"

"This build up...it's messing with my head. Let's just do it and move on."

"Is that what you usually do? *Do it* and move on?"

"None of this..." I gestured around his house, him, the kid in the other room. "None of this is what I usually do. I'm a loner."

"What do you think fucking each other is going to do?"

I flinched at the word. It didn't sound right for us. But I suppose that's what I was suggesting. A fling. A hook up. Fucking.

"Get it out of our systems?"

He stared at me like I was a lunatic.

"It's the curiosity. The buildup. I'm telling myself a story about how good you're going to be in bed, and there's no way you're that good. No way."

"Oh, Genevieve," he said, his fingers spearing into the sides of my hair, holding my head still and looking down into my eyes. Trapping me where he wanted me. "You think once is going to do it? You think I'm going to fuck you and you will be able to walk away like it's no big deal?"

I made a sound, half whimper, half groan – but none of it was an answer. I was mush in his hands. I was hard nipples and trembling muscles and deep pulses of need.

"When I make love to you, and that's what I will do, neither one of us will be able to walk away. I'm going to need a lot of you. Endless amounts of you. Because the truth is I have wanted you from the moment I saw you. Imagining what I would do when I finally got you out of those aprons and into my arms. I have a list of places I need to touch you. Kiss you."

This guy. Nonstop seduction. He was not understanding my mission here. We needed to combust, blow each other to pieces so that there was nothing left standing. Nothing to pull us back to each other. We needed to ruin a good thing so we could walk away and not hurt each other. Too much. Because I knew then, as sure as I knew anything, that walking away from Tony was going to hurt.

Moving off my seat, I invaded his personal space and kissed him. I kissed him so he'd shut up. So he'd stop spinning dreams I had no businesses dreaming. I kissed him like I wanted to hurt him.

Again, I felt that surprise. The startle. Like he didn't like being the one not in control. It was obvious he'd been doing the kissing his whole life. Laying them on beautiful women who were not such unmitigated hot messes.

Well, not with me. I was a hot mess who lit my own matches, thank you very much.

In the echo throughout the house we could hear a door upstairs open and shut. Our cue to step away from each other. Even that somehow wasn't enough. I turned towards the windows, looking out at the ocean and a bruised sky.

"I started the application to be a foster parent," Antony said. "I haven't told him yet, but-"

"What?" I asked, shocked. "But you just met him."

Isn't that what Nick had said? Like we didn't really know him. Except it kind of felt like we did.

He shrugged. "It just feels like the right thing."

"What about the restaurant? Aren't you going to go back to California?"

He sighed. "Eventually. Look, it's a long shot, really." I watched his expression change. Become darker. Somehow I knew what he was thinking.

"You're worried about the video," I assumed.

He nodded. "I'm always worried about that damn video. Which made me think..."

"What?"

"What about you?" he said. He stepped closer and I fought the urge to step away. We needed to keep this quiet. Nick couldn't know what we were talking about.

"What about me?"

"What if you applied to become an approved foster parent? You might have a better chance than me."

I laughed, only it sounded a little hysterical. "Me? I live in my truck. I don't even have an address. And maybe you haven't been listening, but I'm not staying. I never stay."

"So you're just going to keep moving? For what? The rest of your life?"

"I have no plans for a home, or one place where I'm stuck. I never wanted any of that."

Until now. Until these last few weeks.

"Okay," Tony said in a voice that I knew was meant to calm me, but there was no undoing what he said.

Me? A foster parent to Nick? Staying in one place? Forever!

If I did that, if I chose that life, what would have been the point of all of it? Of leaving New York. Leaving Dad.

If I was just going to settle down now?

"I have to go," I said in a rush. Because running, that's what I knew. That's what I did really well.

"Gen, hey, I'm sorry. I shouldn't have said anything. Stay for dinner-"

Only I was already leaving the kitchen, halfway through the living room when I stopped because Nick was coming down the stairs.

"What's going on?" he asked.

"I can't stay," I said in a rush. "I have to go. You guys... have fun without me."

"Did you get into a fight? Was it over me?" Nick asked.

"No," I shouted.

"No," Tony said at the same time, standing behind me. I hadn't realized he'd followed me.

An excuse. I needed a plausible excuse. "Aunt Za's been missing me. All the time I've been spending up here. I should go and cook for her."

"Oh. Yeah. Sure." Nick shrugged. Whether he was bothered by my leaving I couldn't tell. Or maybe he was just getting used to it. Because that's what I did.

I left. I was fucking aces at leaving.

"The potatoes are in the pantry," Tony told him. "Pull out five, okay?"

"Sure. See ya, Birdie." Nick left Tony and me standing there in the living room.

"Genevieve," Tony began quietly. "Look, I didn't mean to put any pressure on you."

I nodded but still kept moving towards the door.

How did I get here? How did I get here so quickly?

Now everything was super messy and I wasn't dealing well with any of it.

"Hey, we're good?" he asked me once I opened the door.

I nodded, but I didn't turn around. "Sure, we're good."

"I'll see you tomorrow?"

I flashed a smile over my shoulder. I wondered if he could tell how freaked out I was in the inside.

"You know where to find me," I said casually.

"I do know where to find you."

17

The Next Day
Antony

"Tillie! Tillie! Go, go, go!"

Nick and I stepped into the Barnes' house, only to find chaos.

"Nora, slow down and stop chasing after Tillie, it only makes her run faster," Vanessa said coming out from the kitchen, with the swell of her pregnant belly leading the way.

The living room floor was covered in kids' toys and dog toys and I was overwhelmed with the sudden understanding of what a real family home looked like.

This house was nothing like the house I was in now and it was nothing like the house I'd grown up in.

"Antony," Roy said, as he picked up Nora to stop her from running. "You must be Nick."

"No, Daddy, down. I have to help Tillie," the little girl said.

"You're not helping Tillie, you're terrorizing her. There's a difference," Roy said. "Meet Nick. Nick, this is my daughter Nora, my wife Vanessa. I'm Roy."

"Uh, hi. Nice to meet you," he said, and wiped his hands on his jeans before he offered it to Roy.

They shook and Nora quieted down as she studied Nick.

"Nick a friend, Daddy?"

"Maybe, we're having a play date to see if we like each other," Roy said.

Nora squealed with excitement and clapped her hands. "Play date! Play date! Down, Daddy. I play with Nick."

Roy set his daughter down and she immediately reached for Nick's hand. "Come Nick, we play dolls with Tillie."

Nick looked at me like a deer in the headlights but I just clapped him on the back. "If you're going to stay here that means playing with the kid."

"You be Dolly and I'll be Nora," Nora said, leading Nick to a corner of the room that was piled with dolls of all shapes and sizes. To Nick's credit, he sat down with his legs crossed and listened as Nora introduced him to each of her dolls.

The dog came back into the room and sniffed around him. Nick just pet Tillie until eventually she sat next to him.

"I can't thank you both enough for doing this," I said.

"We're happy to help," Vanessa beamed. "We've been so blessed with, well everything, it's nice to give back. Plus, I can already tell he's good with Nora."

I looked over to see him with a doll in his hand talking in a high-pitched voice. The dog barked and Nora shook her head.

"No, Nick. Dolly doesn't sound like that. Dolly sounds

like this." Nora used a voice that sounded like a Disney princess on helium.

"Yeah, he'll figure out pretty quick she runs things around here," Roy said, looking down at his daughter, who I knew he'd adopted. "Why don't you go ahead and leave? Let us get to know him on our terms."

"Leave?"

"Beats us sitting here and looking at each other."

"Right. Of course."

It was a good idea. If Nick was going to live here, then they should get to know each other naturally. Not with me looking over everyone's shoulders.

"Yeah, good idea. He's got an appointment in two hours. I'll be back then."

"That's good. I can make him lunch," Vanessa offered. "Nick, are you hungry?"

"Uh, yeah," he said, looking at Vanessa, only to have Nora pat his cheek to bring his focus back on her.

"He's always hungry," I told them. "I'll help with the expenses."

"State helps with that," Roy said.

"Trust me, there is no state budget big enough in the world to feed a growing teenage boy. I'll help with food prep too. It will...give me something to do."

"Food from the country's best chef?" Vanessa said. "Yes, please."

"I like your cooking," Roy immediately told her.

"I know you do you, honey, but trust me, you'll like his better."

"Won't," Roy insisted. Then looked at me. "No offense."

I laughed. "None taken. Okay, I'll get out of your hair. Nick, be cool."

"I'm playing with dolls," he said from his place on the

floor, rolling his eyes. "I'm pretty sure cool left the building a while ago."

"I cool, Nicky!" Nora shouted.

Tillie barked in agreement.

I left the small Barnes' home that was stuffed with love and wondered what that must feel like. What was it like to be Roy Barnes? To have a wife, who he clearly adored. A daughter. Another child on the way.

What did that type of togetherness feel like? I couldn't really imagine it.

But being in that space, as chaotic as it was…it felt sort of nice.

∼

"You found me," Genevieve said, her lips twisted into a smile as soon I got up to the front of the line.

"Told you I would."

I was standing in front of her food truck, because where else was I going to go? She was a magnet in the center of town and if she was here I was here. It was that simple for me.

She'd left in a rush last night without eating. I wasn't sure if we were fighting.

"I thought I could help you work the truck," I said. "You know, because you won't let me have my own."

"Hilarious. Don't you have anything better to do?"

"Not for a few hours. Nick is getting to know Roy and his family."

"Oh!" she said, and then I saw understanding dawn on her. "Oh. Sure. Come on in. But so help me, if you try to boss me around in my kitchen, I'm kicking you off the truck."

"Yes, ma'am."

"I'm serious. I'm the boss, Tony. Say it."

"You're the boss."

I trotted around to the back of the truck where Genevieve had the door open. I hopped in and she handed me an apron that read: *Love is the secret ingredient. Love and Butter.*

"I'm not wearing that," I told her.

"Who is the boss, Tony?"

"Honestly?"

"Honey, I am going to enjoy every minute of this."

I took the apron and put it on. I didn't mind the pink. I looked excellent in pink. It was the layered ruffles.

"Love doesn't make food taste good," I pointed out in protest. "Proper seasoning does. Excellent technique."

"Face me for a second, would you?" she said, and I turned and she had her camera up taking a picture. She grinned at me. "Maybe I'll get an Instagram account just to put that picture up."

"You wouldn't."

"You have no idea what I'm capable of."

"Oh, I think I do."

She shot me an unsure look from under her long eyelashes. It occurred to me that she never seemed to wear make-up. Her skin was a healthy pink and I could see little freckles across her nose. Imperfections other women might cover up.

"I thought maybe you'd be done with me after last night." I blew out a breath I didn't realize I was holding. "It wasn't fair of me to think your plans had changed just because mine had. It'll just be sad to watch you leave."

She turned away, busied herself by stacking her wax paper and brown bags.

I'd never once been in a relationship so doomed for heartbreak.

Wait? Was I in a relationship?

"No, it was me. I panicked. But we're...okay," she said, having pulled herself together.

"Good," I said firmly. For right now I would take okay.

"You stand by the register," she directed me, giving me a little shove in my back. "I'll handle the fryer and sandwich assembly. You take the money, give change, wrap and hand over the sandwich."

"Yes, Chef," I said.

"No. I'm just Birdie or Genevieve. I'm not a chef."

"Yes, Chef," I said, just to piss her off.

"So why don't you have social media?" I asked her as we waited for the customers to show up.

"Why is everyone obsessed with my not having social media?" Her hair was back in a bun today, a bright green kerchief keeping the flyaway hair off her face.

"It's the best way to grow your business. I have a full-time staff member in charge of my social media."

"Of course you do. Ego, much?" Then she shrugged. "I don't really need to grow."

"I get it. But I also noticed you didn't want Levi to take your picture for the paper, either."

"Are you trying to play detective in my life?"

"I'm just trying to get to know you."

Her eyes caught mine in that way that made the already small food truck shrink. I felt like every breath I took smelled like her. Tasted like her.

"It's how my Dad finds me. Pictures on-line. Write ups and reviews. He has a Google alert for Birdies. I try to stay off the map so I can control when I see him and not the other way around."

"What does he do when he finds you?"

"This is the really horrible part," she said sarcastically. "He takes me out for dinner! Tries to ask how I am and if I need anything from him."

"What a monster."

"It always starts off fine. Until he asks me when I'm going to get over this silly food truck business and then things go downhill from there. It's like he still thinks he knows what's best for me even though I'm an adult now."

Daddy issues. Yeah, I knew all about that.

Local shop owners and the folks from town hall showed up. Soon there was a queue of about six or seven people and Genevieve and I got rolling. While she was prepping the sandwiches, I took the cash and made change. She used parchment paper to wrap the sandwiches and brown paper bags if someone ordered more than one. The only other offering was homemade chocolate chip cookies.

"Hey there, Chef. Funny seeing you in a food truck. Should I take a picture?"

I looked down and saw Jolie, who was still wearing her chef's apron and bright green Crocs

"Hello, Jolie. If you take my picture I'll end you." I warned her. "What's the special tonight at the restaurant?"

"Duck confit," she said. "With a truffle infused foam."

"Hmm, sounds good." Maybe I'd take Genevieve there some time. We could enjoy other people's cooking.

"Just make sure you salt it properly," Genevieve said, tongue in cheek, as she personally handed Jolie her sandwich. "Otherwise, Tony over here might give you grief."

Jolie's eyes got wide. "Okay, I'm wrapping my brain around you calling Chef Renard *Tony* and... nope. It's not computing. My head is going to officially explode."

Genevieve just laughed.

"Some chefs have respect for me," I told Genevieve.

She smiled wide. "Good thing I'm not a chef then. Line is backing up."

"See you tonight at poker, Chef?" Jolie asked as she handed over her cash.

I winced. That's right. It was poker night at Mal's house tonight. However, I didn't feel comfortable leaving Nick alone in the house. He was still too skittish and I wanted him to have some sense of consistency.

"Any problem if I bring Nick?"

"Nope, the more the merrier. You should come too, Birdie. Fiona, who runs the dress shop, plays, and when we gang up against the guys it's hilarious. I'm only doing the first seating tonight, so I'll be home around nine. But the guys will go until three in the morning."

"You don't want to play poker with these people, Genevieve," I warned her. "They're sharks dressed up as friendly Calico Cove locals."

"Worried I'll beat you?" she said with a single raised eyebrow.

"Uh. Yes," I answered, like that was a no brainer. "I suck at it."

"All the more reason to play," Genevieve said. "I might check it out. I've always wanted to get inside that lighthouse."

"I promise a tour," Jolie said, and then moved out of the way for the person behind her.

We were efficiently moving sandwiches when a kerfuffle in the front of the line broke out.

"Do you have to stand so close to me?" It was a familiar man's voice.

"Oh, yes, Matt. I'm trying to get as close as I can. Because what I really love is the smell of diesel gas and sea water," the woman who was standing behind him shot back.

She was a stunning red head I recognized immediately as Carrie Piedmont. The big-time actress returned to her hometown to shoot her next film here.

"I would rather smell like something real than some hundred-dollar French fancy water."

Her laugh was shrill. "Please, some respect. It's thousand-dollar French fancy water."

"You could maybe go find someplace else to eat," Matt suggested.

"Oh, I'm sorry, is my being alive inconvenient for you? Let me find the closest knife and stab myself in the chest."

"There's a shortage of perfect breasts in this world... but yeah, go ahead." Matt finished.

"Your *Princess Bride* game is weak," Carrie said, her lips curled in disdain.

Matt clutched his chest and weaved about as if her words had wounded him grievously. Then he placed his order with Genevieve.

"Birdie, how many falafel sandwiches can you make before you have to throw another batch into the fryer?"

"Six," Genevieve answered.

"Yeah, I'll take six."

"That's a lot of falafel, Matt," I pointed out.

"I'm really hungry," he said.

"You. Are. The. Biggest. Ass." Carrie had her arms crossed over her chest and was tapping her foot.

"Sticks and stones," he shot back over his shoulder. "Here's sixty, Antony. Keep the change. Going to see you at poker tonight?"

"Yep." I wrapped up his sandwiches and stuffed them in two separate bags. Meanwhile Genevieve was mouthing apologies to Carrie while she dropped a fresh batch of chickpea balls into the hot oil. They would need at least another five minutes to cook.

Finally, we got another batch hot and ready to serve. Carrie never really lost her frown though.

"Geesh," Genevieve said under her breath, once the actress walked away. "Those two make us sound like long lost friends."

"We're more than friends now," I said. I reached around her and picked up a ball that had cooled to my satisfaction. I bit into it and tried to pick up the flavor combinations. "Are you using a blend of fava beans and chickpeas?"

"I'm not telling you my recipe! It's a secret."

"Also, you should think about adding a side dish. For the competition. They don't include it as part of the judging, but the judges love that shit when you go above and beyond."

"Are you seriously telling me this now? The competition is in a week!"

I smiled. "Just a thought. I have to go. I've got to take the kid to the therapist."

"Please do not let me stop you," she said, clearly exasperated.

I don't know why, but this version of her frustrated and agitated was so attractive to me.

"You want to make out before I leave?" I asked.

"Are you joking?" She laughed.

"No. I just noticed you like to kiss me before you leave, so I just thought I'd return the favor."

"I'm not kissing you in my food truck, Tony."

"Your loss. Are you going to be at poker tonight?"

"You're taking Nick?" she asked, and I nodded.

Everything we'd said to each other last night. Every

heated glance. Every kiss. It was all between us. The air sparked with this undeniable chemistry.

I wanted to shut the awning and have her on the floor of this truck. I wanted to take her to a five-star hotel and lay her down on a king sized bed. I wanted ten minutes alone to fuck her in that lighthouse.

And everything about her, from her dilated eyes, to her parted lips and pink cheeks. Those nipples of hers I couldn't see, but was sure they were hard. Everything about her said she felt the same way.

"Maybe," she said. "Just to, you know,... check out the lighthouse."

"Right. Just to see the lighthouse," I said with a smile.

∽

As I sat in one of the grown-up chairs in the waiting room while Nick was in the office with Ben, Jessie interrogated me.

"What's Bobby Flay like?"

"Nice guy."

"Jamie Oliver?"

"Nice guy."

"Guy Fieri?"

"Super nice guy."

"You aren't going to spill any beans on these guys, are you?" Jessie asked. She peered at me through glasses that made her eyes look huge. It was like being interrogated by an owl.

"No, I'm not. But the truth is, you don't get to be a famous television chef if no one wants to work with you."

"I guess that makes sense," Jessie said and turned back

to her computer. I picked up a Thomas the Tank Engine toy and ran its wheels down my hand.

"Martha Stewart?"

"Surprisingly hilarious," I offered truthfully.

Ben's office door opened and Nick walked out. Head down, hands in his pockets. I jumped to my feet.

"Okay?" I asked him. He looked tired. Young. Fuck, was this too much, I wondered? Did he need a few more days to just sleep and eat before he had to tackle the big shit?

"He's good," Ben said, putting a hand on Nick's shoulder. Nick didn't shrug it away, which was a good sign. He smiled at Ben. Another good sign. "I'm very proud of the hard work you did today, Nick."

Nick practically glowed with pride. I'd told Nick if he didn't like Ben we'd find another therapist. That we'd keep going until he felt comfortable. However, I was relieved that he and Ben seemed to hit it off.

"If you want to schedule him again, this time works. Next week? That okay, Nick?"

Nick nodded. "Yeah, I can do that."

"And Jessie?" Ben said, turning to the receptionist. "Give him a notebook, would you?"

Jessie unlocked a cupboard behind her chair and pulled out a really nice notebook and a package of pencils and pens. Nick took them and held them against his chest.

I handed Nick the keys to the car. "Hey, head down to the car and get it started."

He took the keys, said goodbye to Ben and then to Jessie before walking out the door.

"Before you ask, I can't tell you anything," Ben said, holding up his hand. "Nick asked me to keep our sessions private."

"Okay..." Not okay. Not at all okay.

"Oh my god," Ben muttered. "That bothers you so much."

"I'm fine. Totally fine. I just want to make sure he's okay, right? I mean he's had a rough start, sure. But he's a good kid."

"Nick is a great kid. He's had some trauma and he's young, so developing a vocabulary to talk about his feelings is going to take some time." Ben leaned against the reception desk. "It's commonly believed that humans, when they experience trauma and it goes unchecked, don't grow emotionally from the age they were when the trauma occurred."

"He's going to be sixteen forever?"

"No. He's getting help. You...on the other hand..."

I laughed. "You're saying I'm sixteen?"

"If the shoe fits. Will I see you on the dock tomorrow?"

I'd stopped going the last few days, but tonight was poker and Genevieve might be there. I just had this feeling about tonight, so it was unlikely I would be up at dawn.

"Sorry, Ben. I'm hoping it might be a late night tonight."

And that hope had nothing to do with playing poker well.

18

Birdie

"Does this top look okay?" I turned from the mirror and asked my aunt, who was lounging on my tiny bed, looking more like a teenage friend then a woman in her late fifties.

"For him or for poker?" she asked as she tossed a kernel of popcorn in her mouth.

Popcorn was the one thing Aunt Za could competently make.

"There is no *him,* and what have I told you about eating on my bed?"

"My house, my rules," Aunt Za said. "You wouldn't be asking me how you look in a top if it was just poker. There is most definitely a *him.*"

It was a deep blue silk v-neck. Loose and casual, but the way the v-neck dipped...maybe a little sexy too. This poker night felt oddly like a date. Which seemed strange because it felt like we were already too deep into our relationship to have a first date.

Wait? Was I in a relationship?

Given that under this possibly sexy top I was also wearing my good underwear. Because just in case...all signs were pointing to yes.

"Ugh!" I said, falling back on the bed next to my aunt. "Give me some of that popcorn." She held out the bowl and I took a handful.

"You're over thinking it. He's handsome and entirely into you. Go have sex and enjoy!"

"It's not that simple," I said, popping a piece of corn into my mouth.

"No, it's exactly that simple," Aunt Za said, getting off the bed. Her pink flowy loungewear settling around her. "You're the one making it complicated."

"Because I'm leaving soon. He's staying to become a foster parent-"

"Really? That's so sweet."

"It is, but now there's this kid involved. Tell me how we walk away from this without getting hurt?"

I didn't tell my aunt what he'd said the other night. The way he talked, we would be incapable of *walking* after we had sex. And yes, of course I wanted that. The kind of sex that left you limp and ragged and changed. Every woman wants that.

She patted my shoulder. "Your heart is massive, Birdie. I know this. That's why entanglements aren't easy for you. But you can't spend your whole life avoiding things that might hurt you. That sounds like a life wasted. And another thing-"

"Oh geesh, really? Two sage life lessons in a row?"

"Yes," she said firmly. "It's time to stop running away from your father. He's not a demon on your tail. He's just a stubborn man living in New York. You love this town. You love staying here when you come. Leaving just doesn't make sense anymore. You did what you needed to do. You found your own path. Stop thinking anyone, including your father, can force you to be something you don't want to be."

I thought about what Tony had told me about his father. What little I knew about Nick's situation. There were people who had it so much worse than I did. What if I did reach out on my terms?

Maybe he would understand now that I was my own person. That I wanted my own life. Separate from his.

I mean, it seemed completely unlikely, but maybe it was worth a shot?

"He's lonely, darling," Aunt Za said from the doorway of the bedroom. "He doesn't say it of course. But for him, there was only your mother and you."

"And cooking."

"And cooking," Aunt Za agreed. "Now he has only that. A plate of food, as beautiful and delicious as it might be, will never love you back. Just think about it."

I nodded.

"And your top is divine. I'm thinking a blue-eyed chef will not be able to take his eyes off your fabulous cleavage, which is exactly what you want. All you need to do is admit it."

"Stop with all the wisdom already!"

She laughed at my consternation. "Take my car darling, so you don't have to take the truck. If you're going to make a mistake, it might as well be a good one."

∼

CHAOS. It was absolute chaos. I should have guessed it was going to be more than a quiet night of poker when I pulled up to the gated complex and saw a bunch of cars parked out front.

The front door was open and I didn't think with the noise inside anyone would hear me knocking, so I let myself in. The living room was off to the right and filled with people from town.

Elegant Fiona stood out among the crowd standing near the fireplace.

Matthew was also there, although no sign of Carrie Piedmont, which was a good thing.

"Hey," I said, coming up to Levi, who stood against the wall staring across the room at a woman talking to Lola and Jackson.

"I thought this was just supposed to be poker."

"It was," Levi muttered. "Then everyone found out and just started showing up. Now it's more of a party."

I looked at the woman Levi was checking out, but didn't recognize her. She had dark hair and wore a cute retro style dress covered in books.

"Who is that?" I asked him.

"Who is who?"

"The woman you're staring at."

"I'm not staring at anyone," he said, straightening off the wall. "The woman wearing the dress that looks like something a toddler would wear is Annie Piedmont. I live above her bookstore and I have not once seen her at a poker night. There's no way she knows how to play."

"Why are you staring at her?" I teased.

He shook his head. "Where's Antony? Go bother him."

Jolie popped out from the kitchen, her hands filled with two trays of what looked like hors d'oeuvres.

Only a chef would cook at her restaurant all day only to turn around and whip up something quick for her guests.

"Oh hi, Birdie. Come in and get comfortable. We haven't started playing yet, because it's turned into more of a party than a game night."

"Does that happen often?"

"Apparently," Mal said. He'd followed Jolie out of the kitchen with his own tray. "There was a time I preferred my solitude. Jolie, however, enjoys the chaos of entertaining."

"It's fun," she said brightly. "Don't listen to him, he loves it."

"You're going to ruin my reputation as the Beast of Calico Cove," Mal said.

"Oh, honey," Jolie looked at him with love in her eyes. "I ruined your reputation a long time ago."

When the two started kissing, I caught sight of Tony and Nick standing in the corner and got the heck out of there. Nick had a soda in one hand and a toddler in the other.

"Look at you with a baby," I said.

Nick rolled his eyes. "She won't let me put her down."

"No, no, Nicky. You hold me," she said, with the flat of her hand planted firmly on his cheek. Clearly, she was infatuated. She wore a pair of blue corduroy overalls and white and pink fairy wings.

Roy arrived to our left. "Nora pitched a fit when she found out Nick was going to be here, so I brought her along. Seems she's quickly become attached. Figured I'd give Ness a chance to take a peaceful bath. But we have to get home now. Let's go, Nora."

"No," she pouted. "Stay with Nicky."

"No, you're coming with me," Roy said, his arms outstretched. Nora crossed her arms over her chest and scowled right back at him. Roy sighed. "If you want Mommy to tuck you in bed, you have to come home with me."

Oh, a tough choice, I thought. Her newfound love, Nick, or Mommy. Only it wasn't hard for Nora.

"Sorry, Nicky. I go Daddy and see Mommy."

Nick just laughed and handed her over to Roy.

"Geez, you're getting heavy," Roy grunted. "Stop growing up."

"No, no, Daddy. I a big girl!"

He smiled. "Yes, you're my big girl. You'll bring Nick and his stuff by the house tomorrow, Ant?"

"He'll stay with me tonight in case we're late, but yeah, tomorrow we'll make the move to your place," Tony said.

I could tell already Tony hated the idea of handing Nick off, but the state wasn't going to let him stay with Tony indefinitely. There would be follow-ups, which meant Nick had to be living with Roy and his family.

Roy grunted his goodbye and Nora waved enthusiastically to everyone as they left.

"Okay, are we going to play or what?" Fiona asked, approaching the table that was set up for poker in the middle of the room, while munching on what appeared to be a stuffed mushroom.

She clearly wasn't here just to mingle with the other guests. The woman looked like she was on a mission.

"Relax, Fiona, you'll have my money soon enough." Antony said, then turned to Nick. "Any chance you know how to play poker?"

"Sure," he said. "We played all the time in...you know."

Juvie.

He didn't want to say the word out loud and I wouldn't either.

Tony took out three twenty-dollar bills from his wallet and handed them to Nick. "Sit in for me for a while. I want to show Genevieve the lighthouse."

Nick looked at the money. "For real?"

"Yeah. Anything you make beyond my original buy in we split. Sound fair?"

"Fuck yeah," he said, then looked at Genevieve and blushed. "Uh, sorry, Birdie. Yes, that seems fair."

"Nick is sitting in for me," Antony announced to everyone. "Mal, I'm going to show Genevieve the lighthouse, okay?"

"Yep," Mal said, taking his seat at the table. "It's not locked."

Tony took my hand. "You ready?"

Was I ready? I had no idea, but I was going for it.

"Yep."

~

"Oh my goodness," I whispered, as we climbed the last step and passed through the hatch into the main part of the lighthouse. The lights had been turned on from below so we could see everything as we made our way around the circular landing that surrounded the lighthouse bulb.

"Pretty cool, isn't it?" Tony said.

"I can't imagine what the view is like during the day. You must see so far out into the ocean. Do you think they see whales from here?"

"Mal has. Back when he used to spend more of his time up here. Now that he has Jolie, I don't think they use this space as much."

"That's too bad because this view has to be something special."

A streak of moonlight created a road down the middle of the ocean bathed in white light.

It was beautiful.

Arms bracketed me against the windowsill on either side. I could feel the heat of Tony behind me. See the strength of his forearms, where he'd pushed up the sleeves of the heather gray Henley, my favorite shirt of his, he'd worn over jeans.

"You didn't bring me out here to show me the view, did you?" I asked him.

He pushed my hair off my shoulder, giving him access to my neck. Would I feel his lips or his teeth there first? Was I maybe possibly tilting my head in a direction that allowed even better access?

"No. I brought you out here to seduce you. I'm really hoping you're okay with that," he said, his lips so close to my ear, I could feel his hot breath on my skin.

"Mmmm."

"Your blouse is particularly sexy," he whispered against my neck. Then I felt it, the barest brush of his lips just under my ear. "Makes me wonder, did you wear it for me?"

"No," I insisted, still holding on to this delusion that I was in control of myself when I clearly wasn't. "I wear clothes for me. Of course."

I turned and grabbed onto the front of his shirt, pulling him towards me.

But he held himself back.

"What?" I asked, looking up at him.

"This time I'm kissing you," he said.

"Oh my god, seriously-"

He didn't let me finish before his lips dropped to mine.

He cupped my cheeks in his palms like I was the most delicate piece of fruit he'd ever held. Tilting my head, so he could drop chaste kisses on my lips like he was trying to communicate something. Gentleness. Teasing.

He wasn't kissing me. He was testing me. Looking for some opening in my armor.

"Tony," I whispered as his lips skimmed my jaw. "Just do it already."

"Stop telling me what to do."

"You're savoring me and I'm not a steak," I mumbled.

"Hmm, no. You're something far more delicate than that," he said, tilting his head and grazing his finger under my chin. "Now open for me, Genevieve."

There was something in those words. The command of them. My eyes on his, I did as he asked, opened my lips.

His blue eyes flared and there was a hot, secret communication between his body and mine.

"Wider," he breathed, and look, I don't know what got into me, but I did it.

"Look at you," he breathed. "What would you do if I asked?"

Anything.

He growled like I'd said it out loud, and hell, maybe I had. I'd done it before with this man. Blurted out truths I never would have before. He was in my head and made me feel out of control.

He kissed with his tongue deep in my mouth and I'd known it would be like this. I'd known after savoring me he'd devour me. My first thought was that this...this was what I'd been waiting for my whole life.

I was nothing but sensation and desire. It was like every exchange between us had led to this combustible moment.

I dug my fingers into the shirt at the small of his back. He pressed my body up against his. He was so hard everywhere. His chest, his thighs. I felt the bulge of his cock pressed against his jeans and arched against it. I felt empty. Hungry.

I wanted more. I wanted so much more. I lifted my leg up around his hip and he caught it in his hand. Grabbed my ass with both hands and squeezed. I groaned low in my throat.

"Too much?"

"Not enough."

"Fuck," he growled, and he spun me. Away from the windows and up against something more solid. A bookcase maybe? I was slammed up against it, hard enough to shake the shelves, but I didn't care because the fury of that action on the outside matched the intensity of what I was feeling inside.

Tony released my mouth only to kiss the spot on my neck. I felt his teeth, his tongue. He cupped my breasts, squeezing them with big, wide, rough hands and everything was right on the edge of pain. Everything was right on the edge of our control. I reached my hands under his shirt, wanting more of his skin. His heat.

"Don't," he said, lifting my shirt up, finding my nipple hard beneath my bra and sucking it into his mouth through the silk barrier. My knees buckled and he held me up with his hips. The length of his dick pressed against my hot, damp core. I pushed against him, needing friction. *Needing him.*

"Don't what?" I panted.

He took my hands, locked our fingers and pressed them back against the bookcase. "Distract me."

The movement centered him perfectly against my clit and I bit my lips so I wouldn't scream. So I wouldn't beg.

We were dry humping against a bookshelf like teenagers and it was without a doubt the hottest thing I'd ever experienced.

"Please," I groaned. His head collapsed on my shoulder.

"Fuck, honey, I love it when you beg. Please what?"

"More. Please. I'm..."

"Can you come like this?" he fucked up against me, his hard cock jammed into my jean covered core. All I could do was hold on tight to his fingers.

"Yes. Antony. Please. *Please*."

He thrust against me, harder this time. "It's not enough," he groaned, and snapped his hips again. "Not enough!"

We knocked something over. There was a thump and then a spectacular crash. At the sound of it Tony jumped away from me.

I was so stunned by the absence of him, I almost slipped down the length of the bookcase. I managed to hold myself upright, but I knew my mouth was still open and I was panting to catch my breath. Like I'd just run some extreme race.

"What?" I asked him. "What's not enough?"

But he was shaking his head, running his hand through his hair like he was trying to come to his senses. I reached for him and he backed away.

"Are you okay?" he barked at me. "Did it scratch you?"

I glanced down at where he was looking. A vase had shattered on the floor.

"No, I'm fine. What wasn't enough?" My voice was small and I hated the sound of it. "Me?"

How could something be so big to one person and not enough for the other?

He closed his eyes and covered his face with his hands. When he lowered them, the man I knew was suddenly gone. Like a curtain had been pulled across his actual self and all I was left looking at was his blank expression.

"I'm sorry," he said, his voice low. "I have to go."

"Go? Tony, I don't understand."

I took a step towards him but he held up his hand as if to stop me.

Then he pointed at me in a way I imagined he'd pointed at hundreds of sous chefs in any kitchen he'd ever been in. The way he pointed at that line chef right before he threw the plate.

"You should stop calling me Tony."

Without another word, he turned his back on me and made his way down the circular staircase of the lighthouse into the dark.

19

Antony

"Come on kid, let's go." I was standing over Nick, who was still sitting at the poker table with a sizable stack of chips in front of him. Everything was so loud. So ...sharp. Bright.

After leaving the lighthouse, I'd taken a walk around the property to try and clear my head, but I just needed to be away from people.

Away from Genevieve.

Beyond that, I didn't need to go walking back into Mal's house with a raging hard-on I knew would not go uncommented on by Matt and/or Levi and/or Mal.

"Where's Birdie?" Levi asked.

"She wasn't really interested in playing. So she left after seeing the lighthouse."

I'd heard a car start when I was walking off my frustration. She must have borrowed the car from her aunt and decided not to face the crowd waiting inside the house either.

She probably looked like a wreck. Swollen lips. Marks on her neck. Her hair disheveled.

Like a woman taken hard against a bookshelf.

Fuck!

"She told me to say goodbye for her," I lied. I rubbed my forehead with hands that shook.

It was the night of the kitchen all over again. I was barely hanging onto my control. I was hot and cold. I couldn't feel my fingers. Only instead of throwing a plate against the wall, I'd nearly lost all control with…Genevieve.

"Come on, Nick," I said. I was terrified of what would happen if I didn't leave right now.

"But I just got started," he protested.

"I need to go," I said sharply. I had to get out of here. I couldn't let everyone see the melt down I knew was coming.

It was like I had this monster inside me screaming to get out. A monster I'd always done such an amazing job of locking down, but suddenly it was growing and bursting at the seams. I needed to get control of myself. I needed to do it now.

Instantly, all eyes turned on me. "Sorry," I said to Nick. "I'm just…I've got a migraine."

I pinched the bridge of my nose and closed my eyes, thinking maybe I'd just willed myself into having one, because my head felt ready to explode.

"Yeah, sure," Nick said. "Levi, can you cash me out?"

"Yeah," he offered and quickly turned the chips into cash. I noticed when he handed Nick the money it was significantly more than what I'd given him to start.

"Sorry, everyone," I offered.

"Hold on," Jolie said, getting up from the table. "I have the best stuff for migraines."

"No, please," I told her. "I have medicine at home. I just need to get there."

"We're good," Nick said. "I can drive him."

As distracted as I was, I had no problem with that. With a final goodbye, we headed out and Nick got behind the wheel of the Rover. The darkness helped. The darkness was good. A simple task, getting us home, also good.

"You okay, Antony?" he asked. "You don't look so good."

"Fine. Just...a migraine."

Or just fucking lost it on the most amazing woman I've ever known. Just nearly embarrassed myself during the hottest sex of my life. You know, the usual.

"How much money did you cash out?" I asked, trying to distract myself.

"Two hundred and sixty," he said immediately. "I was going to give you the money, but you seemed like you were in a hurry to get out of there."

"You're that good at poker?" I asked.

"Poker is easy," he said. "It's all about the risk. I was the only one sitting at the table who *needs* money. Well, maybe not the only one. Fiona's pretty ruthless too. Anyway, it makes me play an entirely different game. If you'd let me sit at the table longer, I would have taken all their money. You could have had a better night."

"Great," I muttered. "Not only was I a dick tonight, I invited a card shark to play with my friends."

"You know it's card sharp? Not card shark."

I glared at him.

"Got it, not the right moment for semantics," he said.

We were silent for the rest of the drive until we got to the parking area in front of the house. Nick must have finally pulled together the courage to ask what was really on his mind.

"Did something happen with you and Birdie?"

Yes. I screwed up. I have no idea what she's thinking or how I even begin to explain.

"I'll fix it," I said.

Nick just shook his head and opened the car door. "Man, you are not so good with women."

I gave him another glare, but the sad truth was...he was right.

"I can fix it," I insisted.

I hoped to hell I was right.

∾

The Docks
6:20 am

"You know it's raining," I called out to Ben, who was standing on the edge of the dock.

A bitter wind blew over the ocean. The sky was various shades of grey. Black storm clouds threatened worse weather in the distance, even as steady rain fell over us now.

I hadn't slept much last night, so I'd been up super early. Knowing Roy was an early riser, I wasn't surprised when he answered the text I sent him at five thirty this morning.

He'd told me to bring Nick by so he could show him around the fishing boat.

The kid had still been half asleep when I dropped him off, his entire life shoved into an oversized duffle bag. He'd looked determined though. No pleas to stay in bed longer when I told him to get up, no sad eyes or requests to stay with me.

Nope, he'd gotten up, packed his shit and accepted his fate.

The kid was a fuck ton braver than I ever was.

"You don't say?" Ben answered over his shoulder, then went back to looking at the ocean.

He was wearing a serious set of all-weather gear. I was wearing a windbreaker over my jeans and was immediately soaked through.

"You look like shit," Ben said, when I stood next to him on the dock.

"Well, I'm standing in the rain."

I looked back toward the town square. I hoped Genevieve wasn't setting up in this weather. There would be no customers lining up today, and I knew she hated to waste food.

Heck, she might have left town already. Packed up and put me in her rearview mirror.

I deserved it.

"Feels like you need to talk about something, Antony."

I wiped the rain off my face and it just kept coming. "I was with Genevieve..."

"You were with her..."

"Like, we were together." I gave him a long pointed look and he finally nodded.

"Ah. I get it."

"We knocked a vase over and it smashed against the floor and I..."

Ben was silent. Patient. The rain made tapping noises against his rain coat.

"I freaked out. Said something stupid and just ran away.

I wasn't in control. Not even a little bit. I thought I was getting better."

"Antony, why would you think you were better when you haven't really shared anything?"

I sighed. He was right. I wanted to be fixed, but to do that I had to understand why I was broken.

"Sit," Ben said, pointing to the rain soaked folding chair. "Talk."

I was probably going to get pneumonia, but maybe it would be worth it. I poured off the water that had gathered on the plastic seat and sat down. Ben opened another folded chair and joined me.

"I remember being angry," I began.

"At your sous chef?"

I didn't need to explain what I was talking about. Ben knew I meant that day at the restaurant.

"No." I used my hands to squeeze water out of my pants. "I mean, yes, the lamb was plated wrong, too much sauce, but it wasn't...it didn't deserve that kind of reaction. It had just been a shit day."

"So, what were you mad about?"

"There was this guy..." I stopped. God, why were we in the rain? I wiped more water off my face.

"In the kitchen?"

"No. In the dining room. Some drunk fucking asshole who wanted to be a big shot. He was shouting at his server, but Jenny was a pro. I knew she could handle him. But he must have made some gesture, something, and he ended up breaking a wine glass."

"That made you mad?"

"Of course, it made me mad! That shit is not cool."

"What did you do?"

"I went out on to the floor and got between the guy and Jenny. Made sure she was okay and kicked the asshole out."

"Was Jenny okay?"

"Rattled. But fine."

"From everything I've read about you, you created a beautiful restaurant, where, as far as I can tell, you treated people with respect. You were not a shouter."

"I took a lot of pride in that," I said. My fingers were getting pruny from being in the rain. "My patience. My control."

"Then one night a man came in and ruined it. You want to tell me why?" Ben asked. "Because you already know the answer. You'd just learned that your father was dead, Antony..."

Ben didn't have to say anything else.

"He looked like him," I said quietly. I didn't even know if Ben could hear me over the rain, but it didn't matter. "The asshole. He was drunk and he looked like my father, and for a second I thought...he wasn't really dead."

Ben and I sat there in silence. For a long time.

"Is this... it? Am I done?"

"No, Antony," Ben said with a sad smile. "You're just getting started."

~

> Antony: Can we talk?

I STARED down at the text I'd sent an hour ago, still unanswered. I could tell she'd read it though.

I'd just finished my first appointment with CPS via a Zoom meeting. I knew it wasn't going to be easy and my single status wasn't helping my cause, but I gave the social worker some of my background. Enough for her to understand my interest in doing right by Nick, as well as why I might be an effective foster parent in this situation.

The video didn't come up, but oddly I felt myself better equipped to talk about it. I had some language around what had happened. I could see, in hindsight, it was bad, yes. But there was context. Context mattered.

Now I *needed* to see Genevieve. Explain why I'd botched everything last night. At least now, I thought, I could explain it a little.

I got in my Rover and headed into town. I would wait in the park across from where she usually parked her truck and wait for her line to die down so we could talk privately.

The storm had already blown over, as spring storms did along the coast, so there was no reason any longer for her not to set up shop.

She had asked me something last night. Something about why she wasn't enough and I hadn't understood it at the time. I'd been too much in my head. Or too much in my dick. But I couldn't let her think that *she* was the problem when it was one hundred percent me. If I couldn't fix at least that, I had to let her know that she was beautiful. More than enough.

I'd been the one lacking.

When I got to the center of town her truck was missing from its usual spot.

Panic overtook me. Had I upset her to the point of leaving Calico Cove early? Would she do that without saying goodbye? To me, maybe. But she'd say good bye to Nick.

No, there was no way she would blow off the M vs. A Competition. It was too important. Would she?

Along the edge of the park I spotted Madame Za

setting up her tent. I parked and jogged over as she was writing on a chalkboard the pricing for her various services.

Palm reading, Tarot Card reading. Aura reading.

This woman did a lot of reading.

She looked up from what she was doing and put her hands on her hips. It didn't take any skill to see her aura was pissed off.

"Chef Renard. You are an idiot," Madame Za proclaimed.

I bristled, but she wasn't wrong when it came to Genevieve.

"What did she tell you?"

"Oh no, I'm not sharing secrets. Birdie is a puzzle only you can solve. No clues."

"Fair enough, just tell me she hasn't left for good."

Madam Za pursed her lips. "She decided she needed a day off."

"She's not gone," I tilted my head back, unembarrassed by my relief.

"You were scared," Madame Za nodded. "That's what I thought. Maybe you're not quite the idiot I thought you were. You need to fix what you broke. She was rather...well, she was sad when she came home last night and I hate to see my niece sad."

"Trust me, Madame Za, so do I."

"To understand, Genevieve is to understand her relationship with her father."

"I know he doesn't approve of her life choices. Makes him a dick in my book."

"Hmmm," Madame Za said, pressing her lips together. "She hasn't told you?"

"Told me what?"

"No, that will have to come from her too. But I do think your aura needs some fresh air."

"My aura?"

"Yes," Za said. "Sea air is good for cleaning out the negative energy. That's what I recommend."

She was giving me a clue and I knew exactly where to go.

∼

I FOUND her in the exact same spot we found Nick. She was sitting in the wet sand, her hair free of its normal kerchief blowing gently around her face. She was staring out into the ocean roughened by this morning's early storm as if all the answers were there.

Maybe they were.

I'd found some of the answers I needed today, looking out at that same ocean.

I plopped down next to her in the sand, my ass getting immediately wet, my hands resting on my bent knees, and saw from the corner of my eye, her shaking her head.

"Isn't it obvious I want to be alone?"

"Totally," I answered.

"Then why are you here?"

I shrugged. "I can't seem to stay away. Some people call that golden retriever energy."

"Some people call it stalking," she retorted. "I don't want to talk to you, *Antony*. Whatever. Not until I can get my head on straight about what happened."

My shoulder brushed hers and I let out a defeated sigh.

"I scared you. I'm sorry."

"You didn't scare me," she snapped. "Is that honestly what you think? You scared me? No you idiot, you left me hanging against that bookshelf, pushed me away, said I wasn't enough. Then you just left me there. So, no, I wasn't *scared*. I was pissed off!"

"I didn't say you weren't good enough."

"Oh, yes you did," she insisted. "Trust me. You said, and I quote, 'it's not enough.'"

"You think...you think that was about you? That somehow *you* weren't enough for *me*?" I threw up my hands. "Holy fuck, Gen! Did you get that wrong."

"That's what you said!" she shouted.

"Okay. Okay. Just...listen to me. Everything was going great, right? It was hot."

She lifted a single shoulder. "Maybe."

Maybe. This woman would be the death of me. "Then we broke something."

"A vase. I cleaned that up before I left. By the way, you're welcome!"

"Thank you," I said. "It was the sound. It was like that plate breaking all over again. Apparently, according to Ben, the sound of shit breaking is a...trigger for me. It takes me back to days with my dad. I was out of control with you last night. For me, that's just a scary place to be because I don't want anyone to get hurt."

"Oh," she sighed. "Antony. I'm sorry."

"Tony," I told her, wanting to bash myself in the head for what I'd said last night.

"Tony," she repeated.

She put her hand over mine and I flipped my hand around so we were palm to palm. I spread my fingers wide and hers slipped right between them and we held onto each other. Tight.

"Babe, nothing in my life has been as hot and as out of control as what we were doing."

"Really?"

"That's not how I have sex," I admitted.

"You have boring sex?" she teased.

"No. Of course not. I'm a chef. I like to savor and taste. I like to linger. Easy, slow. Nothing that burns too hot or too fast. And I like to be..."

"In control," she finished for me when I couldn't find the right words.

"In control," I admitted. "I'm good at it by the way. Sex, I mean. You weren't wrong when you thought I might know what I was doing in bed. I'm like *really* good."

She smiled then at my audacity and I knew that whatever sadness I had caused was somewhat forgiven.

"Oh, you are?"

"Everyone says so."

"Everyone? That's a lot of people."

"Well, maybe not so many," I paused. "Why haven't you stood up, brushed the sand from your butt and told me to fuck off?"

"Maybe I'm just waiting to see if you actually live up to your own hype."

I looked at her only to find her grinning up at me. Impish and wise. Freckled and grounded. She was a mix of all the things I'd never valued before her and I was obsessed. Addicted.

"Want to go find out?"

"Right now?"

"Nick is with Roy and Vanessa. My house is empty and you've taken the day off."

"I don't know-"

I didn't let her finish. I grabbed her around her waist and pulled her onto my lap. Her legs spread on either side of mine. I reveled in the weight of her, the heat and shape of her against me. I put my hands in her wild woman hair and brought her down for a kiss.

Her cold hands cupped my face but her lips were warm. Hot, even. She opened her mouth and let me inside and it was everything I remembered and more. I was hard in a heartbeat and she groaned, grinding herself against me.

"Come back to my house," I said.

I could do this. I could have her my way and not lose control.

"Teenagers make out here all the time. It's fun." She pressed wet kisses along my jaw, making her way to my ear. She sucked my earlobe and my toes curled in my shoes.

"We're not teenagers," I said. "I want you naked. I'm pretty sure they don't allow that on public beaches."

Then, in a move that impressed even me, I got to my feet with her in my arms. There was one tiny lurching step when it seemed like I might drop her, she screamed and clutched me.

"Please, Gen. Let me have you," I said into the pink shell of her ear.

"Okay, Tony. Take me to your house," she said.

20

Birdie

He broke every speed limit on the way up to that house. Blew through a stop sign.

"Tony!" I shrieked. "You are going to get us killed or arrested."

"Not happening," he said, looking at me as he hit the gas even harder. "Bobby would never arrest you. He's addicted to your sandwiches."

"He *is* my best customer."

In the cup holder his phone buzzed with an incoming message. Then it rang. He reached down and turned it to silent.

"You can-"

"Not interested," he said. A few minutes later we were parking in front of his house. He was out of the car and around to my side, opening my door.

Would I find that annoying after popping the sex bubble? This old school chivalry he had, with the doors and the feeding me and the warm socks on my cold feet.

No, okay that would probably still be hot.

I heard the buzz of his phone again as he opened the door and let me into his house.

He reached for my hand and I took it, knowing that wherever this was going I was all in for the ride. The bumpy, crazy ride, with a world-famous control freak chef. I couldn't have written a less likely scenario for myself if I'd tried.

His phone buzzed again and I could hear the sound of it, even though he had the ringer turned off.

"Someone is really trying to get in touch with you. You should answer it."

He shook his head. "No. No distractions. I have questions I need answered."

"About what?" I laughed.

"About your freckles. Are they all over your body?" He closed the door behind us and crowded me against the wall. "What color are your nipples. I need to know."

His finger traced the v-neck collar of my shirt, lifting it from my skin so he could see the rise of my breasts.

His phone was still buzzing and I put my hand over his.

"We're not going to have sexy times, if you're wondering what the emergency is."

"You would be amazed at my capacity to block out all distractions to focus solely on sexy times."

"Tony, answer the phone. Put us both out of our misery."

He sighed and turned away to answer his phone. I admired the way his t-shirt hung on his back, over his shoulders. The way his ass filled out those jeans was a crime.

"Yes, Venetia. What's so important...Oh. Really. Hmm. Do we have any time to change...okay. Well, there is no changing it then. It's done. Yes. Of course. I..."

I tried not to eavesdrop or predict who he might be talking to. Someone named Venetia, but I didn't know who that was to him. Not a girlfriend, of course. He wouldn't be here with me if he had someone in his life.

Are you sure about that?

Yes.

That felt good, I thought. To have a gut sense that I knew this person enough to know he wasn't a liar or a cheat. He was too proud for that. If he made something it would be his, not someone else's.

If he had someone in his life. She would be his too.

That was a scary but appealing thought.

"I don't know. I've told you…it's complicated for me," he said into the phone. "Look, there is no point in crying over spilt milk. See that…I made a food reference. Yes, I know I'm not very funny. Sorry. Okay. I'll talk to you soon. Yeah, bye, Venetia."

He was sad, but whatever the emergency was it wasn't life threatening, which made me a little less worried.

He tossed his phone on the couch and sighed. One thing I knew for certain, gone was my charming flirting chef. This man had the weight of the world sitting on his shoulders. I stepped forward and rubbed his back, and strangely it felt like the most natural thing in the world. Like he was mine to comfort.

"The food gods have spoken. The Robin's Egg is officially being downgraded. We've lost our three star Michelin rating and are now simply a two star restaurant."

I gasped. Of course I knew what that meant. The restaurant industry had been my life growing up. I knew exactly how hard and how talented someone needed to be to earn three stars and the ramification of losing it.

Two stars still meant excellence. Two stars was nearly perfection.

But for a chef, a man like Antony Renard, to be downgraded, I couldn't fathom where his head was right now.

"Tony," I whispered. "I don't know what to say."

"There is nothing to say. Nothing to do. That's what I told my business manager."

That's who Venetia was.

"I should go," I said. This was going to be a lot for him to process. He had to want to do that privately. "I can call Aunt Za to come pick me up."

"No, please stay. Please."

He turned into me, his face so close I almost didn't realize what was happening until his lips met mine. This time there were no soft kisses. He wasn't savoring me, he was tasting me full on and I immediately felt the kick of heat through my body.

These were desperate kisses and I got lost in the sensation of it. He was pushing me into the couch and the delicious sinking feeling combined with him on top of me was as exciting as being slammed up against a bookshelf.

His hands were sliding up under the shirt I was wearing.

"Can I touch?"

"Yes," I whispered against his mouth.

"Everywhere?"

His thumb was already rubbing my hardened nipple over my bra. The friction of his finger against the lace was maddening.

"Genevieve," he said as he dusted kisses along my neck. "Everywhere?"

"Yes," I answered, because the threat of him stopping was too awful to consider. His touch was different. I couldn't explain it, or compare it to anything I'd ever felt before. His hands were rough, but his touch was light. Effortless. Like I could feel the scratch of his skin everywhere. Along my sides, my belly, over my breasts and against my clavicle. He pulled me into a sitting position so he could pull off my shirt and remove my bra.

Instantly his mouth was on my breast. Sucking me deep as if he was trying to inhale me. As if I was the best dish he'd ever had. All while teasing me with his touch. A stroke down my spine. Fingers pressed into my lower back that made me arch further into him. Then he was pressing me back down on the couch, his palm warm on my chest.

He knelt between my legs and his fingers went to work on the buttons on my jeans. Pausing only to shove his hand down the back of the pants to squeeze my ass. Like he couldn't wait another second to know what that felt like. He had to get off the couch so he could strip me of my jeans altogether. He was standing next to me, my jeans dangling in his one hand while his other hand ran up and down the length of my body. His gaze landing on my breasts and then the tiny triangle of pink cloth nestled between my legs.

"Beautiful," he whispered. Dropping the jeans, he ran a hand over his mouth, like he was deciding where to start.

Again I felt like some scrumptious meal to him.

"I'm going to lick your pussy until you come, Genevieve. And when you do, I want to hear it. Every bit of it. Understand? Every sound you make, every feeling you have. I want all of it."

Then he was between my legs again, still dressed even as he had stripped me of my last swath of clothing. There was no subtlety in his actions now. He'd told me what he was going to do. But even as he threw my legs over his shoulders and dipped his head between my thighs, I still wasn't prepared for it.

The sensation of his tongue directly on my clit was too much and not enough. Because once again, his touch was light and teasing. As if he was playing with me instead of trying to satisfy me. A nibble on the inside of my thigh.

"What are you doing?" I asked. "I thought you were going to fuck me, not play with me."

His laughter was a deep growl against my chest and he slipped a finger deep inside me, reaching a spot I didn't even know I had. I arched off the couch, bowing against him.

"Like that?" he said.

"You're getting closer," I groaned. He laughed and I reached for him. For the hard length behind his zipper, but he grabbed my hand and pushed it back against the couch. I whimpered, wanting him.

"How about this?" he whispered, and then it was another finger and I was so full. He twisted his hand, used his thumb against my clit. My soul was splitting apart. Pleasure like a bomb in my body.

The sounds I was making. The growling screams. The half-formed words. I was mindless. Animal.

"That's it, Genevieve." He whispered into my ear. "Let me hear you. Do you want to come?"

"Yes, please. I can't take it anymore."

"I don't think that's true. I think you can take quite a bit more."

He shifted so he was over me. His blue eyes all I could see. All I wanted to see. "There you are," he said with a grin. "Right where I want you. You're so wet for me," he groaned. He pulled his hand away from my pussy and sucked his fingers into his mouth.

I shuddered with pleasure. I wanted more. I wanted everything.

I lifted myself to get closer to him, but he pushed me back into the cushions of the couch and spread my legs wide so he could get his mouth on me. He sucked on my clit and the orgasm nearly tipped, from about to happen to happening, but it was like he knew it and backed off.

"Tony," I groaned, my head rolling back and forth on the cushion beneath me. Every muscle was shaking, sweat was pouring off my body.

"Sorry, love, you're just too delicious and too beautiful. I want to taste and watch."

"I want to come," I whined.

"Yes, but I like it too much when you beg."

"Please, Tony. Please, let me come."

He stared down at where his own fingers were spearing into me. With a wicked gleam in his eye, he slipped a finger, soaked in my juices, inside my ass.

I came so hard my body buckled in half.

I screamed and knocked something off a table. Nothing shattered but there was a thud and I caught my breath, watching him to see if he'd react.

He smiled. Kissed my belly. My hip bone. The underside of my breast.

"It's okay. I've got control."

I lost all ability to move once it was over. I was sprawled out on the couch and he was gazing down at my nakedness. I had no idea what he was thinking but every muscle in my body was currently unusable.

"Again," he said.

Again? Again? That wasn't even remotely possible. Was it?

"Tony, no. I can't."

"I think you can," he said, even as he reached down to adjust his erection inside his jeans.

What he'd done to me was all about giving me pleasure. Like I was some kind of dish he'd created and was pleased with. With him in control every step of the way. To the point, he hadn't even taken off his shirt.

"No," I said.

"Try," he pushed, sliding his hands down over my body so that I felt every callus, every burn and knife scar on his hand. Then both of his hands were on my ass cheeks and he was lifting me up to his mouth again.

"No!"

My tone caught his attention and he immediately stopped to check in with me. Lowering me gently back down to the couch and slowly moving his hands off me. "Talk to me."

I rolled off the couch and stood up, my arms instinctively crossing over my breasts even as I looked for something to cover my body.

That motivated him to take off his shirt and he put it over my head. I put my arms through the sleeves and was comforted by the warmth and the smell of him surrounding me.

"I spooked you," he said, as if he was coming to some conclusion.

I shook my head. How did I explain this to him?

"It didn't feel like you were with me."

He moved closer to me and I was fixated on the swirls his chest hair. "Explain, Genevieve. Because I felt like I was right there with you."

He brought me into his arms and I wanted it too much to resist. I wasn't mad, I wasn't hurt, I wasn't spooked. I just wanted this.

"I wanted to be closer to you and it felt like..."

"What?" he pushed.

His deep blue eyes were so freaking intense. "I felt like I was some dish you were creating. Like my orgasm was the point."

That confused him. "Your orgasm *was* the point. I wanted to pleasure you."

"See, that's wrong, Tony. I don't want to be pleasured. I want us to be in it together. I want you to lose your control-"

"No, Genevieve. I told you, that's not how I do this."

"Yes, but last night, until that stupid vase broke, you were in it with me. We were both feeling the same things together. Tonight it was like you were above me watching it all happen, totally in control of every feeling I was experiencing, but you weren't...close to me."

I sound pathetic.

I was standing there in his shirt, wrapped up in his arms, complaining after I had the best orgasm of my life. Complaining because I wanted more. Different.

"I'm not making sense probably," I finally said.

"Genevieve, I told you. I have to be in control when it comes to sex. When it comes to everything. I *have* to be. You see what happens when I'm not."

"Plates start flying?"

He sighed. "I was a very angry kid once upon a time, but I learned through discipline how to keep all of that contained. I need to know that, so no one around me is going to get hurt."

I cupped his cheek in my palm. "No one who touched me like you did could ever hurt me. I'm certain of it."

"God. I wish I had your faith."

"That's okay. I have it for both of us," I smiled at him, feeling closer to him in this moment than I had when he had his fingers inside of my body. "The next time we have sex, I get to be the one in control."

His eyes got wide. "Are we talking ropes?"

"I don't know. All I know is that you're going to do what I say. It will be good for you I think. To turn that over to me, but Tony..."

"Uh oh. Here it comes. This is going to be like the falafels right? You're going to make me work for it."

"You just found out The Robin's Egg lost a star and you turned to me like I could...." s*ave you* was what I wanted to say. But instead I said "distract you."

"I wasn't using you," he argued. "You can't think that."

"No, but are you sure you're not using this town and everything happening with Nick to distract yourself from all the things you need to do in California?"

"You sound like Ben."

"I'm not here to tell you what to do or give you hoops you have to jump through. But you're adrift right now. You have to see that."

I pulled his hand down to my chest and rested it over my heart.

"You snuck in here," I told him. "But if we're doing this...thing...we need to be in it together."

"You should run far away from me," he muttered, running his hand through his hair. "I know this intellectually, and yet I'm fairly certain I would follow you wherever you went."

Yeah, he would. "Take me home?"

"Without pants? I'm pretty sure Madame Za would hex me."

"She doesn't do hexes. Too much negative energy. However, pants are required. We need to find mine. But I'm keeping your shirt. It smells good."

"Fine," he said, bending down to retrieve my jeans and handing them to me. "But then I'm keeping these."

"My undies?" I squeaked.

"They smell nice," he said, wiggling his eyebrows.

21

Antony

This was a dream. It wasn't real. In my head I knew that, but still I couldn't make myself wake up. It was too fucking delicious. I was at a fine restaurant. The Pearl in Manhattan? Where everything was old wood and hushed conversations. Only instead of Chef Edouard Manet's Steak Tartare, which was the only meal I ever ordered when I went to The Pearl, the dish in front of me was mine.

The meal I'd made. Beef Wellington. It had been the first dish I'd deconstructed and made for Francois. This first time he'd grunted at me and nodded his head in approval.

I hadn't realize how much I'd needed it. That approval. The feeling that for once in my life I'd done something right and someone else had acknowledged it. When my father had only ever called me a shithead. A shithead who wouldn't do shit with this life.

His screams wanted back in, but I wouldn't let them. I wouldn't hear them. Just focus on the dish. Focus on what you've accomplished.

Suddenly, the plate was gone and I was back in my kitchen. At The Robin's Egg. There was no one there, it was as pristine as I demanded, except...

"Take me, Tony. Hard."

Genevieve was face down on one of the work stations. Her back arched, her bare ass in the air. All that glorious pale skin and soft flesh, just waiting for me to take her. Claim her. She was wearing her kerchief, a saucy smile and nothing else.

"Take me, Tony. Please! I need you inside me."

And then I was. I slammed my dick into her from behind and it was glorious. Hot, tight, and so wet.

"Harder! Harder!"

No, I thought. I don't do that. I don't let myself take. It's about giving. It's about savoring. It's about her. Not about me.

"Please, Tony. Let go."

She needed to stop saying things like that. I was at the edge of my control. It took everything I had in me to keep my thrusts slow, steady. Pleasing to her.

"More! Harder! Faster! Take me!" She was banging her fists on the work station.

It was like a chant in my head.

Take her. Have her. Let go.

It's okay with her. She wants you. She wants all of you, even the deep down ugly parts.

I let go. I grabbed her hips, my fingers gripping her hard. I would leave a bruise on her ass and I liked that. My mark on her body that she would see the next day. I was rough and needy, thrusting into her so deep and fast. She was screaming my name. I felt the clench of her body around my cock, knew she was coming and then...

Crash!

The sound stilled me. I turned my head and watched the plate crash against the wall. Craig's face. Surprised, fearful. The shards of white china splintering onto the floor.

I did that. I was capable of that. Just like my father.

I sat up in bed panting. My body was covered with sweat, and between my legs I was hard and aching. I wrapped my hand around my dick and squeezed. A groan coming deep from inside my chest. I'd basically been hard all night and jacked off in the shower before going to bed. It wasn't enough. I still had the taste of Genevieve in my mouth. The sound of her coming in my ears.

I pulled her pink panties from underneath the pillow where I'd put them earlier. I hadn't lied. I'd wanted to smell her near me. Shamelessly, I wrapped the panties around my dick and tried to imagine her making herself come still wearing my shirt. No more than three hard pumps and I was coming, but I pulled the panties away first.

I didn't want her smell compromised with my cum. I grabbed a few tissues to clean myself up and shoved the panties back under the pillow.

I thought about what I was going to tell Ben tomorrow.

Definitely not the part about her panties.

∽

"So what's your deal?" Nick asked me as we left Ben's office together.

I had waited in the lobby for his session and afterwards he had waited in the lobby for mine.

It was official. I was now Ben's patient, not just the guy he was talking to on the docks.

Together we walked out of Ben's office, looking

exhausted but a little lighter, I thought. I'd told Ben about the dream and we'd talked a little about what it meant.

True to my word, I didn't mention the panties. Or Genevieve bent over my work station, for that matter.

It was helping. Both of us. I could tell. Like the load we were carrying had been shifted so it wasn't so heavy.

"I have control issues," I said as I tossed him the keys to the Rover.

"You're kidding, right?" He held up the keys. "You let me drive your like billion dollar car. That's not a guy with control issues."

That was true. Really true. It absolutely never occurred to me. Maybe because I trusted Nick. So I probably should trust him with the rest of it.

"Also…my dad used to beat the shit out of me."

"Seriously?" Nick asked me. Like he didn't believe me. Like maybe I was just saying it to connect with him or with his experiences.

I pushed up the sleeve of the hoodie I was wearing. "I tell people I got these in the kitchen. Which is true."

There were three distinct burn scars on my forearm.

"This one," I pointed. "And this other one I got when my dad hit me with a cast iron skillet that was still hot and filled with grease. I'd overcooked his hamburger. I was nine."

Nick nodded and I could see that he was seeing me differently. Not as a rich dude who drove a fancy car and lived in a fancy house. I was more real to him now.

We got in the car and Nick just sat there, his hands on the wheel, the engine off.

"Why are people like that?" Nick asked. "Your dad. My dad. Why?"

"I don't know. Maybe their fathers were assholes."

Nick shook his head. "So, we're supposed to give them a pass?"

"Fuck no," I said and Nick smiled. "All I know is I lost my cool a few months ago and a person I value got hurt. The whole thing reminded me entirely too much of my father. So I have to fix that shit now before I become him."

"You would never do that. To a kid," Nick said, defending me.

"No one who touched me like you did could ever hurt me."

Genevieve's words from the other night echoed in my ear. I wanted that to be true. For her.

I had to be worthy. For both of them.

"Thanks, kid," I said. "Let's go see Birdie."

"You know she's leaving, right? After her big competition or whatever."

I nodded, wondering where he was going with this.

"I was thinking. Maybe we should get her to stay?"

I chuckled, because it really seemed that simple. "I'm working on it, kid. I'm working on it. Let's go see her."

Nick parked the Rover in the town square and there was already a line for Genevieve's falafels.

"Shit, Birdie's backed up," he said, and jogged over to her food truck, I knew to offer help.

She waved him inside with a smile and I realized that smile had become my favorite thing on earth. I also hopped into the back of the truck, which made it crowded, sure, but we were a team now.

She was bent over the service station, her worn jeans hugging the curves of her ass, and it was too much like my dream. Naked, bent over my workstation in my kitchen, begging me to take her.

She turned and saw me in the back of her truck and grinned.

It was ridiculous how happy I was right now.

How do I get her to stay? I wondered.

"Three of us are too many," she complained, shooing me out. "I won't be able to move in the truck. Nick, ring up three sandwiches and a garlic fries."

"Garlic fries?" I asked.

"I'm trying them out," she said. "You said I needed a side."

She wore an oversized flannel shirt on top of her apron. I was disappointed it wasn't my Henley. But maybe she saved that for bed. I planted myself on an overturned bucket she'd most likely used to carry the potatoes. I wasn't in her way, but I could watch her and Nick work.

She was dropping a basket of falafels into the hot oil. Then quickly assembling a sandwich with the falafels she had ready to go, and handing it off to Nick, one by one as he rung up the orders.

A symphony in motion. I waited until the line had diminished before demanding my due.

"Feed me."

She put her hands on her hips, her dark hair as usual pulled back in a kerchief. This one was purple. Now that I could see the front of her, I read her apron.

Bake the World a Better Place.

Yeah, she did.

"Pushy," she said.

"Hungry," I replied.

"Yeah, I could go for some fries," Nick said, looking around the orderly truck. "But I don't see any ketchup."

"No ketchup," Genevieve frowned, even as she used tongs to pull the fries out of the silver bowl where they'd been tossed in a garlic dressing, if my nose was on point.

And my nose was always on point.

She added them to a small brown bag. Then she took a squirt bottle and covered the fries in a creamy sauce. She threw a bunch of herbs on top.

"Try this instead," she said, handing a bag to Nick. I noted he got dibs, but I assumed that was because he was still too skinny.

Then she did the same for me, pushing the sauce covered fries into my hand.

"How much is this going to cost me?" I asked suspiciously. "I only have two twenties in my pocket."

"This one is on the house," she said.

Then because she was close and Nick was distracted with shoveling fries in his mouth, I grabbed her hand and made her bend down to me. "Is that because I gave you an amazing orgasm?"

She quickly looked over her shoulder to Nick who hadn't heard a thing. He was humming, I think with pleasure.

That meant the sauce was good. I was waiting for my fries to cool down just a smidge.

"You're bad," she whispered.

"On the contrary, I thought I was very good."

Her lips twisted into a smile. "I'll have my revenge."

"I'm looking forward to it with every ounce of my being. Come over tonight."

"Is that what you want?" She was asking me if I was ready to move forward. With her. Be with her the way she needed.

"I want you...to grab me some napkins," I added when Nick looked over at us. I held up the bag of fries. "Well?"

"They're fucking stupid."

"Language," Genevieve said automatically. "Is that good?"

"It slaps," Nick said.

"Still uncertain," Genevieve replied.

"He means they're good," I told her. "Man, are you so not cool."

"I'm cool," she objected. "Mostly. Okay, you try them."

I dipped my fingers into the bag and extracted a few fries covered in sauce. But I was able to find a point on the fry to keep my fingers clean. Essential for eating. Like any good fry, the crisp was important. I preferred mine extra crispy and Genevieve did too. I popped one into my mouth and instantly the garlic hit me. I could tell she hadn't just chopped up the garlic. No, there was a roasted flavor behind this. Also, no bites of bitter garlic to distract from the flavor.

Had she infused the oil with garlic, strained it and then used that to marinate the potatoes?

The technique there was solid and somewhat reminiscent of something, but I couldn't place it.

"Genevieve?"

"Yes, Tony?"

"Have you gone to cooking school?"

Her lips pursed and I felt like there was something she wasn't telling me.

"No, not a traditional cooking school like you're thinking."

I threw another couple of fries in my mouth.

There was the tang of the tahini sauce. Sesame, lemon and a little hint of heat. This was a bag of fried goodness in a tangy sauce. Also the herbs were a nice touch.

I grunted. "They're good."

"That's it? I think I like *slaps* better."

"He's messing with you," Nick said. "They're next level. Can I have more?"

"He's going to eat you out of your profit," I told her.

"The fries are pretty cheap," she said, and started to turn to make him another batch, but I grabbed her hand to stop her.

"You'll come?" I asked her. "Tonight."

Her big wide mouth twisted into a smile.

"No, I think you will."

∽

IT WAS STRANGE, I thought. I was putting together dinner, waiting for Genevieve to come over and thinking about how quiet the house was now that Nick was gone.

I'd been in Calico Cove a little over a month, mostly with just myself for company, but with the addition of Nick and Genevieve that had all changed so quickly.

Yes, Nick was at Roy and Vanessa's house tonight, but we all agreed he could spend the night up here every once in a while moving forward.

When I'd asked him how he liked it at the Barnes', he'd said Nora was annoying but he was smiling as he said it.

I missed having him here and really hoped things worked out with the CPS people.

I liked cooking for people who would enjoy my food, without having to perform for anyone. Playing video games at night was way more fun than watching cooking shows by myself.

How had I never known that?

Have you ever been in a relationship?

Ben had asked me that today. It was a simple question. Basic personal facts about me. Of course I answered yes. I had friends. Mal, for one. I'd had lovers. I'd worked with any number of chefs over the years.

"Have you ever lived with anyone outside your immediate family?"

No. I'd answered. Probably a little defensively. I was thirty-five, dedicated to my profession. I hadn't had time to take a relationship to the level of living with a person.

I didn't count Francois. He'd put me up in his restaurant on a cot in the restaurant's back office. That wasn't living with him, that was living with the work.

"Have you ever been in love?"

That had stopped me. It felt like a man my age should have been in love at least once. I'd been in lust certainly. Given all that shit that happened with my dad growing up, I hadn't had the normal teen experience. My first time having sex was with one of the older waitresses at Francois' restaurant.

Nadine. She'd been in her thirties and genuinely just liked to fuck. She'd taught me a lot about sex, but nothing about love.

So no, I'd never been in love. I hadn't had a serious relationship. I hadn't even loved my parents.

All I had was food.

Maybe I needed to get a dog?

The doorbell rang and I felt this wave of heat and happiness fill me up.

Genevieve.

She was going to be with me and eat with me and make out with me.

She was going to make me come, and probably make me laugh, and also probably make me say something stupid because I didn't try to be anything but myself around her. I was going to tease her until her big wide mouth broke into a smile and she showed me her dimples.

I was going to have fun.

"What do you do for fun?"

Ben had asked me that too and I'd laughed.

"What are you talking about? I cook."

That was my fun. That was my pleasure.

That was my whole fucking life.

Until now.

Because tonight I was going to have fun. Actual fun. With Genevieve.

I opened the door and she held up a bottle of wine.

"It's a Merlot, pretty cheap, and I don't want any comments from the peanut gallery. We're drinking it."

Yes, I thought. Tonight was going to be fun.

22

Birdie

"Hello to you," he said, taking the wine from my hand and pulling me up against his chest. He planted a kiss on my mouth. Firm, sexy, but more of a hello and less of a let's continue.

"Is this what we do now? Do we kiss?"

"Yes!" he practically shouted. "And in front of Nick too."

That seemed odd. "Why do you want us to kiss in front of Nick?"

"Not make out or anything," he said over his shoulder as he led me back to the kitchen. Always the kitchen with him. "Like no tongue, but he should see natural adult affection."

"Uh, he's living with Roy and Vanessa. Rumor has it those two can't keep their hands off each other. Aunt Za said Roy knocked Vanessa up a couple of months after some hasty wedding."

"I want him to see what people, who are not his shit parents, behave like."

I nodded. "You want to be a model for him."

"I want to show him it can turn out okay in the end," Antony said. "Just because his life started out shitty, doesn't mean it has to keep going down that path."

"And is it? Turning out okay for you?"

He looked a little grim, but very determined. "I'm working on it."

That made me happy. "So things are going well with Ben?"

"It's kind of one step forward, two steps back."

"Isn't everything?" I asked. I pulled open the heavy refrigerator door looking for a preview of what he had planned for tonight's dinner. I saw a mixing bowl covered with plastic wrap. "What's this?"

"Don't look at that," he said, coming behind me, and taking the bowl out of my hand. "It's an experiment I'm working on, but it's not ready yet."

"Fine. I'll just have wine then."

"I'm making you a riff on Massimo Batturo's Tagliatelle with Ragu."

I grimaced. "I told you I don't like fancy chef food. You don't have to impress me."

"It's pasta with meat sauce," Tony said. "You'll like it. It doesn't measure up to his of course, but it's close. Damn the man for keeping his secrets, secret. But we should talk about that."

"Why I don't like overly fancy food?" I asked him.

"Why someone who has to have had some professional training in a kitchen rejects the art of cooking so thoroughly."

"I'm not rejecting it. Per se," I hedged.

"Genevieve," he said, like he wanted me to just roll over

and bare my belly to him. Just because he was going to therapy didn't mean I was interested in spilling all my secrets.

"Look, I promise at some point I'll tell you the whole sordid story. However, tonight I would really just like to hang out and have fun with you. Can we do that?"

"We can do whatever you want," he said and kissed me softly on the lips. "Sit down. Drink your wine."

I did as demanded, getting comfortable on what I now considered my stool at the island. Happy to have a front seat to watch Antony cook. He boiled water. Put the sauce on to simmer.

"So tell me," I said. "You've travelled all over the world. Eaten food prepared by the best chefs."

"I have."

"What's your favorite? And ego maniac, you can't say any of your own dishes."

"Brat," Tony said. "I can acknowledge there is greatness beyond me. Heck, I have to acknowledge it. I'm no longer a three-star Michelin chef."

I winced. I hadn't wanted to bring that up. "We're not talking about the bad stuff," I reminded him. "Only the good stuff."

"Right," he said, and leaned against the counter, looking like a wet dream in another Henley shirt, this time black, which worked for me on every level. "Noma's Moldy Egg Tart, certainly."

"Sounds delish," I teased.

"This dish I'm making by Massimo is absolutely one of my favorites," he continued.

"You do a lot of riffing on other people's food."

"It's the highest compliment from one chef to another," he said very seriously.

"Go on."

"Don't sleep on Colicchio's braised short ribs. But if we're talking my death row final meal...Chef Edouard Manet's Steak Tartare. So simple, so elegant, so much flavor and richness."

I took a deep sip of my wine. A gulp really. I finished half the glass.

"So you've been to The Pearl in New York?" I asked.

Of course he had, I thought. It only made sense. For years it had reigned supreme in the restaurant world. But it was considered somewhat old-fashioned now. Dishes were simply made and nothing was deconstructed or infused with anything. No dry ice or tricks. So it wasn't as written about as much anymore.

"Chef Manet is one of my idols. He's everything I aspired to be when I was coming up in the cooking world. He doesn't use tricks like many other chefs do. Some call him unoriginal, but I think a man who can make basic flavors sing like he can...that's truly an art."

"Yeah, I hear he's pretty great," I said. "But enough talk about the fancy chefs. We need to talk about my food truck problem."

"What is your food truck problem?" Tony asked. He was plating the dish. Twirling the pasta just so, spooning the perfect amount of meat sauce around it. Then a fresh coat of shaved parmesan cheese and a final swipe of the plate with a napkin before setting it in front of me.

I told myself that I never wanted to eat like this again. I told myself that delicious food couldn't replace things like love, respect and freedom.

But Tony wasn't trying to impress me, or show off how much better at this he was than me.

He was simply feeding me, because that's how he talked to people. I understood that now.

I took a bite of his freshly made pasta with his long-simmered sauce and had to suppress a groan. Then of course, I shrugged and said, "It's good."

"Brat," he said again. He took a bite of his own plate and grunted in satisfaction. "Now talk. What's your problem?"

I sighed. "I'm making too much money."

He blinked. "Seriously?"

"I know. It's sounds like I'm being a jerk, but I've never made this kind of money before. I don't know what to do with it all. Should I hire someone? Should I rent another truck? I mean, who knew Calico Cove had such a thing for falafels? And the garlic fries! My goodness, I had a line of twenty people this afternoon when word got out about the fries. I had to turn away people when I ran out and you know how that goes."

"I do," he frowned. "Genevieve, you make an excellent product that's consistent. You're supposed to make money from that. It's not a bad thing."

I knew that. Of course, I did. "It's just never happened before. I always made enough to get by. I never had to think about..."

"Expanding?" he said, supplying a word that made me scared.

"Expanding means responsibilities, pressure, staff and management. Expanding means being tied down to one place and losing all of my freedom. Expanding means compromising my vision of the life I wanted to have."

"You mean the vision you had when you were nineteen?" he pointed out.

I squirmed in my seat and ate another delicious bite. "You're suggesting I might have been young and immature."

"I'm suggesting you didn't know much about life back then. Fuck, none of us do at that age. But as you go through life, you realize things change. Your wants and dreams do too. I can tell you this, if five years ago my business manager called me up and said I'd lost a star, my ass would have been on a plane back to California immediately. And I would have been in the kitchen twenty-four seven until I'd concocted something so unique, so delicious it would make food critics weep with joy, until I got my star back."

"And now?"

"Now, I'm sitting here on a beautiful spring night, in a small town, with a beautiful woman, eating a fabulous pasta dish and drinking a half-assed Merlot. I'm not going anywhere."

He was looking at me, those blue eyes on fire, like he already knew I was part of his dessert.

"I told you not to be a snob about the wine."

"Can't help it. Occupational hazard."

"I don't know what to do," I admitted. Because I knew the last thing I wanted to do was pack up my truck and hit the road again. Instead I wanted to be here, on a beautiful spring night, eating a fabulous pasta dish with Tony.

Not Chef Renard. Not Antony. Just my Tony.

"I'm pretty sure you know that I can't tell you what to do," Tony said carefully.

"Obviously," I said.

"Then I'll only tell you what business advice I would give to someone in your predicament. When you have something that's working...you expand."

I pursed my lips at him. "So logical," I grumbled.

"So simple," he corrected me. "Do you want more bad wine?"

"Yes, please."

Antony

Hookay. This was uncomfortable. Or not. Or hot as hell, I wasn't sure.

"Not too tight?"

Genevieve was asking me if the hands she currently had tied behind my back with a tie she'd taken from my closet were okay.

No, it wasn't too tight. However, my hands were tied. Technically my wrists, but the point was the same. I couldn't move them. Couldn't free them. I wasn't sure I wanted to free them, but the sensation of not having access to my hands was...unnerving.

It had all started out so simply. I'd asked her what she wanted for dessert and she'd kissed me with *intent*. Now we were in my bedroom and I was sitting on a chair I typically used to put on my sneakers, and my hands were tied behind my back.

Of course she'd asked my permission. And because, let's face it, with the hope of an orgasm in my near future, I'd said yes.

Still, this was different. Strange. She'd said she wanted to be in control, and I was letting her. But I felt agitated. Not just aroused, but like something in my entire body was off kilter.

Oh shit. Was this something I was going to have to talk about in therapy? Telling Ben about my dream was hard enough.

"Tony, talk to me. Too tight?"

"Uh, no," I answered honestly.

She came around the chair, her hands on her hips. "I know this is different for you, but if you're really uncomfortable then it won't be sexy."

"Well, what happens next?"

She smiled and straddled my lap. Her butt on my knees, her legs spread over my thighs. Her skirt hiked up her thighs. I could see the strip of lace between her legs.

"Definitely sexy," I muttered.

"Do you have a safe word?" she asked me, a playful smile on her wide mouth even as she teased the hairs along the back of my neck.

"Do I need one?" I asked a little breathlessly. Was she going to push me past some limit I didn't know I had? Yes please, was the only thought I could muster.

She tilted her head, considering it. "No, don't think so."

She leaned over and picked up the bowl with the cut up strawberries I'd planned for dessert.

"Good. Open." I did as she asked and she placed a strawberry in my mouth. Sweet, tart, ripe.

I watched as she ate one herself, her lips stained red with the juice.

Again, she leaned over and picked up the bowl of whipped cream I'd also prepared. No canned spray cream for me.

She swiped a strawberry through the cream.

"Open."

I did and she placed the fruit on my tongue.

"Good?"

"Delicious, but I would rather be eating something else right now." It was maddening to have her this close and not be able to touch her. Not be able to grab her ass and press against where I really needed her.

"Would you now?" She smiled and set down the bowl, licked some whipped cream off her finger in a way that made me nearly crazy for her. And she knew it, of course she knew it. A sexy grin on her face, she did this amazing and wonderful thing and took her shirt off. With a simple elegant motion, she reached behind her back and her bra was gone too. Those beautiful breasts topped with pale brown nipples. I wanted to touch and squeeze and suck.

Only my hands were tied.

What madness was this?

She further aggravated me by running her finger through the cream and circling each of her nipples.

"What do you think?"

"I think you are a beautiful sexy monster."

She laughed, looking down at her own work. She flipped her hair out of the way and arched forward, toward me, her hands behind her on my thighs.

"You're killing me," I murmured. Finally, she got close enough and I bent my head to taste. She was sweeter than any cream. With my tongue I flicked her nipple. My instinct was to squeeze, pinch and pull, but again my hands were literally tied behind my back. All I could do was tongue and suck and nibble.

Genevieve's head fell back, her hair brushing my thighs.

She was serving herself up as one of the best desserts I'd ever had and I was ravenous for more.

"Your mouth. I want it," I said.

She lifted herself straight and cupped my cheek with her palm, but even as I leaned forward to kiss her, she pulled away.

"You want my mouth?"

I grunted. "Kiss me, Genevieve. I need your flavor. Your taste."

She obliged and the kiss was so much more intense for her withholding it from me. I pushed my tongue in her mouth like I wanted to shove my dick in her pussy. There wasn't a lot of finesse to the act, just raw emotion.

Passion, like I'd never felt before.

And my hands were fucking tied.

I pulled back. Took a few breaths.

"You okay?" she asked, running her fingernails across my head, down to the nape of my neck and back again. Petting me but with an edge.

"Good," I groaned. "So good."

She was a drug I wanted to get addicted to and never recover from.

"You said you wanted my mouth."

Like some exotic striptease act, she slipped off my lap, stood in front of me and pushed off the black leggings she wore for our date. She'd worn leggings and an oversized sweater. Flat shoes. She'd been comfortable and relaxed and I wanted her like that every time she was with me.

Thoughts of future dates fled when she stood before me naked. Her long dark hair over her shoulders obscuring her breasts like some kind of Greek Goddess from my mythological fantasies.

"God, you're beautiful," I told her.

"Thank you."

She bent forward, her hands on my thighs, her breasts swaying. Again, I reached out to touch them only to feel the constriction against my hands.

I might have growled.

"I like that sound," she said, so I made it again.

She kissed me, teasing me with her deft, quick tongue.

Then, sweet god in heaven, she sank to her knees between my thighs.

Her quick fingers untied the string that held my joggers up. Joggers, not jeans, because I too had wanted this to be casual between us.

No, casual wasn't the right word. Intimate. I'd wanted us to be comfortable and warm and easy with each other. I'd craved it. Now she was going to suck my dick, and nothing got more intimate than that.

"Lift your hips," she said. Her words breathy. If my hands were free I would have reached down between her thighs. Made sure she was wet and hot and loving this as much as I was.

Instead, I did as ordered and she pulled both joggers and my boxer briefs down my legs. My cock sprang free, painfully hard at this point. A little embarrassing in its eagerness, but I'd never been so turned on in my life.

She tucked herself further between my thighs and reached for my dick. I groaned as soon as her fingers encircled it. Fuck me if pre-cum wasn't already leaking out of the tip.

"How do you like to be touched?" she asked me, her eyes on my face. I couldn't lift my eyes from the sight of her hand around my cock. Her hand looked so small and my cock looked so big. I was gone for this woman.

Completely gone.

"By you," I grumbled. "Just by you."

"Tony, now is the time to be bossy. I want this to be good for you." Slowly she pumped my cock, her hold not quite hard enough.

"It already is," I said. I wasn't going to give direction. If her touch was too light, that was its own kind of tease. I didn't want to just come. I wanted her to keep touching me.

Just keep touching me like I was the only thing in the world for her.

Her palm ran over the head of my now thoroughly cum-wet cock. She collected it and used it to lubricate my shaft as she pumped my dick.

She cupped my balls in her other hand, rolling them gently in her fingers.

It was the single best hand job I'd ever gotten, and I would have told her that if I could have formed words.

Again, she bent forward, her face hovering over my erection. She waited then until I looked at her, into her eyes, and then she sucked the head of my cock into her mouth.

My jaw dropped. The air left my lungs. She was watching me even as she took me deeper into her mouth. Not very deep. Nothing that would choke her. I had no interest in feeling Genevieve choke on my dick.

I let my head fall back and felt how her tongue circled and teased the head all while her hand continued to pump my length.

I wanted to run my fingers through her hair. I wanted to hold her still and make small shallow thrusts between her lips. I could do none of those because... I. Wasn't. In. Control.

She held me captive. With her fingers, her mouth, her tongue, her fist.

Sucking me to the point of no return.

"I'm gonna come," I muttered. A warning. A fact. I thought about trying to hold back, but why? Why when I knew we would have this again and again.

She released my cock, her lips were red, swollen. Fuck me.

"In my mouth or on my breasts?"

Then she used her hand to sweep my erection across her

tits. The head of my dick teasing her hardened nipples. This was my choice, I thought. My control now. I could make her swallow me. Make her take my cum in her mouth or fuck those pretty tits?

Just the thought ruined me.

"Fuck, Gen-" I started to come, pumping myself shamelessly into her hand, all over her chest and breasts. It went on and on. Waves of pleasure until the sight of her with my cum dripping down her chest, clinging to her nipples, pulled the last of it out of me.

I fell back against the chair, my entire body spent. My head thrown back, my eyes closed, but everything was still spinning.

I could feel her, though. Her breath. Her skin. She straddled me again. I could smell the scent of her wet pussy and it made my painfully sensitive dick twitch. She reached forward, her sticky damp breasts against my chest. Her cheek against mine.

With a single tug, my hands were released. The tie she'd used to contain me, gone.

Instantly, my hands were in her hair, holding her face in place for my kiss. I told her with my mouth, my very being, how completely sexy she was. Completely amazing.

When she pulled away, she was smiling. Like she was the one who'd just had an amazing, life changing orgasm.

"Shower," I grunted.

She nodded and climbed off me. I stood and removed my shirt and together we made our way to the ensuite.

I kept the lights off. The moon through the window was enough to see by. She looked gilded in the marble bathroom with all its modern comforts. Like some kind of siren, brought to torture me with her smile and her perfect body and the way she made me feel.

I turned on the water, waited until it was the prefect temperature, then pulled her in with me. Her back tucked up against my chest. The spray of shower washing away my cum from her skin, as I dipped my head to drop kisses on her shoulders, neck, back.

I poured body wash into my hands and used both of them to touch every inch of her skin. Her breasts, her belly, her shoulders, her ass. All of it was mine and the ease with which she gave all control back to me made my head spin. Her body was mine, her smile was mine.

"Put your hands against the wall," I told her, and she did as I asked. Her palms against the tiles. I pushed the shower head away from her face and slipped my hands between her legs, sipping water off her neck. My finger against her clit, I teased her. I teased her until she was fucking herself back against my semi-hard cock, until the sounds she made in her throat were angry. Until she smacked her hands against the tile and begged.

"Please."

God. I did love it when she begged.

I gave her what she wanted. Two fingers inside her tight pussy, my thumb in her ass. My other thumb riding the ridge of her clit as hard as she could take it. Until she was climbing the walls, shaking and screaming with her orgasm.

She slumped back against me. "You're going to kill me," she breathed.

"I haven't even fucked you yet."

Her eyes opened, interested but exhausted.

A nap, first. Then another round.

We left the shower, both of us so completely mellow we didn't need words. I dried her with a fluffy towel, then myself. Like two sex drunk fools we fell into the massive king-sized bed.

I pulled the coverlet at the bottom of the bed up and over us. Made sure I completely covered her, my thighs behind hers, my dick nestled up against her ass cheeks, my chest pressed firmly against her back, and her breasts cupped in my hands.

This is how I want to fall asleep for the rest of my life.

23

Antony

The sound was coming from a distance. A ringing sound. A familiar sound.

"Tony," Genevieve mumbled in her half sleep state. "Is that an alarm?"

The sound stopped, but immediately it started again and suddenly it clicked that it was my phone. Ringing. I turned my head and checked the clock on the Alexa next to the bed. Just after midnight.

Rolling out of bed, I found the discarded joggers Genevieve had pulled off me and made my way to the kitchen where I'd left my phone.

Where it was still ringing. This wasn't a mistaken call from the west coast not realizing the time. When I saw the name I frowned.

"Roy? What's up?"

"Sorry, Ant, but I'm beat and want to go to bed. When

are you planning on bringing the kid back, or is he staying over?"

I blinked a few times and had to shake off the sleep. "Nick?"

"He's not answering his phone. When I dropped him off tonight, he said you'd bring him back around eleven, I don't know if you lost track of time but it's after midnight."

"Roy," I said grimly. "Nick's not here. Nick hasn't been here all night."

"The fuck. I dropped him off in the driveway. Your Rover was there."

"I had a date with Genevieve. I haven't seen Nick all night."

"The fuck!" This time a little louder.

"Look, it's late. You've got Vanessa and Nora. I'll go look for him."

A deep sigh. "Kid's my responsibility. I should have waited until I saw him go inside."

"Kid's my responsibility," I corrected him. "You're just helping me out. I got this."

"You sure?"

"Yeah. Go to bed. I'll call you in the morning."

"Call as soon as you have him. I'm not going to sleep tonight."

Because that was Roy. He owned his shit, even when it wasn't his shit.

"I'm sorry, man. Sorry I put this on you," I said.

"You didn't put anything on me," he said. "I make my choices. My family, we made a choice. We chose the kid. Now bring him back. If Nora wakes up and her Nicky isn't home, it ain't going to be pretty."

"Yeah. I'll go now." I ended the call. "Fucking stupid, kid. Why?"

"Tony, what is it?"

I turned and saw Genevieve in the doorway. She was wearing my shirt and all I wanted to do was give her some water. Maybe feed her a few strawberries for energy, and then take her back to bed and fuck her stupid. Instead I was going to break her heart.

"Nick's missing."

Instantly, she was awake and worried. "What?!"

Which was more a command for the facts than an actual question.

"Roy dropped him off at some point tonight. Nick told Roy I would take him home. Obviously, it was a set up. Let's get dressed."

She was already scurrying back to the bedroom. In a blur of speed she tossed my shirt back to me, pulled on her leggings, sans panties, and tossed the sweater over her head, sans bra.

"Do you think we should start with the beach again?" she asked. "That seems a little obvious."

"And a hell of a walk from here," I said grimly, following her out the front door.

It didn't make sense. The kid had a roof over his head, food in his belly. He was going to school starting next week, going to therapy and I was working toward being his guardian.

He had people here. People who cared.

"Oh no," she gasped.

I stopped abruptly when I saw what she saw. The Rover was gone.

The kid had stolen the car.

∼

Five hours later
Birdie

"We should drive around again," I said. I paced behind the island in the kitchen while Tony made another pot of coffee.

"We drove around for three hours. There's no point to it. We just have to sit tight and wait for him to come back."

I hated that he was right. It had taken a moment to get over the shock of him having taken the car. Not because he'd stolen it, because it meant he could be *anywhere*.

"Roy said he hadn't been upset? That nothing unusual had happened?"

This was maybe the hundredth time I'd asked that. I felt like a shitty cop on a shitty television show.

"No. He wasn't upset," Tony answered. "And nothing specific happened, but who knows what might have set him off?"

The question that had been burning its way through my soul erupted out of my mouth.

"Do you think this is my fault?"

"What do you mean?"

"Because I'm leaving? After the competition."

"I don't know." Tony pushed another mug of coffee into my hands. My third since we realized he was gone. I was going to be a jittery mess all day from the caffeine alone. The stress was putting me over the top. "We have to consider the possibility he was planning this the whole time. That he was just waiting for the right moment to take off."

No, I thought. I wouldn't believe that. I put my face in my hands, the stress rolling into grief and back again.

Tony put his hand on my back and I was so upset I could barely handle this comfort. Part of me wanted to get in my car and run from this stress. This pain.

"I left a message with Ben. Maybe Nick alluded to something in therapy, but it's doubtful he can tell us much."

"How far can he get?"

"He had a couple hundred bucks from working with you. The Rover had a full tank of gas." Tony shrugged, grim. "He can get far enough."

Tony looked down at his phone like he could will the kid to call. The "find my phone" feature on Nick's phone had been turned off. Nick had turned it off. Because he didn't want to be found.

Was he hurt? Was he scared?

"Maybe we should head to my aunt's," I suggested.

"Why?"

"Aunt Za...well, I know you think her aura reading is a gimmick, but sometimes she just has a sense of things. I don't know how to explain it. She can pick up on the strong emotions of people she knows and Nick must be so scared right now."

"Genevieve," Tony sighed. "Are you listening to what you're saying?"

"Do you have a better idea?" I snapped.

"Then a fortune teller?"

"Tony," I barked. "Humor me. It's almost six, she'll be getting up right about now."

"Okay," he sighed. "It's better than sitting here and doing nothing."

∼

I PUSHED OPEN the unlocked door of my Aunt's trailer.

"That you, Birdie?" My aunt yelled out from her bedroom at the end of the trailer.

"Yeah."

"No morning nookie?" Aunt Za asked. "Tell Chef Renard I'm very disappointed in his lack of stamina."

"My stamina is fine," he said, and Aunt Za poked her head out of the hallway. She was all smiles until she saw our faces.

"What's happened?" she asked.

"Nick's gone missing. He took Tony's car at some point last night and we haven't heard from him since. We've been driving around town most of the night looking for him, but he could be anywhere."

The bread in the toaster popped but she ignored it. She didn't have her scarves or rings on, or dramatic makeup. Just her pink fluffy robe and bedhead. She set her steaming cup of tea down on the table.

"Can you do that thing?" I asked. "You know that thing you sometimes can do. I need to know where Nick is. I need to know if he's in trouble."

Aunt Za nodded and then looked up at Tony.

"Good morning, Chef," she said quietly. "I'm sorry to be so ill prepared for your visit."

"Madame Za," he said awkwardly. "No, I'm sorry for interrupting your morning. Genevieve thought...well, I'm not really sure what she thought."

"Don't trust in things you can't see huh, Chef?" Aunt Za asked him with a raised eyebrow.

"I'm skeptical by nature," he admitted, his hands in his pocket. I'm sure his aura was giving my aunt all kinds of challenges.

"Hmmm," Aunt Za mused. She closed her eyes, her hands palm out in front of her. After several long seconds she opened her eyes. "What if I told you your phone was about to ring?"

I turned to look at Tony. He'd had his phone clutched in his hand all night waiting for Nick to call.

It rang. He stared down at his phone and then back up at Aunt Za. "Is this some kind of a trick?"

"I don't do tricks, Chef. Answer it."

I could see it wasn't Nick. There was no name associated with the number, so it wasn't an existing contact.

Tony answered. "This is Antony Renard. Yes. Yes. Yes, that's correct. No, absolutely I understand I shouldn't have allowed that. I'll be down there as soon as I can. No, I apologize for the confusion. Yes, I understand. You'll text me your address? Thank you, officer."

I could tell by the way his entire body changed, it was relief he was feeling. Relief meant Nick was okay.

I threw my arms around him and his came around me, hugging me so hard.

"The police a couple of towns over picked Nick up an hour ago. He was pulled over on the side of the road. He didn't have a license or registration for the car. Nick told them that I let him drive it all the time. That he was just out practice driving when the roads weren't busy."

"We have to go get him," I said. "Aunt Za, can we hang on to your car for a little while longer?"

"Of course, darling."

I was already headed out of the kitchen when I realized Tony wasn't behind me. Instead he was looking at his phone.

"How did you know it was going to ring? I mean, seriously?"

"Hmm," Aunt Za mused and took a sip of her tea. "Good guess?"

~

THE RIDE to the police station was tense, but one thing was obvious, Nick had the car for almost four hours before anyone realized he was gone. He could have been as far away as Boston or further west. That he got picked up by the police just forty-five minutes outside of Calico Cove said a lot.

He hadn't really wanted to leave. Not really. None of what he'd done had been planned.

As soon as Tony drove into a parking spot, I hopped out of the car. The police station was similar to Calico Cove's. Just an annexed part of what I imagined was their town municipal building. There were three police cruisers lined up in front.

I pushed through the door of the station only to find a relatively empty, very quiet space. An older black woman in a police uniform with a polite smile and calm demeanor sat behind a desk and a thick piece of plexiglass.

"Can I help you?"

"Yes, I'm here to pick up my son," I said. The lie falling off my tongue so easily it shocked me. "I mean, my foster son. I mean Nick. I'm here for Nick Steffens."

"Sure, hold on a second," the woman said. "The office just needs to confirm the license and registration of the vehicle owner."

"That's me," Tony said behind me.

He handed the woman the paperwork and a few seconds later Nick came around the corner. A police officer with a grim face and military style haircut behind him.

"You know this kid's got a record?" the man said sternly.

"I'm aware," Tony said.

"He can't drive unsupervised on a permit."

"Also aware," Tony said. "This won't happen again."

"See that it doesn't," the officer said.

Nick hadn't spoken a word. He'd kept his head down the whole time. I couldn't take it anymore, I threw my arms around him. Hugging him as tight as I could. I felt his muscles tighten and I knew he was going to shrug me off. Push me away, so I held on harder.

"I'm so glad you're okay," I whispered. "I was really scared."

He took a big breath, his whole body rising and then falling against me. He didn't hug me back, but he kind of sagged against me. I thought he'd accepted the hug, but then he said quietly in my ear:

"What the fuck do you care? You're leaving anyway."

I leaned back and he shook himself loose from my arms. I was too shocked to stop him.

The police officer handed Tony the keys to the Rover and together we left the police station behind us.

Tony had already called Roy on our way here to let him know what had happened and that the kid was safe.

"Here," Tony said, handing me the keys to Aunt Za's car. "Drive carefully."

I was numb, my eyes on Nick who was kicking the tires of the Rover.

"Hey, you okay?" Tony asked, ducking his head so he was all I could see.

I wanted to cry, but Tony needed to put all of his attention on Nick.

"Fine. Remember I've driven across this country several

times," I reminded him, pulling up my bravado like a safety blanket.

"Yep. Drive carefully, babe." He bent down to press a firm kiss on my lips.

"Don't be mean. Listen to him." I whispered against his lips.

"Yep."

"Did you just call me babe?" I asked him.

"I did," he smiled softly. "I've never had a babe before."

"Nick," I called over Tony's shoulder. He still wouldn't look at me. "I'll see you at the truck tomorrow, yeah?"

"Whatever." He dipped his head further down, shoved his hands deeper into his pockets.

"He's going to break my heart," I whispered to Tony, unable to help myself.

"Not if I have anything to say about it," Tony said grimly. "I'll call once things are settled."

"He's just scared," I reminded Tony. Willing him to remember how it felt to be that age and feeling like you were alone in the world.

Tony laughed. "Well, the joke's on him, because I'm more scared."

24

Antony

I didn't waste any time once we got in the car. I was driving this time and he climbed into the passenger seat.

"You know, for someone who likes to run away a lot, you're sort of shit at it."

"Fuck off," Nick muttered.

"Oh. We're going to do that?" I said. "Angry teen. Yeah, I know that one. Cool."

"You don't know me," Nick snarled. "Just because whatever happened to you happened, doesn't mean you know what my life is like. Stop pretending like you do. We're not the same."

"Kid, the only thing I have to know, to know *you*, is how it feels to be alone. Really alone in this world. Been there, done that. Done the runaway thing. Done the lash out at the person trying to help thing. Fuck, I stole money from the first chef I worked with, and you know what he did?"

No answer.

"He made me work harder to make up for it. I was waiting for the beating too. Thought he was going to kick my ass. This dude was jacked. I thought, let him try to hit me harder than my dad. I practically dared him. But no. Instead, he let me stay and just made me put in the hours to make up for what I took, and the time he lost coming to find me."

"I'm not staying," Nick said stubbornly. "I'll just leave again."

That made me laugh. "Kid, you had a fully gassed car for *hours*. You didn't get more than an hour away. You didn't want to go. You're just reacting because you can't control all the shit that's inside you. What set it off?"

"Fuck this, you're not my therapist. Pull the car over, I want to get out."

"Not happening."

"Fine." I anticipated his move before he made it. He was about to reach for the door handle as if he would throw himself out of a moving car. I engaged the door locks.

"See this?" I said, pointing to the button on my left-side panel. "Childproof locks. Because that's what you are, Nick. You're a child. It was your parents' responsibility to take care of you, but you lost the parent lottery. I'm sorry about that, but you have a fresh start happening. Right here. Right now."

"What the fuck do you care about my fresh start?"

"What does that mean?"

"Don't you have a restaurant you have to go back to? Jolie was over at the house telling Vanessa all about it. Some famous place that lost a star or some shit. You're leaving just like Birdie. You don't give a shit about me."

We were on a local road in Maine with no traffic, so I

pulled the Rover over. I wasn't having this conversation while driving.

I turned off the ignition, but his passenger door was still locked. He wasn't going anywhere.

"I wasn't going to tell you this until it was a done deal." He was staring down at this hole in his jeans around the knee. New jeans apparently came with holes. It was outrageous. "I've applied to be a foster parent. In Maine. It's going to take a while, so yeah, you have to stay with Roy until then. But my plan is that by the end of summer, you'll be with me."

He looked at me with eyes that were far too old. That had seen way too much disappointment. "You making that up?"

"No. I should have told you. I just didn't want it to be one more disappointment if it didn't happen."

The amount of tension coming off him was suffocating. Staggering. I couldn't tell if it was rage or grief or relief.

"Nick?" I touched his shoulder and he smacked my hand away. His face was red, tears stood out in his eyes.

Rage. So much rage.

"There is no way I get to have this!" he shouted, slamming his fists against the dashboard. "No way! You and that fucking house? Nora says she loves me! What baby says that? What the hell is game night? That's not a thing. That shit happens on tv, not in real life. No one even knows me! I steal shit. I fucking cheated at poker. I take cars and money and do whatever I need to do! And I don't give a fuck about the people I hurt. I don't!"

When the car was quiet I said. "Yes, you do."

"Fuck you!" he snapped.

"You get to have this," I repeated. I would repeat it until he believed me. "You're a kid, Nick. A damn kid, and you get to have people looking out for you, being nice to you, treating you with respect. Now, you keep stealing and cheating them, no. Then you don't get to have those things. You turn yourself into a sorry excuse for an adult, that's a choice you make. But for now, you get the benefit of the doubt."

"That can't make sense," he said, and I could see him brushing the tears from his eyes with his sleeve, but trying to make it look like he just had some dirt on his cheek. "Nothing about this place makes sense to me."

Of course it didn't. Because he'd never had good before. Never had happy before. When you felt those things for the first time, it was too easy to reject them.

"I know. It seems crazy because you've only had it one way. But you didn't pick your parents. You didn't ask anyone to abuse you. You were just a kid and you didn't deserve it. Any of it. Now you got lucky and landed in a place where people are really cool."

"Oh my god, Roy is going to be so pissed." Nick blew out a breath.

"Yeah. And you know what he's going to make you do as punishment for worrying everyone?"

Nick thought about it. The kid wasn't dumb. He wasn't going to get his ass kicked. Just like Francois was never going to kick my ass. Because both men knew they were dealing with someone to whom pain meant nothing.

Pain, physical and emotional, had been a daily event in my house growing up and I suspected it had been the same for Nick.

No, the thing harder than pain was being accountable for your actions.

"Time on the boat," Nick finally said.

I nodded. "Yeah, time on the boat. Some quality time hauling in lobster traps."

"I smell like shit after a day on the boat."

"Yeah, you do. Should have thought of that before you stole my Rover."

"Is it really stealing when you leave the keys in the freaking car?"

I laughed. "Maybe not. How did you cheat at cards?"

"Your friends were shit at covering their hands. I could see Matt and Levi's cards every time."

"Okay, well, we're not going to say anything about that. So help me, I need to win one damn hand at that table. Then I swear we won't cheat again. Deal?"

"Fine. Deal. Whatever," he said, slumping back into the passenger seat. I pulled back out onto the road.

"What did you say to Birdie?" I asked, because I noticed the kid had said something that made her go pale. That set her lips to trembling.

"Nothing that wasn't true," Nick said, angry again.

"What did you say?"

"That she was leaving. That's still true, right?"

"Yeah," I said. But I was going to do everything I could to stop her.

∼

We pulled up in front of the white bungalow with the fresh coat of paint. Vanessa was carrying a crying Nora down the porch steps. She was pointing at the Rover and saying something to the baby.

Roy stood on the stoop, his arms crossed over his chest. His usual pissed off expression somehow scarier. The dog was wagging its tail in excitement while Vanessa crooned to the little girl, who'd reached the hiccup stage of crying. Nora's face red and blotchy. Her shoulders lifting up and down with each gasp of air.

"Best to get on with it," I said.

To his credit, Nick didn't hesitate. He just got out of the car and walked up the path to the porch.

"Nicky! Nicky, go bye, bye! Not like! Bad! Bad, Nicky!"

I could hear Nora screaming from here and thought that having to listen to those cries was worse than any lobster trapping Roy was going to have the kid do.

Nora held out her arms as soon as he approached, and Nick, because I knew instinctively he was a good person, scooped her into his arms and carried her up the porch steps. The dog barking and circling his legs.

Roy gave Nick a chin nod and I was certain Nick was apologizing based on his expression. Eventually, Roy gave him another nod and Vanessa followed Nick inside.

I got out of the car and Roy met me at the edge of the walkway to his house.

"Didn't get very far," Roy said. "Tatem's only about a fifty minute drive from here."

I nodded. We both knew what it meant. Nick was struggling. There was no question about that. But he also knew Calico Cove was his best option. He just had to find a way to accept it. That was going to take more time.

"You okay?"

"Me?" I asked. "Sure. I'm fine."

"Kid's under your skin," Roy said. "Him bolting like that has to have you rattled."

"I...uh no, I'm fine."

But Roy was right.

I wasn't fine. Now that the job was complete. Nick was safely back with Roy and his family, I could feel the absolute terror wash over me. What if he'd kept driving? What if we'd never been able to find him? What if I had to call the police and instead of being safely inside that house with Vanessa probably fixing him something to eat, he'd been arrested instead?

I'd had no control over any of it. Not Nick, not the outcome. None of it.

I felt...I felt...I felt like I was coming apart at the seams.

There was only one thing I could do. One place that might restore some semblance of balance.

I needed Genevieve.

"Hey, Roy. Do you know where Madame Za lives?"

∽

Birdie

I'D STARTED PACKING my bags ten times. Ten times. I'd packed my favorite jeans and shirts. Then unpacked them. Ten times.

They didn't need me. Nick and Tony? They didn't need me hanging around like a ticking time bomb. The smart thing would be to just leave. Nice. Clean. Neat. No goodbyes. No scenes.

It would hurt them for a minute and then they'd move on.

But somehow, I couldn't make myself pack up those jeans again.

I opened Aunt Za's good rum and sat at the little table in her trailer and felt bad for myself.

The sudden pounding on the door scared me so bad I

screamed. Then Tony stuck his beautiful blonde head in the door and I was nearly overcome. So damned happy to see him.

"Tony?"

"You alone?" He looked around like Aunt Za could be hiding somewhere.

"Yeah. Aunt Za went to work at the square."

"How long?"

"Are you okay?" I asked. "Did Nick-"

"How long will she be gone?" He asked, coming into the trailer and filling it with electric energy. With dark intent. My nipples were suddenly very hard.

"A while," I said. "Hours."

"I need to be with you," he whispered, like it was a sacred confession.

He yanked me up out of my seat and against his chest, his hands buried in my hair. He was hard against my stomach.

"Genevieve," he muttered against my mouth. "If you knew...if you knew how I fantasize about fucking you. Ruthless, endless. Like some damn Viking who could pillage and claim you. I shouldn't have come here. You shouldn't be around me when I'm like this. I could hurt you."

My heart beat heavy in my chest. There was also a throbbing between my legs. Apparently, Viking porn was a thing for me.

But this wasn't about some role-play kink. Tony was coming apart at the seams and maybe he needed to know that was okay. Maybe he needed to see that no matter what he felt, he could control himself when he needed to.

I took a step back and tossed off the sweater I'd thrown on this morning. Still not wearing a bra underneath.

"Try," I said.

"Try to hurt you?"

"You won't. You can't. You can fuck me as hard as you want, but you won't hurt me."

He let out a slow breath and then fell to his knees in front of me. His hands reaching for my breasts, even as he pressed his forehead against my stomach.

"If I take you, it won't be easy."

"I know," I whispered.

"I'll fuck you so hard and I won't be able to stop."

"I know," I said. "I want that, Tony. I want all of you, unleashed. I don't want to be some recipe you play with in your kitchen. Someone you seduce. I want to be the woman in your bed. The one who makes it okay for you to lose control. Because it's me and I…"

I didn't get a chance to finish. He pulled me down onto the floor. Surrounded by crystals and gauzy scarves and half burnt candles, under the wise eyes of a Dolly Parton poster. On top of a rag rug Madame Za made herself.

This was urgent and needy and I was ready for all of it. Even the rug burns on my back. But before I could take off his clothes, he was pulling off his soft long sleeved Henley. He pulled me up and laid the shirt on the rug underneath me.

Out of control, but still taking care of me.

I shimmied out of my leggings. At some point, I'd managed to put on a pair of panties. I was about to slip out of those too, when Tony stopped me.

"No," he grunted. "I want to strip these off you. You're mine to make naked."

He shook his head, like he wasn't even aware of the words coming out of his mouth, but I let him have his way. I stretched out in front of him, my legs spread on either side of his kneeling body.

I absorbed the view of his broad naked chest. So thick and powerful. His arms heavy with muscles. In that second I was reminded of how much stronger he was than me. How truly at his mercy, I was. It made me the opposite of nervous.

"Hurry," I whispered.

He pushed his fingers inside the elastic of my panties, shoving the material down my legs and sliding them off my feet.

To make me naked.

He loomed over me, all his weight on his forearms, his bare chest barely touching mine. I arched my back, pressed my tight nipples up against him and the sound he made... God. The sound he made.

Feral. Dark. I felt a rush of arousal so powerful. Like maybe he could tease the orgasm out of me with his smell, his heat. His very existence.

"Tell me you're on the pill, Gen."

Gen. As if my full name was too much for him in his state.

I nodded. "It's been over a year for me. I'm clean."

"Me too. You'll let me come inside you?"

I nodded again and he smiled again. Wicked. Pleased.

"I'm going to pump you so full of my cum you'll never be rid of me."

Oh my god. Could I come from his words alone?

He plunged his hand between my legs, his fingers finding my softness.

I gasped as he slid a heavy finger inside. I was so wet he slid in fast and deep and I wondered if that's how it was going to feel when he finally came inside me.

"I'll play with you later," he muttered, as he rose up on his knees. "Later I'll make you come so many times you'll faint. But now, I need you. I need you so damn bad."

With shaking hands, he unbuttoned his jeans. He reached inside his briefs and pulled out his heavy cock. I knew his shape, his size, how incredibly thick he'd been in my mouth. He'd stretched my lips. My jaw still ached a little.

It was probably going to hurt. When he finally came inside me he was going to stretch me so tight and I'd be so full of him.

I couldn't wait.

"Hurry." I arched my body off the floor. Desperate. Needy.

He pressed his hand down against my stomach, as if to hold me in place, his other hand gripped his cock fitting himself against my slit.

"Ready?"

I nodded.

He pushed in so hard and fast I gasped. That feeling of being opened. Penetrated. A feeling I hadn't felt in so long. There was pain, a stretching pinch, but it was overwhelmed by the intensity of knowing Tony was inside me.

Those deep blue eyes met mine.

All of this went beyond the physical. I was overcome in a way I'd never been during sex. That emotional connection was so strong. Like we were two parts of a puzzle finally fitting together. I wrapped my legs around his hips and squeezed. I wanted to wrap my arms around his back and hold on.

Only he wouldn't let me. He was still above me. His weight resting on his hands and knees. He thrust hard against me and I watched his face change into an expression of almost agony. Like he was desperate to hold on to something.

"Let go," I told him. "It's okay to let go. I've got you."

His eyes held mine, even as he started to pump his hips

into me. Hard and fast without any kind of sophistication or rhythm. He was fucking me across the room. This was a man out of control. This was a man who was taking me because he couldn't stop.

I gasped when he slammed home. Again and then again.

"Fuck," he said pulling out.

"No, no, no, don't stop." I was close. I could feel it. I'd never come from penetration before, but the thick heavy weight of him inside me took me to the edge faster than I'd ever been. Because I wasn't holding back.

Because he's not holding back.

Sex had always been enjoyable. Something nice and fun. This wasn't nice or fun or sweet or innocent.

This was intense. Elemental.

He flipped me over onto my stomach and brought my ass up high, my weight now resting on my forearms.

"This ass," he said, even as he smacked it. "I'm going to fuck this ass someday, darling."

Then he was inside me again and I screamed with it. With the pleasure and the pain and the beauty of it all.

I pressed my face into my palms and felt every inch of him inside me. Thrusting over and over again, the slap of his hips against my skin. He put his arm under my chest, between my breasts and lifted me up and back against him. I was sprawled out, my back against his chest, my legs spread out on either side of his heavy thighs. He had his weight back on his haunches and pressed my head against his shoulder. Even as his cock still speared me.

I was basically mounted on him and I'm sure there was a word for this position, but all I could think of was that he was so totally and completely in control of my body right now.

"Slower now, honey. Slow," he crooned. "I never want this to fucking end."

"I think you're going to kill me," I breathed against his neck.

He played with my sweat-slick breasts even as he kept his thrusts slow and steady. Tugging on my nipples with his fingers, which fired off every nerve down to my very core. I arched my back against him and it only drove him deeper.

"Ahh, Tony, Tony…I'm so close."

He slid a hand down my body and his finger against my clit while his hips bucked up into me.

My orgasm hit me like a punch. I wanted to fold myself over, but Tony wouldn't let me. He held me pressed against him and I could feel the tension in him. His muscles were hard, clenched. There was a desperation in his body. The need to release.

Reaching up and behind me and I ran my fingers through his hair.

"Let go, Tony," I said, and it felt like giving him permission.

He shouted and I could feel the hot pulse of his cum shooting inside me. His hips snapped uncontrollably against me. Filling me in a way that was…profound.

Life-changing.

Tears filled my eyes.

"Genevieve," he breathed, as he bent his head to kiss my neck, my shoulder. Anywhere his lips could reach. "You've destroyed me."

"That's only fair," I whispered.

He pushed me forward so he could kiss the spot where my neck met my spine. I curled my fingers through his and brought his hands to my mouth.

"What happens next?" I asked him. The question was

about now. It was about later. It was about how we got off this floor and what I should do with my half-packed bags in that little room I called a bedroom.

"We go back to my place where I have a bed, and I show you how much stamina I have."

I was right. He was going to kill me.

25

Antony

I was lying on my side in bed and watching Genevieve sleep. Physically, I was exhausted. Mentally, I was drained. Still, I couldn't sleep. Because Genevieve was in my bed sleeping. Breathing softly. Her body rising and falling against mine.

She was art. Poetry. A beautiful song. My best dish. I wanted to consume her over and over again. We'd fucked for hours until finally she'd collapsed into sleep. I knew what she tasted like now. I knew what made her come. I knew how much she liked it when I took her hard and fast and how frustrated she got when I took things slow and easy.

I knew about the birth mark she had underneath her left ass cheek. I knew what she looked and sounded like when she slept.

Never had I paid that much attention to a woman.

Usually when the sex was over, I either left or fell asleep, but this…watching Genevieve, counting her extremely long eyelashes was endlessly fascinating.

"I want you," I said softly. She didn't stir. Her eye lashes didn't flutter open. This wasn't just sex. "I want everything. I want tomorrow and your bad dreams. I want to get you pregnant and help you expand your business. I want to take you to Paris and eat oysters and fuck you in the sunlight."

Was this love?

I'd certainly never felt anything like it before.

I swallowed the words I wanted to say because I wasn't an idiot. She had one foot out the door and I wanted to coax her back in. But I couldn't not express this feeling. It was too big. I was too transformed by this feeling. It needed recognition.

Celebration.

But I couldn't say it.

Food. Your love language is food.

∽

Birdie

THERE WAS nothing in this world as wonderful as waking up to the smell of coffee and bacon. Still naked, I stretched out in the soft sheets and couldn't contain my shit-eating grin.

That was a proper fucking.

My body felt used, a bit abused, but in a good way, and if I squeezed my legs together tight and remembered what he'd felt like inside of me, I could come just from that.

I needed food and fluids, because I wanted one more

orgasm before I returned home to unpack my half-packed bags, get my truck and set up shop for the day. I would swing by Vanessa and Roy's place to check on Nick. Try and make him understand that I wasn't leaving just yet. Not until I knew he was settled.

Then maybe the four of us, Roy and Vanessa, me and Tony, could come up with a plan to make Nick feel more secure. More safe.

But first coffee.

Bacon.

Sex.

Then all the serious stuff.

I got out of Tony's big bed and scrounged the floor for the leggings and t-shirt I'd worn over here. My panties? No clue. Maybe I'd left them in the living room?

In the ensuite, Tony had left a toothbrush out for me and I wondered when he'd thought to pick up a new toothbrush. Or was he a guy who always had extras? I imagined him having toothbrushes for the women who stayed in his house in California.

I frowned, but then I remembered what he'd told me yesterday. That it had been a year since he'd had sex with a woman. Yes, he was rich. And charming and as handsome as a movie star, but he was also someone who kept a tight control on elements of his life. Which meant he didn't let a lot of people in.

I was the exception, not the rule.

He must have been lonely. He must have been lonely like I was lonely.

This was scary, I thought. These feelings. So big and so strong. All so soon. Was it even possible to feel this much in such a short amount of time?

I was leaving! The competition was next week and then I was gone!

Right? I had to tell myself that. I had to.

I finished up in the bathroom and walked barefoot down the smooth hardwood floors to the kitchen. He was deep frying something, which seemed a little extravagant for breakfast, but I wasn't going to be picky.

He was also barefoot, wearing joggers and a t-shirt that fit him so I could see the outline of his back. I approved.

"Good morning," I said. My voice croaky from all the screaming and begging last night.

He looked over his shoulder and his smile was nearly blinding.

He's relaxed.

Happy.

So at ease in his body, in his home. It was touching. Moving, even. I'd known this guy for a few weeks and I'd never actually seen him relaxed.

I did that.

"You look like a guy who got laid last night," I joked with my sex-ravaged voice. He lifted an eyebrow at me.

"You sound like a woman who screamed my name last night."

True. All true.

"Sit. I'll pour coffee. Cream right?"

"Yes, please."

I took a seat at the island and he set the coffee down, along with a plate of two measly strips of bacon.

"Yeah, I'm going to need more than that," I told him. "You remember what you did to me yesterday, right? And last night? And when you woke me up at three in the morning because you had to have me again?"

His smile was evil and he dropped a heavy kiss on my lips. "Yeah, I did. But I let you sleep in and now I plan to feed you, but it's a surprise. The bacon is just to tide you over."

"A good surprise?" I asked him, as I reached for the bacon and my mug of coffee.

"I hope so," he said with his back to me as he worked on the counter next to the sink.

This, I thought, was heaven. I felt pampered and the coffee just seemed extra delicious.

"How did it go with Nick on the drive back to Roy's place?"

He blew out a long breath. "Emotional. I mean, the kid is just fighting for his life, you know? I should have told him I was applying to be a foster parent right away. Let him know how invested I was from the start."

"You didn't want to get his hopes up," I said.

"What the fuck do you care? You're leaving."

I took a sip of coffee, my heart hurting all over again remembering what Nick had said to me.

Could I blame him? He wasn't wrong.

"Well, the kid could use some hope. I talked to Shelia this morning actually. I was on a conference call with her and Nick's new case worker. Things are looking good and they both think everything should be squared away by summer. Then he can travel with me back to California."

My back stiffened. "California?"

"Yeah," Tony said with a heavy sigh. "I mean, I've got to go back and get that star back. I can't just let The Robin's Egg fall into obscurity. Not to mention it will be good for Nick to see a little of the country. Start to understand some of the opportunities I can provide. I'll train him to be on the line or in the dining room. Wherever he fits best." Tony turned to face me, his expression sober. "The kitchen is a good place to find focus in life."

The words had such a familiar ring to them, I bristled. "What are you talking about?"

He looked surprised at my tone. "It's not forever," he said. "Just until I get the star back. I'll be back in Maine by the time he starts school again."

"Have you talked to him? About any of this?"

"Uh. No. I've been with you all night. Obviously."

I blinked at him. He blinked back at me.

"What if he doesn't want to work in your kitchen?" I pressed.

"I just meant it's a place that can teach him discipline."

"He's a kid!"

"Who could use some discipline. Genevieve? Why are you upset? You can come too-"

"Oh, can I? Thank god Nick and I have you to make these decisions for us."

I was having painful déjà vu. The number of times I yelled at my father and it never did anything. Never changed his mind. Never made a bit of difference. My father wanted to break me until I fit into his mold.

Now Tony was doing the same damn thing with Nick.

Tony looked confused. "Genevieve, I'm giving Nick an amazing opportunity to have a great summer job, learn some skills and find his place in the world. That's all."

"As long as it's your place in the world? On the other side of the country."

See, this was why I couldn't be trusted with big feelings. That urge to leave, to run, to get as far away from the conflict as I could get, pressed in on me.

"Can you tell me why you're so mad? Is this about your father-?"

A kitchen timer went off and Tony stopped mid conversation to open up his oven.

"Et Voila," Tony announced, in a quiet voice. He set a white soufflé dish in front of me. There was a drizzle of dark green along the top – I could smell the herbs. The hint of heat beneath it.

He wouldn't?
Would he?

"I've been working on it for days," he said, studying me closely. "I couldn't make it work, not the way I wanted. Not until this morning. I know we have things to talk about, but...I made this for you."

This was every awful moment from my childhood, but made worse. So much worse. I couldn't breathe. It felt like I was invisible.

"It's beautiful," I said. Because of course, it was. He handed me a fork and I took it with shaking fingers.

I broke through what was a crispy layer, into the soft center. The smell of garlic and coriander. I dug out a forkful, already afraid of what I was going to taste.

And I was right.

Chickpeas. Tahini. Tarragon. Maybe ten other elements that hit my tongue so perfectly. It was soft and fluffy. Crispy on the outside. The zhoug across the top gave it sharpness and tang that was softened by the texture of the inside. It was fresh and comforting. Satisfying and intriguing.

It was perfection on a plate.

It was my falafel deconstructed into something else. Something...better.

"Well?"

I swallowed although it was difficult. He looked so expectant. He had to know it was delicious. He had to know it was better than anything I could ever put together in a food truck.

What he didn't know was that he was breaking me in half.

"It's delicious," I said numbly.

My answer seemed to please him. In that moment he looked like a proud lion, his head lifted while I stroked his mane and gave him his due. He looked so much like...so much like my father, I couldn't bear it.

"I have to go." I scrambled off the stool.

"Go?"

"I have to go home and shower and get ready to open this morning. You know I need the money from the truck to live, Tony. It's not some hobby I have."

He blinked. My tone caught him off guard.

"Of course, I know that," he said softly. "I just thought we could enjoy this together."

I shook my head. "Sorry, it's delicious, it really is. But I can't sit around here all morning playing the part of your girlfriend. I need to get to work."

I was at the kitchen doorway when I heard him say.

"*Playing* the part of my girlfriend?"

Yeah, it was a shitty thing to say, but I didn't know how to stop this crazy beating in my chest.

"Hey, Genevieve," he said, catching up to me in the living room even as I searched for the shoes I'd kicked off when we got back here. There, near the door. "You know I wasn't trying to show you up or anything, right? It's a riff on your falafel. A compliment-"

"Stop!" I shouted at him. "Just stop."

As soon as I got in my car I was going to cry hot sloppy tears. For now though, I had to hold it together. I lifted my head, focused on giving him my best fake smile and turned to face him.

"Look, last night was fun and all but...well, you know I'm leaving after the competition next week, so maybe we should just call this a one and done."

"Genevieve," he whispered, and I could see how badly I'd hurt him. Like a knife straight to his heart, only I was the one bleeding. "What the hell is happening right now?"

Well, I hurt too!

"See you around, Tony."

The shock on his face might have registered with me, if I wasn't already spiraling so far down the drain.

I slipped into my shoes, shut the door behind me, sent a silent thank you to past me who insisted on following him up here in Aunt Za's car.

I got into her old sedan that smelled like sage, and a little bit like weed, and didn't once look in the rearview mirror as I drove off.

Well, I thought, wiping the tears off my face. Yeah, I had fucked that up as badly as a person could.

Which was my cue to leave.

26

Birdie

"Aunt Za, are you here?" I called out as I opened the trailer door.

"I'm here," she said. "I got a ride home last night from that lovely Levi...oh no."

She got sight of my face and stood up from the table to pull me into her arms.

"What happened?"

A sob worked its way out of me. "I had the best sex I've ever had. And I'm pretty sure I'm in love. For real love, for like the first time. But then I woke up this morning and Tony's taking Nick back to California to work in his stupid restaurant without even talking to him about it. Just deciding everything for him. And then..." Another sob. "He made me a de-constructed falafel soufflé that was better than anything I could have ever made!"

"Oh no." Aunt Za breathed. "Not a soufflé."

I nodded as tears streamed down my face. "He was so proud of it. Said it took him all week to get it right."

"Did you tell him why that might upset you?" Aunt Za asked me.

"No!"

She pursed her lips and gave me a knowing look.

"Let me guess, did you shut down emotionally and hightail it out of there, which is your norm?"

The floodgates opened and I just started bawling. There wasn't any way to stop this pain. All I could see was Tony in every iteration of himself, and the idea of him just being gone from my life was too much.

"Yes!" I screeched. "I didn't know what else to do."

"Hmmm."

I pulled my t-shirt up to wipe the snot from under my nose. "Don't say *hmmm* like that."

"I'll say hmmm if I want to say hmmm."

"You're implying it's my fault," I said trying to get ahold of my breath.

"Because instead of confronting a man directly and honestly, and telling him what you were feeling and why, you chose to run away instead. No, Genevieve, that doesn't sound familiar at all."

She was calling me Genevieve. That meant I'd really messed up. I blew a wet, tearful raspberry.

Aunt Za sighed. One of those deep worldly sighs like she had all the secrets to life.

"Do you love your father?"

It hurt. It hurt so bad because I *did* love my father.

"I wasn't enough for him. You know that, Aunt Za. I was never good enough."

"That's not what I asked," she pointed out.

"What does this have to do with anything? We're talking

about Tony!"

"We're talking about love. About loving difficult driven men. The man made a soufflé, my guess, to impress you, instead it triggered you. I get that. I do. But honey, you should have talked to him. Have you even told him your last name?"

I sniffed. Took a shuddery breath.

"That's what I thought. You didn't say a word about your father, or your life. Instead, you circled the wagons, bundled up all your hurt feelings and ran away. Back here to me. My guess, and this doesn't require any psychic ability on my part, is you're already packed in your head."

"I have to go. I messed everything up. It's too much."

"Well, you're a grown woman. I'm not going to stop you, but the result of that will be that Antony and Nick will no longer be in your life. Is that what you want?"

No!

Every fiber of my being, every string in my heart rebelled at the idea.

Of course, it wasn't what I wanted but I didn't know how to fix any of this. Not now.

"I need to leave. And don't you judge me," I said before she could. "I just need some time to clear my head and think it through. I'm not running away."

"Hmmm."

"I'm not!"

Except an hour later, I was all packed up in Old Blue and we were headed west.

As I merged onto the highway to head out of town, I looked at my hula girl on the dashboard and I could tell even she was disappointed in me.

～

Antony

I KNOCKED on the door of the trailer. "Genevieve!"

Nothing. So, I knocked again. This time harder.

"Genevieve, you get your fabulous ass out here right now!"

This time the door opened and Madame Za stepped out. She was in a pair of sweatpants and hoodie and looked less like a psychic than anyone I had ever seen.

"Hold your horses, Chef. I'll spare you the shouting. She's gone."

No. That couldn't be right. Not after everything we shared. No way she would have just left.

"I love my niece, but sometimes she makes me want to strangle her," Za said, only I wasn't listening.

I couldn't really hear anything over the pounding of my heart.

"I made her a soufflé and...she left me? This can't be happening. I'm a very good cook."

Za was patting my shoulder even as I dropped onto my ass on a deck chair in front of a fire pit. I looked up and noticed there were fairy lights strewn about the trees above. Of course there were.

She took the seat next to me and passed me a flask that she held in her hand.

Unthinking, I took a sip and the whiskey went right to my chest.

"I was expecting you," Za said.

"She left. Without a goodbye to me. To Nick?"

Now I was pissed off. She knew how that was going to make Nick feel. Like she'd rejected him.

"She's scared. Petrified really, and Birdie's first instinct is always to run. She was twelve the first time she did it. When her father and I had to sit her down and tell her the news that her mother was gone. Like she couldn't just sit there with all those big massive emotions. I'll never forget it. She just opened the front door and started running as fast as her legs would carry her. It was hours before her father finally found her."

I took another hit of the flask.

"Why is she scared of me?" I asked, confused.

"Because she loves you, stupid. And you love her back, which is probably even scarier for her. But this time...I know my niece pretty well, and I think this time she's going to figure it out before she ruins what could be a very good thing."

I was trying to take hope from that. Trying to hold onto the idea that this wasn't even close to over.

"Do you know where she is?" I asked Za. "Because I'm not letting her go. I'm just...not. I need her. Nick needs her and...she needs us."

Za nodded. "Yeah, she does. No, I don't know where she is. But I know where she's going."

It took a few seconds for it to click. "The competition. Of course."

I stood up like I could somehow teleport myself there.

"Hold on," Za said, grabbing my hand. "There's something you should know. Something my niece was too stubborn to tell you, but if you're going after her, you need to know what you're up against."

Five Days Later

Portland, Maine
Masters vs. Apprentice Food Truck Competition
Birdie

"I WAS AN IDIOT." I read the text message I'd typed out in my phone.

I was sitting in my truck in the middle of a municipal park in Portland. A place usually reserved for soccer tournaments and field hockey matches that was now cluttered with food trucks. I was among the best in the world and I'd never felt so bereft in my life.

"That's not enough," I muttered, erasing the words. I tried again. "I was so wrong about everything."

I had started and stopped about a hundred texts to Tony. A hundred over the past five days.

Nick, I'd already texted. Told him I needed to get to Portland for the competition ahead of time and that I was sorry I hadn't had a chance to say goodbye in person.

He texted back: Okay.

I felt every ounce of his disappointment in that okay.

"I was scared and stupid and I'm sorry," I said, even as I typed out the letters. "Can you ever forgive me?"

Press send. Just press send.

But every time I tried, I froze up.

Because what if he said: no.

No, I don't forgive you. No, I can't believe you just bailed.

I could hear the commotion around me of trucks pulling into their allotted slots. I was in an area of six trucks dedicated to vegetarian options. Five of the trucks were run by professional chefs, only one of us was an amateur.

Me.

I had to cook today and the idea filled me with utter dread. I didn't care about this stupid competition. I didn't care about proving anything to my father. He didn't even know I was here.

What was the point to any of this?

A knock on the back door of Old Blue startled the crap out of me. It had to be someone from the competition with directions for the timing of the cook.

Except when I opened the door, the first thing that hit me were a set of the bluest eyes I had ever seen.

And boy was he pissed.

It felt like hope seeing him again. It felt like everything I'd ever wanted and told myself I could never have. I stopped myself, pulled up on my foolish heart.

"Tony," I said breathlessly. "What are you...one of the masters?"

My breath shuddered.

"No," he said. "I'm not here to compete."

Please. God. Please let him be here for me. Even though I didn't deserve it. Even though I'd run.

"Gen," he said. "You need to breathe. Passing out in this truck-"

"Why are you here?" I blurted. Then, like the child I still was in so many ways, I closed my eyes. Like I could stand here and not run, but only if I didn't see the pain coming.

"Open your eyes," he whispered, his hands closing around mine. Gathering up my cold shaking fingers. I'd been so cold the last five days. So cold and so lonely.

His blue eyes weren't mad anymore. I saw myself in them. The way he saw me. Strong and talented. Foolish, yes. But important. I saw all of that on his face.

"I'm here for you," he said.

I couldn't talk. I couldn't think. I did the only thing I wanted to do and jumped into his arms.

He caught me, hard and sure and steady against his chest. Rock solid, this man. "I'm sorry," I wailed in his arms. "I don't know what happened to me. I just got so scared and everything got so big inside, I didn't know what to do. So I did what I always do and I ran."

He pulled back, his own eyes were watery. "You don't think I was scared too? It's love, Gen. The real deal. But I wasn't running away from it. Or from you. Not for a second."

I nodded. He was right. He made me a souffle because he wanted to show me he cared and all I could do was bolt like an idiot.

"I'm sorry," I said again.

"You're forgiven," he said and kissed my nose.

I hiccupped. "It can't be that simple. You must be so mad. I was such an asshat to you that morning."

"One and done?" he said, repeating my words to me. I winced. "Yeah, I get to hold that over your head for a while, but you're still forgiven."

"I am?"

"Because I love you," he said gently. "Now man up, put your big girl pants on and tell me how *you* feel."

I smiled through my tears and sniffed a few times, so when I said it, snot wasn't dripping from my nose.

"I love you, too."

"Yeah, you do." He was beaming. "Why didn't you tell me who your father was, Gen?"

"You know?"

"Za spilled the beans. She said you're here at this competition to finally prove something to him. He was the one who trained you?"

I nodded. "From the time I was thirteen I was meant to

be a great chef in his image. To take over the restaurant. To take over his life really. But I was never good enough. My food was *never* good enough. I worked so hard until one day, I just gave up. Told him I didn't want his life, his dream, any of it. I wanted my life."

He brushed the hair that was sticking to my cheek away and tucked it behind my ear. "He should have listened to you."

"I should have...I should have tried harder to explain too. You might not know this about me, but I have a tendency to bolt when things get heavy."

His eyebrows shot up his forehead. "What?" he said in mock surprise. "No. You?"

I swung at his shoulder without any heat. "Don't make fun of me. I'm really vulnerable right now."

He kissed my lips gently. "Okay. No making fun."

"Nick's mad at me. I can tell," I admitted. "I let him down too."

"Good thing for you Nick and I are total goners over you. And we'll get to him in a second, but babe, I've got something to tell you."

"What?"

Because I didn't think I could take anymore. I was in love. I was forgiven. I was pretty sure nothing mattered beyond that.

"Ladies and gentlemen! Let me have your attention while I announce this year's Masters vs. Apprentice surprise judge."

"Uh...Gen-"

"Hold on a sec, Tony. They're announcing the judge. It's always a big surprise."

"Yeah, it's going to be," he muttered.

"Seven time James Beard award-winning chef with over

twelve Michelin stars to his credit and former Masters vs. Apprentice winner...Chef Edouard Manet!"

I gasped. Then I let out a squeak. Then I saw stars in front of my eyes.

"Tony!" I shouted, grabbing his arm.

"Yeah, babe. This year's judge is your dad."

27

Birdie

"Tony, I can't do this. I have to leave. There is no way I can cook for my father."

In my head, I was already packing up my knives, packing up the truck. Sure, there were issues I needed to work through with my father, but now was definitely not the time. In a food competition? I mean, talk about the universe getting it a little on the nose.

How many major life events could a person handle in one day?

I couldn't tell Tony I loved him and deal with my dad!

Tony, however, looked like a man who already knew how this was all going to play out. He pushed me out to arm's length and smiled at me.

"Babe...damn I like calling you babe. We've got this."

We absolutely did *not* have this. I hadn't cooked for my father in almost eight years. Any dish I had ever made for him had been picked apart and broken down until it was just a list of every element I had gotten wrong.

The worst part was Dad was right.

My cooking never rose to the level of what he could do. I preferred easy flavors, comfort food, things that settled in your stomach well and made a person feel good. As opposed to things that looked amazing on the plate and broke new flavor boundaries.

Tony put two fingers between his lips and whistled.

"What are you doing?" I asked, cringing from the sound "Who are you whistling to? Don't call him over here!"

Nick's lanky frame came jogging over to us and my heart collapsed into my stomach. He was wearing a pair of new jeans and a fresh t-shirt. It had only been five days and I could tell he'd put on some weight. He smiled at me like I hadn't broken his heart. Like I hadn't been a selfish asshole.

"Hey Birdie, Tony said you might need a hand." His eyes glittered and he looked so confident standing there. Tony had given him that.

I started crying again. "I'm so sorry, Nick! I shouldn't have left like I did. I know texting you wasn't good enough. I was just being such a jerk. About everything."

I hugged him and every muscle in his body tightened. It only made me hold on tighter and cry harder.

"Uh. It's okay. I understand. Tony explained everything to me on the ride over here," he said. His hand patted my back tentatively, like I was a bomb that might explode. "Oh no. Birdie, please stop crying. Nora does this to me all the time. I can't take it anymore."

That made me laugh through my tears.

I pulled away and looked at him. "Thank you for coming, but we're leaving. We're going back to Calico Cove right now."

"No, you're getting back in that truck and kicking some

professional chef ass," Tony said. "Nick and I will help you prep."

"Tony, you don't understand!" I cried. "He's not going to like my food. He's never liked my food! Being here will not change that, it will just be humiliating on a larger scale."

"Wow, between the three of us we've got some serious daddy issues," Nick said, hopping inside the truck, completely ignoring my temper tantrum. "I'm going to grab an apron and get started on the salad prep."

I watched Nick throw on an apron and knew, just knew, that he was supposed to be mine. Like really mine. Not Roy and Vanessa's. Despite how I'd messed up, he belonged to Tony and me. We found him first.

How was this all happening at once?

"Gen," Tony said, his hands wrapped around my upper arms. "You've cooked for your father to impress him. You've cooked for your father to try and win his approval. Did you ever just cook for him with love? The kind of love that made the people of Calico Cove stand in lines around the block to get your falafels?"

I tried not to roll my eyes. "You're the one who said love wasn't an ingredient. He's a chef, Tony! He demands technique, precision, and execution."

He wiggled his eyebrows. "Do you trust me?"

"Yes?" I said it like a question, but the truth was, I did trust him. I trusted him with my heart, which seemed so incredibly fragile right now.

"That didn't sound very convincing" he said, calling me out. "Let's try this again, do you love me?"

"Yes," I said. Because I did. I really, really did.

"Better," he agreed. "But you know it's in the rules. If you love someone you have to trust them. I wouldn't tell you your food was up to Chef Manet's palate if it wasn't. It's good and you can do this."

He hopped into the truck beside Nick, and I watched the two of them jump into action.

Cook for my dad?

Could I actually do that?

My falafels were really good.

Tony wouldn't lie to me and tell me they were good enough just to placate me. He knew what my dad's standards were. There was no way Tony would set me up to fail like that.

Maybe if I wasn't trying to recreate Dad's legendary tartare. Or any other dish he'd made famous. What if instead I was going to give him food I loved?

Food that I thought tasted great. Food that the people of Calico Cove lined up for every day.

Food that Tony and his exacting standards said was delicious.

"I know what you're doing," I said to Tony, even as I got in the truck. He was holding out my favorite *May The Forks Be With You* apron for me. "You're trying to boost my confidence."

He dropped a kiss on my mouth and said quietly. "I want everything for you, Genevieve. Now let's impress your dad, win this thing, then we can go home and fuck like bunnies."

My eyes went wide and I tilted my head towards Nick.

"He's got his ear buds in," he said with a mischievous wink. "Kid can't hear a thing."

"Yeah," Nick agreed. "Can't hear a thing."

∽

TOGETHER THE THREE of us prepared the falafels, the sauces. Fresh salads. I made pita on the flat top, showing Tony my trick with the domed aluminum lid.

He grunted in approval.

Nick dressed the fries.

It was time. I assembled the plates for judging. My father would be here any minute with the officials from the competition.

What would he do? He wouldn't yell at me, those days were long gone and there was an audience. But he'd sigh, that disapproving sigh that made me feel like a child. He'd take a bite of the falafel and sniff like it was all wrong. He'd taste one of the sauces and flick his fingers like he wished someone would remove it from his sight.

"They're perfect, Genevieve. Just like always," Tony said, his arm around my waist, holding me up when it felt like I might fall down.

"What about the salt?" I asked him, eyes narrowed.

"You were right," he said, and I pretended to have a little heart attack.

"Hey, he's coming!" Nick said, ducking back inside the truck.

"Ah!" I squawked, feeling overcome with nerves.

Tony put his hand on my shoulder and said, "Duck."

"What?"

"Trust me," he said. "Duck!"

Because I did trust him, I squatted down inside the truck, completely invisible to the people who were approaching. I heard my father's booming voice.

"Chef Renard! I didn't expect to see you here."

It was a blind competition. My father wouldn't have been given any of the contestants' names in advance, but of course he would recognize them once he was here. And he would certainly recognize my truck. I imagined my father's brain was exploding.

Or maybe he wouldn't recognize my truck. Maybe like so much of who I was, the blue truck and the yellow bird outside would be completely beneath his notice.

"Chef Manet," Tony said. "It's good to see you again."

"Heard about your troubles at The Robin's Egg."

I winced. My father could be utterly exasperating when it came to things like Michelin stars.

"Soon to be corrected, I assure you," Tony said easily.

"Well let's get to it then. I'm told falafels are the order of the day at this truck."

"Yes, sir."

I don't know why, but I closed my eyes even as I heard the sounds of Tony handing over the plate of food to my dad.

"Nothing fancy," Tony said above me. "Just good and filling. I hope you don't mind, Chef."

"Food is meant to be delicious," my father replied. "It doesn't always have to be foie gras."

Now you say that.

"I'm glad you feel that way," Tony said. "I agree."

My father had a ritual. He would find a place to sit. He didn't believe in eating food standing up. There were picnic tables set up in front of each truck, probably just for him.

He would take the plate there, unfold a napkin in his lap to start. Then he would carefully spin the plate first, taking in the visual quality from all sides. Color and contrast. Was the dish pleasing to the eye? Then the smell test.

I stood up and peeked out over the side of the truck. The awning provided enough shade that I could watch him eat without him seeing me.

He picked up a single fry, sniffed it, then popped it in his mouth with a satisfying crunch.

He set his attention on the sandwich. First he bit into the falafel. Chewed so thoughtfully, much like Tony had when I'd finally allowed him to try them for the first time.

Again that rush of love filled me up.

How in the world had I fallen for a man who was so much like my father, when I thought my father was everything I didn't want for my future?

I'd been short sighted and so stubborn.

Having that time away from my father, figuring life out on my own, it made me into the person I was today. A person I was proud of. A person Tony loved. No, I wouldn't regret that. But if I could have my dad back in my life without the pressure of trying to be something I could never be, then it felt like there was nothing I couldn't do.

But, if he couldn't be in my life without trying to make me into something I wasn't, then I knew I had the strength to let it go. To let his disappointment wash over me.

I didn't have to run anymore.

Minutes ticked by while my dad finished everything on his plate.

"Is he supposed to do that?" Nick whispered. "Doesn't he have like a ton more food to eat?"

"He knows good food when he's eating it," Tony said, and I patted his ass in gratitude. He patted mine too. Nick rolled his eyes.

Instead of moving on to the next truck, my Dad turned back to Old Blue and I ducked down again.

"Well, sir?" Tony asked when he approached.

"I have to say that was special, Chef. Thank you."

Special! My dad never thought my food was special.

"No critiques?" Tony asked him. "You know it's okay, I welcome them."

"Perhaps, just perhaps, a little more salt."

Damn chefs and their salt, I thought.

"On that," Tony said with a smile, "we'll have to agree to disagree. No other critiques?"

"Yes," My dad said crisply. "It was delicious. Good flavor, balanced ingredients, excellent preparation. The garlic infused oil on the french fries, quite unique without being overpowering. The zhoug sauce is transformative. The tahini is perfectly matched. It's elevated street food and nothing less than what I would expect from an award-winning chef. Very impressive."

My dad said that. My dad said that about my cooking. I could feel the tears well up again and dropped my face into my palms.

"Oh no," Nick said groaning. "There she goes again."

"There who goes again?" my dad asked. "Is there someone else in the truck with you, Chef?" I tried to read into what he was thinking just by his tone of voice and I got nothing. That was my father's great skill – he showed nothing he didn't want to show.

"Yes, sir. The person who actually made the food today. I was just on prep," Tony tapped me on my shoulder. "Come on, Gen. Time for the big reveal."

I stood up and turned to face my dad. He looked the same as he had when I saw him back in New York. Impeccable posture, stern mouth, my eyes staring back at me, receding hairline, large belly, wearing an immaculate white chef's coat.

Always *The General*.

I lifted my hand and waved, waiting for his thunderous disapproval. He wouldn't like being duped.

"Hi, Dad."

He blinked, blinked again, and then, to my surprise, he smiled. And for a second he was the dad of my youth, before Mom died. When we were really happy. When all I had to do to please him was be myself.

"I was scared I'd gotten it wrong," he said.

"Gotten what wrong?"

"Gerald, the organizer, told me you'd been invited. It's why I signed up to be the surprise judge. I saw the truck and I was sure it was yours."

So much for blind competitions. I tensed and Tony put his hand on my hip. A reminder that I wasn't alone. I remembered that day on the beach with Nick when he'd said he would protect me. It didn't seem funny now. It seemed nice. It seemed like love.

"Why?" I asked. "To tear apart my food in front of more people?"

"To apologize," he said. "My sister called me and explained to me what perhaps I should have understood a long time ago. I'm so sorry, my sweet Birdie. Your food is delicious. It always has been. Yes, I was hard on you, but of course it was just because I knew how much potential you had. I am desperately sorry if I ever made you feel like you weren't enough."

Oh my god. It was all too much. Like honestly, how was I supposed to survive all of this?

"Here," Nick whispered, and pressed a napkin into my hand.

"You're right, sir. Your daughter made all of the food," Tony interjected. "She's quite talented. The people of Calico Cove love her food almost as much as they love her."

"Of course they do," my father said, like it was a given.

"She's brilliant. Clearly. So explain all this. How do you know my daughter, Chef Renard?"

"Oh, I'm her boyfriend," Tony said with a huge smile, even as he wrapped an arm around my shoulders.

I winced. I was pretty sure Tony didn't know what he was in for announcing that to my father.

"Her *boyfriend*? Genevieve, is this true?" My dad asked, looking at me with this steely gaze.

"Yes, Dad," I said, and felt so much of the tension I usually felt in his awesome presence just melt away. "Tony is my boyfriend and sous chef and this is Nick, my other sous chef. We made this food together. Really, it's the first time I cooked for you without trying to impress you. I just made food I love."

His stern face softened and he smiled. "My darling little cook. We need time to talk. Really talk, Genevieve."

"I agree," I said. "We have a lot to talk about."

"Yes," he said. "Good. Then I change my mind. Not a dash of extra salt was needed. It was perfect in every way. Now get out of that truck and come give your father a hug."

"Yes, sir."

I hopped out of the truck and my dad met me around the back. I hugged him and he hugged me back, squeezing me tight like he didn't want to let me go.

"I just missed you so much, honey," he said into my hair. "All I really wanted was for you to come home."

I pulled away from him then. "About that, Dad. My home is not New York City. I have a different home, now."

He looked back at the truck. Both Tony and Nick were stepping out of it. They looked so cute in my freaking aprons.

"With those two?"

"Yep. Wherever they go, they're home now."

"Sweet!" Nick said with a fist pump. "She's staying in Calico Cove. Did you hear that Antony?"

"I did," Tony said.

My father threw his shoulders back and trained his entire focus, which could really be a scary thing, on Tony.

"Dad, be nice," I hissed at him.

"Chef Renard!" he barked. "So you are dating my daughter?"

"I'm *in love* with your daughter," he corrected him, and it filled me with warm gooeyness.

"Two stars? Really?" my father asked like it was a challenge.

"It will be three again. I assure you."

"Your James Beard count?"

"Five. Emerging, California State, California State, Chef and Chef."

My father sniffed and the gesture was so typical of him it made me want to laugh.

And cry.

"Can I call you Edouard?" Tony asked him.

"You can call me Chef Manet," my father said. "At least until I've tried your food. Now I have this little matter of judging to finish up, but I will be heading to my sister's place for a nice long visit. I imagine we'll be joining you at your home for dinner. I would like to see where my daughter's boyfriend calls home."

"Uh. Okay," Tony said, but I could hear him audibly gulping.

My father looked at his watch. "After all this food, I don't imagine I'll be hungry again for at least another five, six hours. Which means you'll have plenty of time to prepare. So maybe something a little more upscale than street food.

Perhaps a five course tasting. Nothing too heavy. Does that work for you, Chef Renard?"

Tony audibly gulped and I could see the wheels in his head turning. He wasn't going to get away with tacos or pasta aglio e olio with my father. Right now he was wondering where we were going to find white truffles on the drive home.

"Yes, Chef."

"Excellent answer. My sister and I will be around at eight. Does that suit?"

"Yes, Chef," Tony said. "I'm sure I can put together something."

"With my help," I said, moving from my dad to Tony. I wrapped my arm around Tony's waist and squeezed. "Because we make an excellent team."

"That," he agreed, "we do."

28

Later that Night
Birdie

"Oh god," I whimpered. "Oh god!"

I brought my fist up to my mouth and bit down on my thumb even as Tony's tongue slid across my clit. My legs were draped over his shoulders while he feasted between my thighs.

I'd promised Nick he wouldn't hear all the sex we'd be having, and he was staying in the upstairs guest room on the other side of the house.

But still, I needed to stay in some kind of control.

Except Tony was clearly ravenous as he plunged his tongue deep inside me and twisted it. I lifted my hips against him, wanting basically to smash his face against my pussy.

Fuck, when had sex ever felt this good?

He was stretched out between my legs, naked, one hand

pressing down on my stomach, his other hand wrapped around his cock, jerking himself off hard. So much that I could hear the slap of his skin against his hand.

"I want you in my mouth," I whispered. "I want to suck you again, Tony. Please."

The words spilling out of me, I wasn't sure if they were nonsense or made sense. I was a creature of feeling and being and existing. No thought. No worry. No tomorrow. No yesterday.

It was delightful.

He pulled back and nipped at the soft skin on the inside of my thigh.

"Stop that," he growled. "Talking about sucking me. It will make me come too fast."

"You already made me come once," I whined, and he was working me toward my second very quickly.

He got to his knees, his cock still firmly in his hand as he looked down over me. His eyes on my naked breasts. So entranced he lost his hold on his dick and bent over to suck my nipples. First the right, then the left, as if he didn't want either to not feel worshiped.

He braced his knees on the bed by my shoulders and I lifted my head, trying to catch the head of his cock between my lips, but he pushed me back down. He tapped my nipples with the head of his thick cock, watching himself as if it was the most profoundly erotic thing he'd ever seen.

"Squeeze your tits together," he demanded.

"Like this?" I whispered, pressing my breasts together for him.

He nodded even as he stroked his cock in the crevice I'd created between them.

"Hot as fuck, Gen."

He thrust forward and I licked the tip of his cock. The groan that came out of him made me wild.

"I told you what would happen if your father liked at least one of my dishes."

Yes, he'd warned me. The lobster sashimi had been nothing short of miraculous. I'd smiled through every bite knowing my father could find absolutely no fault with it. But I would have smiled through Kraft with hot dogs. I could have smiled through anything with Tony beside me. Nick watching all of us with wide eyes and the sixth sense of a kid who knew there could be trouble.

But there'd been no trouble. Just a family around a table, figuring things out.

We were going to make mistakes. Lots of them. But I wasn't running ever again. Not from Tony. Not from Nick. Not from my family.

"How do you want it, babe? Because it's going to be hard and rough and I'm not stopping until I make you scream."

Shamelessly I pushed him back and lifted my leg up and over his head and rolled onto my stomach. Hopefully I looked sexy as I got to my knees and arched my back and buried my face in his pillow.

I felt him press in between my thighs, felt the heat of his body against me, his erection pressed between the cheeks of my ass.

He bent over me and whispered into my ear.

"You want it like this so you can yell into your pillow?" he asked.

I nodded into the pillow.

"You did that so Nick wouldn't hear you scream when you come?"

I nodded again.

"I love you, Genevieve. For that and everything else you are."

He didn't slam himself inside me like he'd promised. He pressed into me so slow, so I could feel every inch of him sinking deeper and deeper into my soul.

"So fucking hot and wet. Squeeze me tight babe, yeah, just like that."

I was getting louder so I bit down into the pillow. Tony's hands were wrapped around my waist, pulling me back against him even as he was thrusting deep. He was fucking me like I was the prize he'd won.

Take me. Use me to get off. Fuck me hard for your pleasure, only your pleasure. I'm yours to have.

The inner monologue was running through my head, turning me on even more. Then his magical chef-calloused fingers found my clit and pinched just hard enough.

"There's my good girl. Come for me now."

I came so hard I screamed, loud and into the pillow, as he endlessly and relentlessly continued to fuck me. Not letting me come down even a little before he was stroking my clit again, holding himself pressed deep inside before he started thrusting again.

I might have come again, or it might have been the single longest orgasm in the history of orgasms. I didn't know which.

He slapped my ass cheek, once, twice, then snapped his hips until I could feel the pulse of his cock releasing inside me. Hear his animal-like grunts as he continued to pound me through his own orgasm.

Finished, he collapsed on his side next to me. "Give me your leg, babe."

I knew what he wanted. I turned on my side, and lifted my leg so it was draped across his waist. His still semi-hard cock nestled against my core, wet from both of us. He liked to fall asleep like this, his hand on my ass, my face pressed into the spot between his chin and neck.

"Tony," I muttered against his warm manly smelling skin.

"Yeah, babe."

"This makes us a family now. Right?"

There was a painful beat while he didn't answer.

Then he squeezed me tight into him.

"Yeah, Gen. You're my family now."

∾

Antony

IT WAS EARLY in the morning, just after six. Chilly, but warm enough that I could sit on the back deck and take in the view of the cliff and the water beneath it. I lifted the mug of coffee to my lips and felt a serenity I didn't know was possible.

All that control in my life – all it had given me was a void.

This, losing control, it brought me peace.

I felt love. I felt worry and concern. I felt profound sadness for the loss of the family I'd never had, but at the same time, I felt a joy so keen I'd cried softly after Genevieve had drifted off to sleep for the family I had now.

What had I done to get me to this place? Or maybe more importantly, what did I have to do to keep it?

"Anything," I told the morning sun as it rose over the water.

I heard the patio door sliding open and looked back over my shoulder.

"Hey," Nick said, lifting his chin in my direction.

"Hey. You're up early," I said, as he fell into the Adirondack chair next to me.

"Roy's been getting me up in the morning super early to go fishing. Guess I'm just used to it."

"Want coffee?"

"Nah, I'm good."

I nodded. "You get enough to eat last night?"

"Yeah, Birdie hooked me up with extras of the...what did you call it? Pasta course?"

I smiled. "Good. Were you impressed?"

He smirked. "You slayed and you knew it. You could tell. Birdie's dad doesn't strike me as someone who says well done a lot."

"Definitely not," I agreed, feeling the satisfaction roll over me again. He'd been looking for faults and could find none.

"So what happens next?"

"Once all the paperwork is finished, you come live with me here. It's what I want. Mal is going to sell me the house. The lawyer is expediting the paper work. Starting in June I will be approved for full-time guardianship. How do you feel about that?"

"Like I won the lottery. Like I went from having no luck to all of it."

I snorted a laugh and took a sip of my coffee. "You say that now. I haven't lived with anyone since I was your age. I might be total shit at it. You leave dirty plates in my sink, I will hound you until you clean them."

"Okay."

"And you should make your bed in the morning because it's a good habit."

"Or maybe just don't go in my room," Nick returned.

"When we were cleaning up after dinner, Birdie said she's going to come live with us."

My head swiveled in his direction so fast it almost made me dizzy. "She did?"

"Yeah. Is it true?"

"I'm going to ask her, yeah. That she said it, means she's going to say yes. I didn't think it was going to be that easy."

"She's into you," Nick said.

She was more than into me. She loved me. I was loved.

"Yeah."

"So you, me and Birdie are just going to hang here and cook and clean and live and shit?"

"Yes, after I get back from California. I've got to go fix what's wrong with The Robin's Egg or I'll never really win her father's approval."

I could see his face fall. Almost as if everything was too good to be true and then suddenly it wasn't.

"Not any time soon, Nick. I'm not leaving until you're done school. We're going to go out to California together. If you want, you can work in the kitchen or on the floor so you can make some money while I salvage my reputation."

"Oh. California?"

"Napa Valley. Wine country. It's beautiful. Peaceful like this, but something different."

He shook his head and muttered, "The lottery."

"We have to work on Genevieve though. Convince her to bring her food truck out there for a few months. Now that she's decided to make Calico Cove her home, it might not be easy to get her to leave."

"Did I hear my name?" Gen asked, as she came outside in sweats, thick socks, and one of my shirts. Fuck me, she was hot. Her hands were wrapped around a coffee mug, and because there were only two Adirondack chairs, she plopped into my lap and I shifted her butt against me so we were both comfortable.

"Nick and I want you to come to California with us. We can drive your food truck out there together."

She blew out a breath. "Old Blue might not be up to the challenge."

"I'll say nice things to her the whole way," Nick said.

She smiled. "Then we're golden."

"Road trip. Solid," Nick said.

"Solid," I agreed, and because it had been too long since I'd kissed Genevieve, I leaned forward and placed a kiss on the spot underneath her ear. She shivered and I felt the reaction all the way down to my dick.

"Gross," Nick groaned. "You guys are going to be doing it all the time, aren't you?"

"All. The. Time. Deal with it kid," I told him.

Nick pulled himself up out of the chair and stood, but he didn't leave. Even though I was still nuzzling Genevieve's neck.

"What if..." Nick said, then stopped. "What if we don't like it?"

"Like what?" Genevieve asked him.

"Being together. Being a family. What if it sucks?"

"Well," I said, as Gen looked at me expectantly and Nick looked at me cautiously but also hopefully. "There's only one way to find out."

EPILOGUE

Six Months Later
Antony

"Genevieve!" I called out as soon as I stepped inside our home.

Pure chaos greeted me. Tillie, the Barnes' dog, rushed up to the front door and was either barking at me to leave my house or welcoming me home. It was hard to know. Then Nora came running after the dog with Nick close on her heels.

"Oh no you don't, kiddo," Nick said, scooping her up before she tripped and planted herself face first into the step and down into the foyer. Something she did whenever she was chasing after Tillie. Or Nick, for that matter. Nick plopped her on his shoulder and twirled her around until Nora was laughing.

"Birdie volunteered to watch Nora and Tillie," Nick said. "Roy and Vanessa took the baby to the doctor."

I frowned. "Anything wrong?"

"Nah, just normal checkup stuff."

"I big sister!" Nora announced, her head upside down as she hung over Nick's back.

"You are," I agreed.

"Baby Chawlie is my sistah!"

"So I heard," I smiled. And saw for myself with the eight hundred baby pictures Roy brought to the poker game the other night.

"Imma a good big sistah!"

"I have no doubts."

"Nicky, twirl me!" Nora demanded, and like the good babysitter he was, he did as she asked.

Genevieve walked out from the hallway that led to the kitchen with a somewhat sheepish expression.

"Sorry for the chaos," she said as she approached me for a welcome home kiss.

I didn't mind. I loved the chaos of a busy house. I bent down and planted a kiss on her luscious mouth and both Nick and Nora made kissy noises behind our backs.

"Mature much?" I said to Nick, who realized he was making the same sounds as the two year old.

"Come on, Nora," he said. "Let's leave them to their kissing. We need to take Tillie out to pee."

"And poop!" she said, then immediately started laughing. "Poop, poop, poop."

Nick shook his head and opened the door for Tillie, who sprinted out to find the nearest patch of grass.

Nick closed the door behind him and quiet was restored.

"Well, did you hear?" Genevieve asked me.

I had, but I wasn't ready to share that news yet. Because the minute after Venetia called me to inform me we had in fact been granted our third Michelin star, something became instantly apparent to me.

Something so clear, so evident, I didn't know why I hadn't seen it before.

For the past six months Genevieve and Nick had become the family I never had. They were all the emotions I never let myself feel. In so many ways we acted like it was all a done deal, but it wasn't. Not really. We'd all been too busy.

Nick catching up with school, me with the restaurant, Genevieve with her truck. We forgot something vitally important.

"We need to formally adopt Nick," I announced. "I know he's going to be eighteen soon, and maybe he won't want that, but I feel like legally he should be ours so we can help him with college if he changes his mind. So he always has a home to come back to. "

Genevieve blinked a few times. "Oh. Okay. Well, we should ask him first. Then we'll need to call your lawyer... what are you doing?"

What I was doing was getting down on one knee, but the tile in the foyer was brutal. I winced and shook my head. "No, I don't want to be in pain while I'm doing this."

"Tony, are you doing what I think you're doing?"

I stood up, took her hand, and made her follow me into the living room where there was a plush rug that covered the hardwood floors.

"Are you seriously doing this now?" she said, trailing after me.

I got down on one knee again.

"Pretend to act surprised," I told her.

I took out the ring box I'd shoved in my back pocket. The ring I'd spent the last two hours selecting, once I heard the news. It needed to be practical because she needed to be able to cook in it. I didn't want her to have one of those over-the-top rings she would always be having to take off and put in some dish by the sink.

"Genevieve Manet, I love you. And the second I heard they gave us back our star-"

"Oh my gosh, we got it! We did? Really? All those late nights coming up with so many recipes. All your hard work and the entire team. I'm so proud of you, Tony."

"Focus, Gen. I'm proposing here."

"Oh, right. Sorry. Please proceed."

"Genevieve, I love you-"

"You said that part already," she said, even as she started to bounce a little on her toes.

"Uh, you're sort of interrupting this whole speech I have planned."

"I want to see the ring! And I want to say yes! Hurry up!"

"You've been the best part of me these past six months," I continued, unwilling to accommodate her impatience.

"I know that already. Get to the good part."

"You know social media has really messed with our attention spans."

"Tony!" she shouted. "Now!"

I smiled, pretty confident in her answer at this point. "Gen, will you marry me?"

"Yes!" she screeched, now officially jumping in place and clapping her hands.

I popped open the ring box and tried to explain my selection process, but she wanted to hear none of it. Instead, she got down on her knees in front of me and took my cheeks in her hands.

"Tony, you're the best part of me too."

Yeah, I was. Together we were unstoppable.

"Love me forever?" she asked, looking into my eyes.

"No," I said. "Forever's not long enough."

~

Turn the page for what's next...

~

Want a little more of Tony and Gen? Bonus epilogue right here!

BONUS EPILOGUE

Coming soon in June....FLIRTING with Disaster.

Pre-Order Now!

ACKNOWLEDGMENTS

Because it takes a village we just wanted to give a shout out to our amazing cover artist Ecila Media. The fastest copy editor in all the land, Andrea Stocks. And our assistant, proof reader and all round go to person, Becca Habina, who catches things like wrong titles on covers!

Thank you for making Hailey Shore 2023 work!

ALSO BY HAILEY SHORE

Happily Ever Maybe?

Not My Prince Charming

The Grump, The Bride & The Baby

Fake Date For Christmas

Can't Take The Heat?

Printed in Great Britain
by Amazon